TALKING TO TREES

TALKING TO TREES

"Great characters, a fascinating world,
a scary villain, griffins and talking trees, what more can a
reader ask for in a good Fantasy novel?"

—*Carrie Masek*
***Author of* A Dragon's Tail**

"What do you mean, 'it's found you'?" Jody asked. "That's just smog!" It was odd that there was such a small patch of it, but there was no reason for Twyl and Rafi to act as if it was something serious. They had made her frightened of it, too, but that was only at first, before she realized what it was.

Twyl stared in horror at the swirling brownish gray mist. "The life-destroyer. This is what it used before."

Jody looked from the small cloud to Twyl. Did she really think a cloud was going around looking for her?

"Run!" Rafi ordered. He sneezed, but continued to flap at the cloud with powerful strokes. Jody blinked. The cloud actually seemed to be held in place by the flapping. And it seemed to be shrinking as well.

Twyl tugged at Jody's arm. "He said run!"

Jody pulled away. She was tired of being dragged all over the place. Anyone could see this wasn't dangerous. It was just a patch of smoke. "Don't be so worried. Rafi is blowing it away."

The smoke thinned to mere wisps. Suddenly one wisp darted past Rafi straight at Jody.

Jody opened her mouth in surprise. The tendril of smoke clamped over her mouth and nose. Startled, she tried to take a breath, but couldn't. She tried to pull whatever it was off, but her fingers slipped through the mist. There was nothing there, but she couldn't breathe!

She could see Twyl and Rafi staring at her as, struggling to breathe, she fell to her knees. Rafi pushed Twyl behind him. He reared up and began fanning his wings at her. Her vision turned red, then black...

ALSO BY KATHRYN SULLIVAN

Agents And Adepts
The Crystal Throne

TALKING TO TREES

BY

KATHRYN SULLIVAN

To Doug & Helen
two great travelers

[signature]

AMBER QUILL PRESS, LLC

http://www.amberquill.com

TALKING TO TREES
AN AMBER QUILL PRESS BOOK

Amber Quill Press, LLC
http://www.amberquill.com

Layout and Formatting provided by: ElementalAlchemy.com

PUBLISHED IN THE UNITED STATES OF AMERICA

To my sisters: Karen, Nancy and Rose.

Thank you to my early beta readers and language/fashion references: Abby Shusis, Betsy Leighton, Alexina Gardiner Chai, Deb Walsh, Sheri Frey, Lauren Leighton, and Rose Shusis.

A shout out to the House 6West of 2004-5 at Winona Middle School.

Thanks once again to my sister, Rose Marie Sullivan Shusis for the wonderful map she created for The Crystal Throne *and to Trace Edward Zaber for the modifications.*

PROLOGUE

TWYLGALIT

She looked over the devastated land, at the groves of trees buried by landslide, and leaned again into the embrace of her grandmother. "They can't all be gone!" she sobbed.

"We are the only two remaining. The next strike will be soon."

There came the rattle of small stones down the side of the hill, almost unnoticed in the pouring rain. Thunder growled like an angry voice.

Her grandmother lightly touched her hair. "You must go."

Tears mixed with the raindrops streaming down her face. "I can't leave you!"

"You cannot stay. You must find help for us."

Twylgalit stepped back, looking wildly across the wasteland outside their sanctuary. "How? Where?"

"Only a human can help us. I have spoken to the Watcher of Gates. He knows of our plight. He will ensure you will be sent to one who can help. Now come, give me a hug, dear twiglet, and I will send you on your way."

Twylgalit fiercely hugged her grandmother. She felt the rough bark against her face for a moment, and then suddenly, she was elsewhere.

CHAPTER 1

JODY

Jody Burns saw the green-haired girl step out of midair.

At first she didn't realize she'd seen anything unusual—this was the mall on a Saturday, after all—but then it struck her that this couldn't possibly be some advertising trick. The girl hadn't been there a second ago. The air had suddenly *rippled* and she had stumbled through. She was dripping wet, her hair and clothing clinging to her. She looked as if she had been crying, and Jody could hear a half sniff/half sob as she glanced around at the crowded mall.

The girl shook her head and Jody expected to see droplets of water fly everywhere, but instead she only heard a faint rustle and the short hair suddenly looked dry, lightening to a sea green in color. The water beading her light brown skin and soaking her shirt vanished as if absorbed. The girl hugged her bare arms below the short sleeves and looked around as if she was searching for someone.

Jody quickly looked back at the window display before her. Summer pastels were such a relief after the gray winter drabs. She said as much to Amy Evans, but Amy was looking elsewhere. "Well, check out the new style."

"Eww, seaweed," Brittany commented.

Jody turned with the rest of the group. The green-haired girl was heading directly for them. She wore a loose, almost knee length, brownish smock and dark brown leggings. The smock had a pattern that reminded Jody of the paneling in the family room. Light and dark wood grain swirls, and the neck and sleeve trim even resembled bark. Close up, her brown skin seemed to have greenish undertones. *Wonder if she's ill,* a small thought began before Jody crushed it.

The girl stopped before them. Small beaded cords that held short tufts of hair at each temple clattered softly as she bobbed her head. "Excuse, please. Do you know where dwells a hero?"

"Hero?" Amy echoed.

"Or a wizard. A demon slayer would be best."

Jody wondered why the girl was looking at *her.* Maybe it was because she was the tallest of the group of twelve- and thirteen-year-olds. She knew she was dressed more in fashion than the others, but then the city stores she used to shop at were much better than those in small town malls. *She seems about our age. Too old to be playing little kid games.*

"You mean...The Slayer?" Brittany asked, emphasizing the name. "Someone obviously watches too much television," she added to the group.

"Weird," Sadie commented. She made a circling gesture by her temple, and the other girls giggled.

The girl looked from one to the other and finally returned her attention to Jody. "Please. I need help."

"Definitely," Amy agreed. "For one, that hair color is so *out.*"

"Out where?" She seemed puzzled when several of the girls laughed.

Jody actually thought the girl's hair color was interesting—sea foam, she thought the shade might have been called. She tried to remember if she had seen any outfits in that color; it would definitely suit her blonde looks. Unnervingly, the girl focused on her again. "Please. We've held back the evil as long as we can. We need help."

Why was she asking *her?* "Uh." Jody looked around. Weren't there any security guards in this mall? She'd settle for an older teen or an adult, if she could get anyone's attention. But everyone seemed to be in a hurry, walking past or around the group of girls.

"And that outfit." Amy tsked. "Long baggy T-shirts are so *yesterday.*"

The girl tilted her head as she looked at the girls. "I don't understand your words. The Watcher of Gates said that the first person who saw me would be the one to help." She looked again at Jody, who tried not to squirm. "Will you help?"

"Yes, Jody," Amy said with an unfriendly smile and a glance aside at the other girls. "Will you help?"

Jody could feel the other girls watching her as they waited. Somehow it felt as if everyone in the mall was watching her. This girl might be serious about asking for help, but what could she do? Better to make a big joke of it, as the rest were, and go back to window-shopping.

Jody opened her mouth to speak—and suddenly felt overwhelmingly bored. *So bored. I want to walk away.*

"I'm bored," said Amy. She turned and walked away. The rest of the girls followed. Jody started to turn as well, but a brown hand closed about her wrist.

The green-haired girl looked closely at her. "Will you help?" she repeated.

Jody looked down at the hand around her wrist just above the silver bracelet. She was so *bored*. She should leave now…and yet, there was something odd about that grip around her wrist. She felt as if there were two voices in her head; one demanding *go*, and the other *stay*.

"Hey, Jody."

Jody looked up to see Jeanne Tucker, her brother's friend, coming toward them. She really should leave; Amy and the other girls were already several stores away. Jeanne Tucker was not one of the popular crowd and never followed the trends. For example, as usual, the dark-haired girl was wearing jeans and a plain sweatshirt more suited to a barn than the mall. Fashion disaster. Amy always said Jeanne Tucker was odd, that she had *powers*. Jody vaguely remembered something strange about Jeanne last October, something about her spotted horse and a tree… But there was someone holding her wrist.

Jeanne Tucker looked at Jody, at her wrist being held by the green-haired girl, then finally at the green-haired girl. "Yes," she said softly, "I thought I sensed…" She looked closer at the green-haired girl and smiled. The strange girl smiled hesitantly in return. "But you're not a dryad, are you?" Jeanne continued.

"No," the girl said slowly. "My ancestor was human."

Jody's boredom vanished as if it had been switched off. *What* had she said?

"That explains it," Jeanne said, although Jody didn't think it did. "I'm Jeanne, that's Jody, and you are…."

"Twylgalit."

"Twyl-gaa-lit," Jeanne repeated slowly. "Is that right?" The girl

4

nodded and Jeanne smiled again. "Twylgalit, why don't you let Jody go, and you and I can talk."

The green-haired girl shook her head, the cords in her hair clacking. "No, the Watcher of Gates said that the first to see me would be the one to help us."

"I...see," Jeanne said slowly. Then she nodded. "Sorry, Jody, looks like you stay here for the moment."

"What?" Jody's temper flared. *Don't I have a say? And why am I still standing here? This girl is smaller than me; I could shake off her grip and go join—* But before she could complete the thought, it was gone.

Jeanne acted as if Jody had not spoken. "How did you get here?" she asked the strange girl. Jody tried to remember her name. Twillow—something.

"Grandmother sent me to where I could find help."

Jeanne tilted her head. "Grandmother?"

"I call her Grandmother. She's actually"—the girl spread the fingers of her free hand—"great-great-great—"

"We get the idea," Jody muttered. Jeanne glanced at her and Jody had the urge to stay quiet.

"She's very ill. I think...I think she's dying." Twillow-something wiped her eyes with the back of her hand. "Being closer to the magic, she has the power. She 'spoke' to the Watcher of Gates and sent me through"—the girl waved her free hand—"to this place. To where the person who could help us would be. I found her." Her grip tightened around Jody's wrist.

"She does have the choice, though," Jeanne said thoughtfully. "You can't force her to help against her will."

Jody wanted to say something, to tell them to stop talking about her as if she wasn't there, but Jeanne eyed her and she couldn't. The dark-haired girl glanced again at Jody's wrist. "And, actually, you might have the wrong one. Jody, is Peter here?"

Suddenly she could talk again. "How should I know? We don't actually hang out with the same crowd." Jody tossed her hair back, remembering the last time her twin had commented about her friends.

"Yeah, I know. He needs to hear this, though." Jeanne closed her eyes and took a deep breath. "So much fear," she said softly. "And something follows. I can feel it. It's—" Her eyes snapped open. "No wonder you're scared."

Jody took one step back from Jeanne even as her captor moved closer. "Yes! You understand! It hates life. It will destroy all the lands if it gets free—"

"Hey, Jody!" a familiar call came. Jody relaxed for a second—*Peter would know what to do*—and then immediately scowled. *Know-it-all Peter.*

"Jody, Mom's waiting by— Get away from my sister!" Jody turned to see Peter suddenly break into a run toward them. He was staring at the green-haired girl with a furious expression. Just as he reached them, though, Jeanne stepped before him.

"She needs our help, Peter. Her grandmother is very ill and there's something after her. Twylgalit, this is Peter, Jody's brother. Peter, Twylgalit."

Twylgalit had released Jody's wrist at Peter's shout. She rubbed her hand and bowed slightly.

"What's a dryad doing here?" Peter growled, still glaring fixedly at Twylgalit.

"Not dryad," Jeanne corrected. "Human."

"That hair isn't— Jeanne, I see a tree."

"You see a human," Jeanne said firmly.

Peter attempted to pass Jeanne, but the dark-haired girl blocked him again. He frowned at her and gestured at Twylgalit. "But it—" Jeanne shook her head and he corrected himself. "She...Human? How?"

Jody looked from one to the other. Why was Peter talking about a tree? He was glaring at Twylgally-something again. She looked at the green-haired girl as well and saw nothing strange about the girl other than her hair color. The greenish undertone to her skin was more pronounced than before. Maybe Peter's comments were making her sicker. *Hope she doesn't throw up on me.* She backed a step away from her.

Twylgally-something glanced at Jody, then back at Peter. "My ancestor had magic."

"Obviously." Peter crossed his arms. "So what's the story? Why are you here?"

Jody looked from one to the other. Jeanne and Peter acted as if the strange girl was making sense. She suddenly realized that Amy and her friends were no longer in sight. Maybe she could find them. "I'll just go—"

"No, you won't," Peter disagreed. "Mom's waiting for us outside. I want to hear this first." He nodded at Twylgally. "Go ahead."

"My ancestor's ancestor imprisoned a powerful being." Twylgally glanced at Jody again, faltered, then continued. "His magic was not enough to defeat the evil, but he had knowledge enough to know how to keep it confined until it could be defeated. He created us for that." She looked pleadingly at them. "We have waited so long for help to come. And now we can no longer wait. There is only my grandmother and myself. And I don't have the wisdom. Once Grandmother is...gone, it will be free to turn all of the Lands into a wasteland like the one it now rules."

Peter raised his hands. "And you come to us? What's wrong with the wizards?"

Jody stared in amazement. Peter was not only buying the weird story, but he was adding to it! Wizards? But Peter didn't believe in magic—or at least the Peter she used to know hadn't.

"We had no way to reach them." Twylgally frowned. "They aren't...nearby."

"And we are?"

"Peter," Jeanne said softly, glancing aside at the crowded mall, "she's telling the truth. Her grandmother sent her here for help. She found Jody."

Peter lowered his voice. "Jody? Why Jody? No offense, twin, but you aren't someone I'd ask for help."

"What?" Jody scowled at him.

"Um, you might be the one they were looking for." Jeanne, Jody was irritated to see, seemed amused. "Take a look at what's on her wrist."

Peter took one look and exploded. "My wristguard! What were you doing in my room? How dare you take my stuff!"

Jody shrugged. He didn't frighten her; she was still taller than he was. And it wasn't like him to make a fuss over jewelry. "You weren't wearing it. Besides, it looked good with my outfits." She'd had the argument about his fancy bracelet ready for months, and it still sounded strong. He hadn't missed it in all that time. Mom would see her side.

Peter didn't. "Hand it over. You don't know what you're messing with."

Jody shrugged again and obeyed. She'd wait for him to forget it again and get it back.

Twylgally looked from Jody to Peter as the bracelet was passed. Peter flushed and ran a hand through his sandy hair. "Sorry I was angry," he said to the floor. He looked up at the green-haired girl. "Your grandmother sent you to the wrong twin. Not her fault. Jody was wearing something that belongs to me. This"—he held up the silvery wristband—"came from—" He said something in a language Jody didn't understand. Twylgally looked impressed.

Jody wasn't. "Oh, yeah, like it's my fault you leave it lying around."

Peter scowled at Jody and put the silvery band around his right wrist. "Where's Amy and the rest of her shadows?"

"Oh, they had a sudden attack of boredom," Jeanne said. Peter eyed her, and Jody recognized the you're-not-telling-me-everything look even when it wasn't directed at her. Jeanne grinned and shrugged with open hands. "They were hassling Twylgalit."

"Good thing for Twyl you were nearby, then." Peter glanced at his watch. "Mom's waiting for us. Jody and I have to go."

"Meet later by the Watcher?" Jeanne suggested.

Peter nodded. "We'll need to get some supplies. Where is your grandmother?" he asked Twylgalit.

"In the wasteland."

"Where's that in location to? Wait, my map's at home. Right, we have to go home, get the map, get supplies—" He shook his head. "Why didn't the wizards spot this thing sooner?"

"The Flood may have awakened it," Twylgalit said helpfully. "There was the Great Forgetting and it seemed to sleep—at least we have not been troubled by it for some time."

"And it woke up when the curse was broken?" Peter asked.

"If that stopped the Forgetting, then, yes."

Peter glanced at Jeanne. "You're right; it's our responsibility, then."

"I do not understand," Twylgalit said. Jody mentally agreed.

"We broke the curse that caused the Forgetting," Jeanne said softly.

"Oh." Twylgalit looked from Jeanne to Peter and Jody felt very jealous at the awe in the girl's eyes. "You must be most powerful, then."

"Lucky is more like it," Peter disagreed. "You mentioned a flood; did this thing cause it?"

"No. It is trapped on the wasteland. But from the top of Grandmother I can see water where a desert used to be during the Great Forgetting. Before that she told me it was a wondrous grassland."

Jeanne nodded. "Near Windgard, then. The wizards were going to cause a flood to restore the plains."

"That's a long way from the Watcher. It'll be a walk then."

Jody couldn't believe this conversation. What Peter was so casually talking about sounded as if it would take days—what about school? How was he going to convince their parents? And he was bossing everyone around as usual. At least she wasn't going to have to worry because *she* wasn't going along.

As if he caught the thought, Peter turned to her. "Coming, Jody?"

Jody opened her mouth to reply, but Peter wasn't looking at her. He had turned back to Jeanne and said something in that weird language. Then he looked at Twylgalit. "Twyl, you coming with us, or going with Jeanne? We'll all be meeting later to get back to your world."

Twylgalit edged closer to Jody. "Please, let me go with Jody."

Jody sighed and hoped no one she knew would see her with the green-haired girl.

*   *   *

Mrs. Burns was used to sudden additions of passengers. "Coming with us?" she greeted the new arrival. "My, what a lovely shade of green, dear."

Jody rolled her eyes. Was she the only one who found this situation strange?

Peter frowned at his sister. "We need to go to the woods later today, Mom. Got a project...for Science. I'll be meeting my study partner there. This is Twyl, Jody's study partner."

Jody stared at Peter in shock. Peter never lied—yet here he was telling their mother these big fibs without a qualm! And he was scowling at her as if ordering her not to say anything about what was really happening! As if she knew.

She made sure to grab the front seat beside Mom. Not that Peter noticed. The entire ride home he kept whispering to Twyl, occasionally drawing on a notepad and showing it to the green-haired girl. Their voices weren't loud enough to carry, but Jody was sure she heard that strange language again.

Jody looked out the window, not really seeing the passing scenery. She and Peter had been so close once. They were twins; they used to do everything together, even finish each other's sentences. They used to have their own language, too—"twin speak" as Dad called it. All that had changed in the past year—suddenly boy stuff and girl stuff were more important than twin stuff. Had it started when she began getting taller? She knew from health class that girls matured earlier than boys, but it didn't seem to be that. Peter had no time for her anymore, and no interest in what she and her friends thought important. If he wasn't at gymnastics practice, then he was at the stable helping Jeanne exercise her brother's horses. The horsy smell clung to his clothes when he returned home. Jody thought it was a disgusting smell.

When they got home, she followed her brother into his room and, despite her worries about smells, shut the door. "Peter Robert Burns! You lied to her!"

"Well, what am I supposed to say? 'Hey, Mom, we're off to defeat an evil creature in another world and if we're successful we should be back by dinner?' You think Mom would say, 'yes, dear, go ahead,' to that?"

"Well, no, but—"

Peter was opening drawers in his desk, not even looking at her. "Mitch could probably get away with it, but he's a role player. Think she'd buy that from me? This way, she knows where we're going and we have a reason to bring a backpack. Now stop complaining and pack."

Jody felt stunned. "Pack?"

"Yeah. It'll be a hike. So we'll need food and water."

Jody mentally sighed. Her brother and food. He was always hungry lately. For a moment she had thought he was serious about packing.

"Oh, and map!" Peter pulled a large folded piece of paper out of a drawer and spread it open on his bed. Jody recognized the project their father had helped Peter with during the winter.

"You told Dad that map was for a friend."

Peter was intent on the map. "Yes. Jeanne."

Jody tried to be reasonable. "Jeanne's not a role player."

"Neither am I."

She looked at the map, remembering how he and their father had worked on the computer and the long discussions they'd had on the placements of mountains and woods and rivers. Surely Peter would drop this...joke soon. She recognized names on the map from earlier comments as Peter traced a route with his finger: the Watcher, Windgard... "That place is real?"

"Ask your friend. That's where she came from." Peter looked around the room. "Where is she?"

There came a knock at the door, and their mother's voice outside it. "Dear, your friend is going to get muddy wandering around the garden like that."

Jody found Twyl outside in the remains of the vegetable garden. When they had moved into the house last August, her father had been delighted to find a vegetable and flower garden in the side yard. He planned to continue it this year and had begun preparing the ground for planting. Jody had been drafted to help rake away the previous year's debris. She was determined to miss any further planting or weeding chores, even if she had to join an after-school club. Maybe she could join the cheerleaders, since there wasn't a girls' soccer team.

Yellow and white daffodils and crocuses bloomed already in the flower side of the garden, and fat buds of tulips promised to open soon. Twyl stood with feet buried in the mud and smiled happily at Jody. She flung out mud-streaked arms. "The soil here is so…rich!"

Jody eyed her warily. "Uh huh. You're going to track mud into the house."

Twyl's shoulders slumped. "Must I enter? It seems like the dwelling in which I found you. There was so much deadness all around. Even the light was dead. How could the small trees of that place endure it?"

Jody tried to figure out what she was describing. "You mean the mall?" How could anyone not like the mall? "But it's wonderful there! Well, not as wonderful as the malls in the city, but the stores are much better than downtown."

"If you say so." Twyl slowly began to pull her feet out of the mud.

"Hey, Twyl. Ready to go back?" Peter set his backpack on the walk and checked his pockets, tucking his Scout knife into one.

Jody glanced at him and sighed. He was wearing what Jody called his "nerd" jeans. They were covered with pockets and zippered flaps and loops for tools as if he was some carpenter. He even had a roll of duct tape hanging from one loop. Plus he was tugging an oversized gray sweatshirt on over his T-shirt. "You're not going out like *that*, are you? You look ridiculous."

Peter pulled down his sweatshirt and shrugged. "This is comfortable. Not that it'll matter. The last time the elves insisted we wear their clothing. I like pockets better." He pointed at her shoes. "You're not going like that, are you?"

Jody looked down. What was wrong with her sneaker clogs? They were perfect for the mall. His words suddenly sunk in and Jody looked up. "I'm not going."

"Suit yourself." Peter picked up his backpack. "Twyl, we're going to have to walk, so…"

Twyl anxiously grasped Jody's wrist. "But you must come! The Watcher of Gates said that you would help!"

Jody carefully pulled her sleeve out of the girl's muddy grip.

Twyl's belief in her was rather touching but scary. On the other hand, Peter didn't seem to want her along. She eyed him in sudden suspicion. His whole ridiculous story about elves and wizards could be just that, a story to make sure she didn't come with them.

She started for the house. "I'll just be a moment."

CHAPTER 2

PETER

Peter wished Jody would stay home. First she couldn't decide what to wear. Then she didn't see why they had to bring food with them. Peter had juice, crackers, cheese, and small bags of his father's favorite mix of pumpkin seeds and sunflower seeds in his backpack, but he wondered what Jody had in the small tote bag she carried. *Probably not food.* Then she didn't want to walk.

"Can't we take our bikes?" she complained. "Or, maybe Jeanne could bring one of her horses."

Peter shook his head. "Her brother's horses. They stay here." He glanced at Twyl. It had been hard enough talking the girl into getting into their car. Somehow he didn't think she would handle riding on the handlebars of a bike very well. The forest wasn't that far to walk. "You can load up your bike if you want. I'm taking only what I can carry myself. Less chance of losing it." *Especially since I can't see the Watcher letting us bring bikes into the Lands.*

The Free Lands. He couldn't believe he was actually going back there. After what happened last October, when he and Jeanne Tucker had been kidnapped by the Watcher to break the curse on the Land, he had avoided going anywhere near Wilson's Forest and the haunted tree. Just in case the tree being had other plans for them. *And I was right.*

Twyl seemed happier as they left the sidewalks of the subdivision behind and walked along the bike trail through the park. Or maybe it was because the trees were bigger. *It's almost like walking a dog,* Peter thought with a slight smile. *She has to visit every tree.*

He studied the green-haired girl as she darted away to pat the trunk of a large black walnut, wondering why Jody and his mom hadn't noticed anything different about her. *Maybe they only see what they expect to?* Ever since Jeanne had told him he was looking at a human, Twyl had changed somewhat from his first impression of her. Now he had to look closely to see that her hair wasn't quite hair and that her skin had greenish undertones. But how could even Jody miss seeing that she had no eyebrows and that her clothing seemed to be made from bark?

As they approached the town-side entrance to Wilson's Forest, he was glad to see Jeanne seated on a boulder beside the open gate, waiting for them. He had been worried that she would have taken one of the bridle trails and gotten to the haunted tree before them.

Jody had seen the girl as well. "I don't see why she has to come along," she muttered with a toss of her pale blonde hair.

"She'll be more use than you," he retorted. "Jeanne's a Sensitive."

"A what?" Jody snapped back.

"A healer," Twyl said in wonder, rejoining them. "She can help Grandmother?"

"A healer," Jody mimicked. "Riiiight."

"Right," Peter agreed. "Didn't you wonder why fewer people at school got sick since we got back?"

"No, I didn't—" Jody frowned. "Got back? Got back from where?"

Peter sighed. He had forgotten that the Watcher had erased Jody's memory of their disappearance and reappearance. "Remember last fall when we had to write a report about the haunted tree? When you frightened Jeanne's horse?" He looked closely at her, *willing* her to remember, just in case he could affect the Watcher's spell here.

"I—" Jody started, then stopped, her mouth still open. "She fell..." She looked toward Jeanne in amazement and fear. "The...the tree..."

Peter grimaced. In all those months, Jody had never asked him about what had happened. *Probably never even thought about what she did.* "Yes, she did fall through the tree. The haunted tree is actually the Watcher. It pulled me in as well. It's a...door, to another world. That's where Twyl comes from."

Jody still seemed stunned. "But...she just appeared. In the mall."

"The Watcher of Gates sent me to where I would find help," Twyl reminded her, as if that explained everything. Peter could see from

Jody's face that it didn't.

"But...the mall. She appeared in the mall. Why did we come to the woods?"

"Because this is where the Watcher is." Peter saw disbelief crossing Jody's face, and added, "Make up your mind, Jody. Either you saw her appear out of thin air or you didn't."

Jody's mouth snapped shut, and she glared at him.

Jeanne slid off the boulder as they neared the entrance to Wilson's Forest. "It was hard for us to accept, too, Peter, when it happened to us." She picked up her backpack. "I brought extra water; anyone need some?"

Peter nodded. "I'll take one. Thanks."

"I'm not thirsty," Jody said, in the tone of voice that implied that Jeanne had brought the wrong brand.

Peter mentally sighed. "You will be later. Why don't you put one in your bag anyhow?"

He expected her to argue, and she glared at him as if she would, but she also took the water Jeanne held out and put it into her bag. He glanced closer at Jeanne. His friend gave him the innocent "who, me?" shrug and he suspected she had mentally nudged Jody, just as she had done to Amy and her clique at the mall. He grinned back and whispered in the Common Tongue of the Lands, "Can't you make her go home, or something?"

Jeanne shook her head and replied in the same language. "It's your own fault she's here. She's tagging along because she knows you don't want her along."

Peter knew she was right. Jeanne was not only a healer, but an empath who could sense the emotions of others. Once he would have known his twin's feelings himself.

"Besides," Jeanne continued, "the Watcher did send Twylgalit to her. And, I think I sensed a compulsion spell on Jody earlier."

"Compulsion?" Peter turned on Twyl. "You have magic, don't you. Did you try to force her to come?"

Twyl shook her head, her eyes wide. "No. No, Grandmother has the power, not I."

"Hel-loo," Jody interrupted in disgust. "Mind letting me in on the conversation?"

Switching back to English, Peter kept his attention on Twyl as he answered. "Jeanne sensed someone using a spell on you earlier, one that would have forced you to come with her."

"Oh, puh-lease," Jody groaned. "More magic? So why are you two here? Did someone put a spell on you?"

"We've been there before," Peter replied. "We can actually do something to help."

Jody scowled at him. "Fine. Whatever. You two go ahead, then. I'll just go home." She looked from one to the other. "After I see this haunted tree, Watcher, whatever, for myself. Then I'll go home." She brushed past Jeanne into Wilson's Forest. Twyl hurried after.

Peter glanced at Jeanne. The dark-haired girl shook her head. "That was Jody speaking. No compulsion."

Peter sighed as Jeanne pulled her backpack on. "I don't know how much help she's going to be."

Jeanne shrugged. "I probably won't be much help either. Remember, I don't have the Ring of Calada anymore. Just this one." She raised her hand and a ring of the same silvery material as his wristguard caught the light. Gifts from the High Council of the Lands, the objects would allow them to re-enter the Lands. Peter didn't expect they would have to use that magic to enter the Lands, though, since the Watcher controlled the Gates and it had sent Twyl to them for help.

Jeanne nodded at Twyl, ahead of them. "If the Watcher sent her here, then it's probably for your abilities. Disbelief and belief. Did Twylgalit tell you anything more about what this thing is?"

"It's big, it wears armor..." He shook his head. "She was so scared of the car I wasn't sure if she was talking about the car or whatever it is she's running from. I've got a vague idea where her grandmother is. I'll point it out to you on the map later. Did you bring your copy?"

Jeanne raised her eyebrows. "You didn't give me a small one, remember? Mine's still on the wall of my room."

*   *   *

Peter was glad of his sweatshirt as they walked deeper into the forest. Outside the lawns were turning green with new grass, but in the shadows under the trees it was still early spring, with the chill of the few remaining patches of snow. Here and there he could see a crocus or a snowdrop amid the dead leaves and mud. He glanced ahead on the path. Jody's pale blonde hair and blue denim jacket were easy to spot against the trees, but Twyl seemed to all but vanish whenever the path curved.

Before too long they had reached the bushes that in summer would mask a faint side path. Jody waited impatiently by the path that led to the haunted tree. Peter looked for Twyl and finally saw her patting a nearby maple.

Jody uncrossed her arms and tossed her hair back. "This forest is creepy. I'm cold and my shoes are getting all muddy. Can we go back home now?"

Peter shrugged. "You can if you want to. Jeanne and I are going to help Twyl." He waved at Twyl to follow them down the path. Soon he had entered the small clearing before the haunted tree.

"It's waiting for us," Jeanne said softly beside him.

Peter scowled at the gnarled old oak, willing to see behind its disguise of a spooky tree with dangling clawlike branches. Nothing changed, but he had the impression that it was watching him.

"What has happened to the Watcher of Gates?" Twyl ran up and leaned against the large trunk. "Why do you wear this shape? Please, how is Grandmother?"

"That's it?" Jody said scornfully.

"That's it," Peter agreed. He adjusted his pack and patted his pockets to make sure everything was secure. He glanced at Jeanne and saw she was doing the same with her belongings. She finished and nodded. "Go ahead," he told Jody. "Touch it."

"You want me to touch that nasty old tree?"

Peter mentally sighed. Had she already forgotten everything they had talked about? Maybe he should just push her—

Jody screamed.

Across the clearing, the trunk of the Watcher shimmered. Twyl was already halfway into the brownness.

Jody started back a step, and two branches whipped forward to encircle and push her, still screaming, into the trunk.

Silence fell in the small clearing as Jody vanished.

"Guess it did want her there," Peter said, surprised. He had been so sure that Twyl had the wrong twin. *What can Jody do there?*

"You want to go next and calm her down?" Jeanne asked.

Peter shook his head. "No. You go."

She chuckled. "Coward. She's your sister."

"That's why you go next. She'll just keep screaming until I 'save' her."

"See you on the other side." Jeanne stepped through the brown shimmer. The swirling shimmer slowed.

Peter reached forward, expecting his hand to go through the Watcher.

His palm met solid wood. The door was closed.

CHAPTER 3

TWYLGALIT

Twylgalit looked about the wide meadow, wondering at the huge expanse of greenness. This was all so beautiful, and so rich with life. On the other side there was life, but it was only beginning to awaken from the slumber of the cold season. Here it was long awake, and singing with the joy of growing. Off in the distance she could see green hillsides, their forests beckoning to her. She flung out her arms and spun, giddy with the growing song. She stopped, facing the Watcher of Gates, here once more fully arrayed with leaves as it had been when they met.

"I was so worried," she said, starting forward.

A leafy branch swung down to gently bar her from the shimmering trunk.

"What—" she started, when she suddenly heard a high-pitched sound coming closer. She covered her ears, trying to shut out the piercing cry. Was it a hawk? She saw nothing in the sky, no shape diving from the clouds. Whence came that sound?

The yellow-haired human girl fell through the Watcher and pitched face forward into the soft grassy ground. The sound stopped.

The branch moved away and Twylgalit approached cautiously. Jody had been the source of that cry?

The girl raised herself up. "Euuuww," she complained.

"Are you all right?" Twylgalit asked.

"Of course I'm not all right. There's grass stains and dirt all—" She suddenly rolled over, looked at the Watcher behind her, and emitted the piercing cry.

Twylgalit clapped her hands over her ears again. "What is wrong?"

Jody pointed a shaking finger at the Watcher. "That—that *thing* swallowed you! And me! Where are we? Where's the forest?"

Twylgalit was puzzled. "Back in your world. We have stepped through the Gate into the Lands."

But Jody wasn't listening. She climbed to her feet. "Peter and Jeanne were behind me. I'll bet *she* pushed me. Where are they?"

"They should be arriving now." Twylgalit looked toward the Watcher, expecting to see the other two humans emerge. However, the shimmering Gate was gone. In its place was solid bark.

"No!" Jody ran up to the tree and began pounding on the trunk. "Let him out! You let my brother go! Peter!"

Twylgalit listened as the Watcher of Gates spoke, but Jody did not appear to hear. "He says that you do not need him now. We are to gather more help."

"No!" Jody hit her fist against the trunk. "I want to go home! You hear me? Send me back!"

In answer, a branch swung out, pointing stiffly across the meadow. "We are to go in that direction," Twylgalit translated helpfully.

"No way." Jody crossed her arms. "You might as well send me home. I'm going nowhere until you release Peter."

Another branch swung out to join the first.

"You will not help?" Twylgalit felt a rush of sadness. "You must. You are the only one who can save us."

"Me? Yeah, right."

Twylgalit nodded eagerly. "Yes, right. You are the one the Watcher sent me to find. Please come. The Lands need your help."

Jody looked from the trunk to Twylgalit and back again as if expecting the Watcher's Gateway to reappear. It did not. She sighed loudly. "Oh, all right. After all, it can't be too hard if Peter expected *her* to help."

Twylgalit was awestruck. Peter had said that Jeanne was a Sensitive, and Jeanne had said that she and Peter had broken the curse of the Great Forgetting. If Jody felt those meant little, then she was powerful indeed. The Watcher of Gates was right. This human—not the others—was the one to stand against the Evil One.

The Watcher rustled its leaves. Yet another branch swung out to

19

join the other two, pointing toward the forest-covered hills.

"All right, all right, I'm going," Jody muttered. She stamped off in the direction the branches indicated.

Twylgalit delayed only long enough to bow to the Watcher of Gates and give thanks for its help. Then she hurried after the human girl.

*   *   *

They walked in silence for a while.

Twylgalit was still amazed at how the grasses and the flowers and other plants covered the ground as far as she could see. Her home had only the few patches of grass and one small pocket of flowers that had continued to survive the influence of their neighbor. And she knew not to *walk* on them! But here, as in the land beyond the Gate, there was no way to avoid stepping upon green life of some sort. At first it was hard to do so, but the protests and complaints from underfoot were grudging and resigned, and soon she no longer winced at the small voices.

Jody did not appear to hear the tiny protests beneath her feet. Or, if she did, she didn't comment on them. "This had better not take long," she muttered suddenly. "I'm supposed to meet Amy Evans and our friends on the bus tomorrow. I should have been there, at the mall, in case anyone bought anything. They want my opinion, you see."

Twylgalit did not see. "Your opinion?"

"On clothes. On *style*. You know, fashion?" She glanced at Twylgalit, then shrugged. "Amy Evans says I have excellent taste. I found the perfect blouse for Amy this morning. She said so. And I saw this darling skirt this morning that would go so well with several tops I have, but I don't have a jacket to go with it. I was hoping to find one when you arrived." She waited.

"I am sorry," Twylgalit said, sensing some apology was necessary. She tried to puzzle out this "fashion" idea. "Do you mean you all choose to look alike?"

"Of course not. Who'd want to do that?"

"But—" Twylgalit started.

"Now, take your own outfit. Where *did* you buy it?"

Twylgalit looked down at her kirtle. She smoothed the front self-consciously. "My mothers made it for me."

"Oh, you poor thing. Hand-made clothes are so old-fashioned. No one sews anymore. But I suppose if you're from a broken home, you can't afford good clothes, can you?"

Twylgalit looked again at her kirtle. How else was clothing made,

20

but with care and love? She remembered the amusement of Little Mother explaining how Gruff Mother placed spells in every seam, and of watching Graceful Mother intent on matching every swirl in the pattern. She hugged the memory of them close, of their gentle smiles and the caress of their leaves in her hair. She felt tears welling. Her mothers were gone now.

"There, there," Jody said. "I don't mind what you're wearing."

Twylgalit did not have an answer for that. She walked on in silence, struggling not to cry. She missed her mothers. She also missed her fathers and aunts and uncles, but she had always been *aware* of her mothers. The empty space inside her, where the awareness had been, now held only a faint and distant echo. Grandmother! She increased her stride. Grandmother was depending on her.

"Hey, wait up!" Jody called behind her.

Twylgalit did not stop, but she did slow her steps.

The human girl soon caught up. Twylgalit kept her gaze on the forest ahead, willing it closer.

Jody sighed loudly. "This is boring. Why do we have to walk? If it's so important that we get to…wherever it is that we're going, why do we have to walk?"

Recalling the metal beast that had brought them from the mall place, Twylgalit shivered.

"I'm hungry," Jody said. "And I'm thirsty, and I'm tired." She stopped.

Twylgalit continued walking. Soon she heard footsteps behind her once again.

"Didn't you hear me?" Jody asked.

"I heard." Twylgalit walked on. "Don't you still have the water that Jeanne gave you?"

"No, she didn't."

Twylgalit was puzzled. Perhaps the girl had forgotten. "You put the water in your bag."

"No, I didn't." Jody opened her bag. "Hey! Who put that in there? I didn't want her old water."

"Does it matter when you are thirsty?"

"Yes, it matters! This isn't flavored—I don't even recognize this brand." Jody scowled and pushed the bottle back into her bag. "Are we going to stop soon?"

Twylgalit pointed to the forest. "The Watcher of Gates said we would be safe within there."

*   *   *

By the time they reached the forest's edge, Twylgalit felt overwhelmed with information. She knew so much now about Amy Evans and clothes and what various other girls at someplace called school had done recently. But she was afraid she would not be able to remember it all.

A nearby beech commented that birds drove away their rivals with their songs. Perhaps all this talking was the girl's manner of defense—to drive away enemies with sound. The idea suddenly explained much which had puzzled Twylgalit. It was true she had heard small creatures departing when they came within hearing range of herself and Jody. Perhaps Jody would not require her to remember everything about Amy Evans and school. Twylgalit felt relieved at that. She thought this "defense" also explained Jody's piercing cry when she had arrived in the Lands. Twylgalit touched the beech's leaves lightly in thanks as she passed.

"Finally!" Jody said loudly. "We're reached the woods. Can we rest now?"

Twylgalit stopped and looked back at Jody. The girl had barely entered the shade of the beech. "Just a bit farther?" Twylgalit asked.

Jody scowled. She opened her mouth, but whatever she started to say was drowned in high-pitched roar from overhead. Her mouth stayed open as she stared with wide eyes into the sky.

Twylgalit dashed out from under the sheltering tree and scanned the sky. The sound had been a mixture of a screech and a roar. Whatever it was, it was angry. She spotted the golden-furred gryphon as it circled and flew back in their direction. It roared again.

Jody pointed and screamed her own piercing cry.

Twylgalit darted behind Jody and pushed her toward the beech. "The trees will protect us!"

Jody at first seemed to want to scream back at the gryphon. Then she suddenly began to run. She ran past the beech, and continued running. Twylgalit glanced back only long enough to be sure the gryphon was not following them. Then she hurried after the girl.

Twylgalit kept the girl's long yellow hair in view as she followed cautiously. In the shadow of the trees it would be easy to overlook exposed roots or loose stones until you tripped over them. The shadows could also hold other surprises for unwary passersby. Perhaps the gryphon wasn't following because it had a partner waiting in ambush.

Jody ran as if she feared no such dangers. She ran so fast that

Twylgalit began to worry she would lose sight of the human girl.

Suddenly Jody stopped. She screamed.

Twylgalit caught up with the human. Covering her ears in an attempt to protect them from Jody's piercing cries, she looked for the cause. But she saw only trees and brush. "What is wrong?" Twylgalit shouted.

Still screaming, Jody pointed at a nearby cluster of young trees.

Twylgalit cautiously edged up to the concealing cluster. She braced herself in case anything attacked, then looked around the saplings. There was nothing behind them. She straightened and looked back at Jody.

Jody stopped screaming. She looked all around, then hurried to join Twylgalit. "There was something there! The bush moved!"

"You must have frightened whatever it was away," Twylgalit agreed, happy her previous idea had been confirmed. She looked closer at the ground. There were impressions in the loose soil, a jumble of prints as if more than one being had stood there.

"I don't like it here," Jody said, looking from one tall tree to another. "And I'm not waiting for whatever it was to come back." She glanced in the direction they had come, shivered, and began walking in a different direction.

Twylgalit looked after the human girl, then down at the prints again. The faint line of footprints went in the same direction the girl had chosen. As Jody had said, she wasn't going to wait for their owners to return. She was going after them instead. Twylgalit smiled as she started after Jody. She had definitely found the right hero.

CHAPTER 4

PETER

Peter pushed on the unresponsive bark, not wanting to believe what he saw and felt. "Hey!" He knocked on the trunk of the Watcher. "Hey! You forgot me! Let me through!"

The bark remained solid.

"I don't believe this," Peter muttered. He glanced upward as a branch creaked threateningly overhead, then returned his glare to the rough bark before him. "I don't believe this," he repeated in a firmer voice. He concentrated, reminding himself how his disbelief affected things in the Lands. *The bark is only an illusion; behind the illusion is the doorway to the Lands. I will walk forward and* through *to the Lands.* Holding that thought firmly in mind, he closed his eyes and walked forward.

He collided with an unyielding surface.

Rubbing his forehead, Peter scowled at the trunk and took a step back. There was another way. He pulled his sleeve back, exposing the silvery elven carvings on the swordguard. He studied it for a moment, remembering what the Elder had said about the swordguard and Jeanne's ring. *"These but serve as keys to the Door from your land. The Glen itself formed these for you, to permit your return to this land, should you wish it."*

"Well, I wish it." Peter looked from the wristguard to the tree, unsure how to use it. He finally laid his arm against the tree so that the

24

band was in direct contact with both the tree and himself. Peter concentrated, willing the entrance to the Lands to open. He felt resistance and pushed harder, fighting also the impression that the tree was glaring at him.

The bark beneath the wristguard shimmered, and the shimmer slowly spread until it was door-shaped. Peter stepped through—

—and found himself in a very familiar small clearing. He was back where he had started.

He turned to face the Watcher again. "Very funny. I *am* going with them."

The shimmering doorway had vanished. Peter placed the wristguard against the trunk again. "Now, send me where Jody and Jeanne are."

The resistance was there again. He was reminded of the time he tried to open a door that Jody was holding closed. Peter kept pushing with his mind as he leaned against the bark, and suddenly he fell into the trunk.

He fell a short distance, then his feet splashed into shallow water.

"What?" Peter looked around. He was standing in a creek, the water murmuring as it swirled around his feet and over the rocks and pebbles on the bottom. The Watcher was behind him, leaning crazily over the creek. The grass-topped bank on which it stood was deeply undercut by the swiftly flowing current. Peter looked again across the creek. The trees on other bank looked familiar, although shorter.

"This is Raccoon Creek!" He scowled back at the Watcher. "What are you playing at?"

The bank beneath the Watcher looked too steep and unstable to climb, so Peter waded further down the creek for an easier spot to climb back onto dry land. Over the murmur of the creek, though, he began to hear voices approaching. They seemed to be coming from the Watcher's side of the creek. He scrambled up the opposite bank and behind the trees.

"It's still there!" a boy's voice shouted.

Peter cautiously peeked out to see the speaker. He saw three boys on the opposite bank. All three were shirtless and barefoot. The two brown-haired boys wore overalls while the black-haired boy wore brown trousers held up with suspenders. The youngest one in overalls pulled a slingshot out of his back pocket and shot a pebble into the creek. "Told you it'd still be here, Jason Tucker!" he shouted.

Peter pulled back as the two older boys approached the bank's edge and looked down at the exposed roots. *Jason Tucker?* He knew one of

Jeanne's brothers was named Jason, but these boys were too young. Jeanne's brother Jason was a senior in high school.

"It won't be here for long, though," the black-haired boy said. "Pa said the Wilsons are going to cut it down. Said it's too dangerous now. And if'n they wait for it to fall, it'll stop up the creek."

The youngest boy shot another pebble into the creek, and Peter's stomach dropped with the *plonk*. He cautiously looked at the black-haired boy again. He remembered Jeanne had once said that her grandfather told her stories about when the Watcher was on Raccoon Creek. Could that be Jeanne's grandfather? If so, the Watcher had sent him back in time!

But why would it send him here? His backpack jabbed him as he leaned back against the tree hiding him, taking stock of the differences from where he had been. When he had entered the Watcher it had been early spring, with no leaves to be seen. Here leaves were out on the all trees, except for the Watcher, but that was normal for the "haunted tree". He was beginning to feel hot under his sweatshirt and the backpack, and all three boys had been shirtless. It had to be summer here. He could hear bird songs over the murmur of the creek. If Jody was here, he would have heard her by now—she wouldn't have gone far. So the Watcher had sent only him to this place and time.

A butterfly fluttered by, and Peter glanced back toward the Watcher. The boys were no longer in sight. He looked toward the trees past the Watcher, checking to be sure they were gone, then emerged from hiding.

The creek was too wide to jump across, so Peter walked along the bank until he found a spot on the opposite bank that looked easy to climb. He hurried back to the haunted tree.

He studied the leaning Watcher. Even tilted, the trunk was still wide enough that he could enter without crouching—once he got the doorway to reappear. He placed the wristguard against the gray bark. "Now, send me to Jody and Jeanne," he ordered. "And no tricks this time."

Branches creaked, but Peter closed his eyes and "pushed". *I'm going with them.*

He heard a gasp behind him. His eyes snapped open, and he saw the black-haired boy standing nearby, gaping at him. But the shimmer had reappeared as well. Peter jumped through—

—and landed in long grass.

Peter climbed to his feet. He was standing in a great meadow. "All right!"

He looked toward the ends of the meadow. In one direction were hills covered with green and golden leafed trees. In another, across the long browning grass, was a large woods. "Wait a minute," Peter said, turning back toward the Watcher. "It's late summer! You sent me to the wrong time!"

The leafy branches of the Watcher swayed slowly, but there was no other response.

Peter scowled at the tree, then looked across the meadow. He could see no one heading toward Lytleaf Forest. He walked around the Watcher and stopped, staring at a trail leading from the Watcher through the waist-high grass. Making the trail across the meadow, heading toward the distant hills, was a tall figure.

"Hey!" Peter broke into a run. *Wonder where Jeanne and Twyl are?* he thought.

The figure did not stop, so Peter called again. "Hey, wait up!"

He was almost to the walker before he realized two things. First was that the person he was following was much taller than his sister. Second was that a long pteradon-like shape had appeared in the sky. The Watcher had sent him back in time again!

Peter stopped. "Witch hound!" he warned. "Get back to the Watcher!"

The figure stopped and turned to look back toward him. "What did you call me?" the slender man asked politely.

Peter pointed up at the approaching witch hound. "That! It's dangerous! Get back to the tree!"

The man looked skyward just as the red-violet creature opened its beak and shrieked. He stared. "What is—"

"C'mon! It's calling backup!" Peter yelled.

The man turned and began to run.

Peter ran back toward the tree. "Watcher!" he shouted. "Call Graylod! Now!"

A distant chime sounded in response. Peter glanced back to make sure the man was following, then returned his attention to the ancient tree. "Why didn't you call Graylod as soon as he arrived?" Peter complained loudly as he ran. "You're supposed to protect him until a wizard arrives—that's what you did for us! The witches *know* when humans enter!"

The hound shrieked again and Peter saved his breath for running. He could hear the man's pounding footsteps behind him.

Finally Peter gained the safe shelter under the tree branches. Panting, he turned to see if the man had joined him.

The witch hound swooped downward, talons extended. The man wasn't going to make it to safety.

"Get down!" Peter yelled. He looked frantically for a rock or something to throw at the witch hound.

The tree behind him rustled. Long branches whipped out directly in the witch hound's path. The creature tried to pull up, but more branches closed over it from above.

Peter danced excitedly. "Yes!"

Face down on the ground before Peter, the man cautiously raised his head. He rolled over and stared up at the struggling witch hound held captive above him. He looked over at Peter. "Who are you?"

A branch smacked against Peter's chest and swept the boy backward. He fell into the shimmering trunk.

CHAPTER 5

JODY

She recapped the water bottle and shoved it back into her bag. She was *so* tired. They had been walking for hours and hours. Why had that old tree sent them in this direction? There was nothing but trees and bushes! She gingerly adjusted her seat on the fallen log and looked at the green-haired girl standing with her feet buried in the dirt.

Jody studied her own shoes. Her feet were tired, but she didn't care how "refreshing" the dirt might be. "I'm hungry," she complained. What was that girl's name again?

The green-haired girl opened her eyes and looked at her. "Why don't you root yourself in? The soil is very tasty here."

"Tasty? Eeuuww! Are you...eating dirt? Through your feet?" Jody felt queasy. "Was that what you were doing in our garden?" Jody wasn't going to eat any vegetables from *there* ever again!

"Not dirt. The nutrients in the soil." The girl looked from her buried feet to Jody's shoes. "So that is why Peter talked of bringing food," she said sadly. "You do not absorb nourishment as my people do. I did not understand."

Reminded of her twin's orders, Jody looked again inside her bag. Other than the bottle of water, which she had *not* packed, everything inside was what she had brought—her comb, her brush, hair ties and scrunchies, multi-colored bracelets, gum and fruit snack candies. She decided to open a fruit snack before that girl started offering her dirt.

Obviously she wasn't going to get any real food here. "Whatever. I'll eat this." Jody broke off a strip of the candy and put the rest back in her bag.

The girl nodded. She closed her eyes again. Her green hair rustled in the light breeze.

Jody looked around at the trees as she nibbled on the strip. "You know what I think, ah…" She still couldn't remember that girl's name. Till..will.. "Willow. I think we should—"

The girl's eyes snapped open. "My name is Twylgalit. Not Willow. Not Gally. Twyl-gaaa-lit."

Jody was surprised. Why was she making such a big fuss? It was only a name. "Hey, sorry. It's only a name."

"But it is *my* name. My name is important to me. In the language of my people it defines me."

"It does?"

"'Twylgalit' means 'twilight wood.' It means I am the last of my people."

"The very last?" Jody shook her head. "Creepy."

Twylgalit studied her. "Doesn't your name mean anything? What is a jody?"

Jody shrugged. "I don't know. It was one of my grandmothers. Peter was named for one of our uncles. Thank goodness, otherwise we might have been stuck with some cute twin names."

"Twin names?"

"Names starting with the same first letter. Like…oh, Brittany and Brian. Actually, I think I'd rather be called Brittany. Or maybe Caitlyn. Then Peter would have been stuck with a 'C' name like Cedric or…Clarence." She snickered. "He would have hated that."

"Even if it was his name?" Twylgalit shook her head. "I do not understand."

"Whatever," Jody said. "Anyhow, your name is too long."

Twylgalit eyed her. "Brittany is just as long."

Jody rolled her eyes. *Why doesn't she understand?* "Okay, your name is too hard to remember. Can't I call you something else?" Jody tried to remember the name her twin had used. It was a type of fabric or a pattern— "Peter called you Twyl. Would that be okay?"

The girl raised her head and slowly turned to look behind her.

Jody scowled. All this fuss about her name and now she wasn't even listening to her! "I said—"

"I heard." Twylgalit turned back. "It…it is acceptable." She lifted one foot. Clods of dirt fell away from it.

Euuww. Jody turned away so she wouldn't have to watch. She saw movement beside one of the trees, as if something had ducked out of sight.

Jody screamed.

Bushes rustled violently behind her, and Jody sprang off the log. She ran past Twylgalit, then stopped and screamed as a tall figure emerged from the shadows before her.

She turned to run in the other direction, but two girls had appeared—one atop the log, the other next to Twylgalit. They froze, their dark eyes and mouths open in round *o's* as they stared at her. Both girls had green hair similar to Twylgalit, but both were totally green!

"You—you have green skin!" Jody faltered.

The girls looked at each other, then back at Jody. "Of course," said one. "Why don't you?"

"Look what she wears," said the other. She jumped off the log and straightened, eyeing Jody. "How...odd."

Jody's mouth opened in astonishment. The two girls wore loose green smocks similar in cut to Twylgalit's brown one. The closer girl had a yellow-orange belt with small bags dangling from it. Their hair color was a darker green than Twyl's but still a light green in shade. Both girls had a tiny little bag-like pendant around their necks.

Jody blinked. She had the strangest impression there was something different about their eyes—they seemed almost completely black—and that neither girl had eyebrows. But of course that couldn't be so.

Twylgalit stepped forward. "We're looking for help. My grandmother and I—"

"This is your grandmother?" asked a voice behind Jody.

Jody turned. Behind her stood a tall, green-skinned girl. She wore a knee-length dress that seemed to be woven out of leafy vines. Curls of tendrils and red and green leaves stood out against the weaving, forming their own patterns.

"Maybe she's ill," one of the girls whispered.

"Of course I'm not her grandmother!" Jody said indignantly. "Some old watcher thing sent her and—"

"You refer to the Watcher of Gates?" the tall girl asked. Her hair rustled as she turned toward the other girls. "The mother grove will know what to do."

The two girls nodded, their hair rustling loudly as well. "Yes, the mother grove will know."

"The mother grove," Twylgalit repeated softly. It sounded important, the way she said it, but when Jody glanced at her, Twyl turned away and brushed at her eyes.

"Come," said the tall girl, striding past Jody. "Follow us to the mother grove."

"Yes," said the other two, beckoning to Twyl. "Come. Follow us."

Jody hurried after the tall girl. It was a struggle to keep her in view—she kept vanishing into the leafy greenness. Then Jody would catch sight of movement against the dark trunks of the bigger trees or a splash of red in the patches of sunlight. "Hey, wait up!" Jody called. *She's not even looking back to see if I'm following*, she thought angrily.

Finally she lost sight of the girl completely. Jody stopped, feeling hot, tired, and exasperated. "Do you see her, Twyl?" she asked. She glanced behind her, expecting to see Twyl there. But all she saw were green leaves and brown and black trunks. "Twyl?" She couldn't see Twyl or the other two girls. "Not funny, guys." She turned slowly, watching the shadows. They were probably hiding and soon they all would jump out and yell "Surprise." She waited. They should have jumped out by now. "Guys?"

She heard faint giggles overhead. Jody glanced sharply upward, but all she could see was the waving branches of the nearby trees. "Helllooo," she drawled. Where were they?

Leaves rustled all around her and Jody was sure she could hear soft whispers and more giggles. "Twyl? This isn't funny."

"Why have you come?"

The tall green-skinned girl had reappeared. She stood close to one of the smaller trees, her arm draped over its branches as if around the shoulders of a friend.

Jody wanted to say *I followed you*, but decided not to. "I told you, some old tree sent us. Well, he sent Twyl first. She said she and her grandmother need help. Where is she?" Not that Jody totally cared, but she had gotten used to the girl's presence.

"The mother grove wished to speak to she who is named Twylgalit first." The girl tilted her head to one side as if studying Jody. "She does not seem well. Are you well?"

"I'm hungry and I'm tired, if that's what you mean." Jody deliberately did not glance at the nearby shadows. The giggling had stopped, but there seemed to be more voices whispering than before. Well, she would just ignore it. That would show them. "We've been walking for hours."

The tree next to the green-skinned girl swayed slightly, its leaves rustling. The girl nodded, her hair rustling almost as in answer. She stepped away from the tree and beckoned to Jody. "Come, I will show you where you can find food and rest."

Jody hesitated. "I don't eat dirt," she said warily.

"We have other food for visitors. You will see."

The shadows were deepening as Jody followed the green-skinned girl to a huge willow. Its drooping yellow branches swept almost to the ground. The tall girl parted the curtain of green leaves, gesturing Jody inside.

Within the shelter of the willow's branches was a large comfortable space. From the inside, the leafy curtain appeared blue-tinted, giving Jody the impression that she stood within a vast tent. Heaps of leaves dotted the dirt floor, and the tall girl indicated the closest. "You may rest there. I will have food sent."

Jody watched as the girl departed through the leaf curtain. Then she turned her attention to the heap. She cautiously sat, half-expecting to sink into loose leaves. The heap seemed to consist of springy branches and leaf fronds, rather than just leaves. It was more comfortable than she had expected. She leaned back and settled herself. She looked up at the faint light playing between the branches. The soft wind whispering through the leaves was very soothing.

The light changed as someone entered the willow shelter. Jody glanced toward the curtain, expecting the promised food, then recognized Twyl and relaxed again. "I was wondering where you were, Twyl."

"I have discussed our plight with the mother grove," Twyl said, coming to stand next to Jody's seat. She sighed, the beaded cords in her hair clanking softly. "I do not think the mother grove understood."

"What, couldn't they check with that watcher thing?"

"Evening approaches. The pren are not able to go far from the grove yet."

"Pren?" Jody wondered what the word meant. "Why don't they talk to the Watcher like your grandmother did?"

"Grandmother has strong magic and her need was great." Twyl looked toward the leaf curtain, and Jody followed her gaze. The two smaller girls were entering. Twyl sighed. "They are so beautiful."

Jody was surprised. Beautiful? "Yeah, right. If you like that overall green look." She still thought there was something wrong with their eyes. She studied them as the girls approached. Their eyes were totally black, with no white around the iris. She shuddered. Still, there was something very graceful about how they moved. She looked back up at the branches overhead. Almost like the way the branches swayed.

Jody shook her head and looked back at the girls. Each carried a broad leaf in both hands like a tray. The girl with the orange belt reached them first. "I bring you fresh berries and mushrooms." She carefully set her leaf on the ground. "The berries are very sweet." She smiled at Twyl.

Jody recognized the dark red and purple raspberries, but the tiny orange globes were new to her. Mushrooms were for topping pizzas or steaks. Still, they couldn't be too weird alone. She started with a few raspberries.

The second girl, moving very carefully, set her leaf tray down as well. On it were small bundles of wrapped leaves and…flowers? The girl pointed to a small bark bowl in the center of the tray. "The honey is for dipping." She demonstrated with one bundle and licked her lips as she finished. "Mmmm."

Jody ate a few more raspberries as she thought. She had encountered different ways of eating salad in the city. She'd show these girls she was no uncultured farmer.

Jody picked up one of the leaf and flower bundles, dipped it in the honey, and took a bite. "Mmm," she echoed. It *was* good, if a trifle sticky. She finished off the bundle, alternating bites with berries to help with the stickiness.

Twyl hesitated. "Go ahead," Jody encouraged, waving a second bundle. "It's all good."

"Please," said the second girl. "We prens only feed that way"—she pointed at her feet—"if no other nourishment can be found."

"It can't be healthy to starve yourself that way," the orange-belted girl agreed. She snatched up the berry and mushroom tray just as Jody was reaching for another berry and held it out to Twyl. "Try just one."

Jody eyed the mushroom in her fingers. She had managed to grab that when the tray had moved. She popped it in her mouth and chewed slowly. Rather than being tasteless, it had a slight meaty flavor. "Go on, Twyl. You don't want to be different, do you?"

Twyl carefully picked up one orange berry. She held it between thumb and forefinger and eyed it as if it were some strange alien object. She gingerly placed it inside her mouth.

"Go on," Jody persisted.

Twyl closed her eyes. A second later they flew open again. "Oh! So that is what "sweet" tastes like!" She picked up several more berries and crammed them into her mouth.

The orange-belted girl laughed and placed the tray back on the ground. Both girls fluidly sat on the ground beside Jody's leaf heap and began to eat as well.

Soon Jody leaned back against the leaves, contentedly full. She watched Twyl scrape the last of the honey out of the bowl. "Well, that was good. Thank you," she told the girls. "I'm ready to go home now."

Twyl stared wide-eyed at her, one sticky finger in her mouth.

"Oh no, you can't leave now," the orange-belted girl said. "Not at night. It's dark."

"And dangerous," said the other girl.

"But it can't be night," Jody protested. "I can see—" She stopped, looking about at the clusters of tiny lights now shining from the tree trunk, leaves or even hovering in midair. The change in lighting had been so gradual she hadn't noticed. "Oh, that's pretty. How do you get the lights to hover like that?"

The nearer girl tilted her head to look at Jody. "That's how they fly."

"Your lights fly?" Jody was looking right at one cluster when its lights suddenly winked out. A few seconds later, the lights winked on again in another spot. She had a sudden memory of Peter dragging her into the backyard one evening, pointing at flickering lights and talking excitedly about— "Fireflies? Those are fireflies?"

"How beautiful!" Twyl turned slowly, smiling as she gazed at the clusters of lights. "We have no lights like this at my home. At night there is only starlight and sometimes moonlight."

"Must be...dark," Jody commented.

"Yes," Twyl agreed. "And also beautiful. We can see so many stars. My mothers would tell me stories of the stars and of the dark places between." She sighed. "I miss them."

The two green-skinned girls exchanged glances. "We can see the stars, if we climb to the top of the tree," one offered. "I can show you."

Twyl shook her head. "No. These lights are pretty to watch. I will see the stars again another night." She glanced at Jody. "After we save my grandmother, I will show you how beautiful our night sky is."

Jody looked away from Twyl, reluctant to remind her that she was only along to find help. Twyl just didn't seem to understand. She noticed the two green-skinned girls exchanging glances again. Jody had the impression they weren't saying something as well. "Hey, where's the other girl? Um, the tall one? With the leafy dress? What are your names, anyway?"

"You won't like them," said one.

"You don't like long names," said the other.

"Well, I've got to call you something," Jody insisted. "I'm Jody and she's Twyl."

"She is called Twylgalit," said the girl with the yellow-orange belt. "We heard you talking."

"You can call me Brittany," said the other girl. "I like the sound of that name."

"And I like Clarence," said the girl wearing the belt.

"I can't call you Clarence," Jody protested. "That's a boy's name."

"But I like it," the girl insisted. She looked over at the other girl. "Brittany."

"Clarence," said the girl now called Brittany. Both girls started laughing and pointing at each other.

I don't see what's so funny, Jody thought. She heard a muffled sound from Twyl, but when she glanced up at the girl, Twyl was studying the lights in the branches above them. Jody struggled to her feet and stalked over to the blue-tinted curtain. Pushing aside the leaf fronds, she peered outside the shelter. It was definitely night. And very, *very* dark. She could barely make out the shapes of the nearby trees. A lone firefly flashed as it flew past her to join the clusters inside. She looked back at the two girls still pointing and laughing at each other. "Whatever."

"They are outers," a voice said from outside the willow. Jody looked at the tall shadowy shape and thought she recognized the voice of the third girl.

"So?" Jody asked.

The girl turned toward her. "They enjoy being different. For the sake of being different."

Jody scowled. "They're laughing."

"Everything is a game to them." The girl tilted her head as she studied Jody. "You understand the importance of fitting in. Belonging."

"Don't they?"

"No. They want to be different. Unlike. That is why they are outers. They do not want to fit in. To belong." She paused, and Jody had the impression that she was listening to something, though Jody heard nothing but the wind through the leaves.

The girl turned toward the willow. "My friends want to meet you.

Tomorrow."

"Your friends?"

"They are not like those outers. You will like them."

Still holding the curtain open, Jody stepped back as the girl approached. "What about Twyl?"

Entering the shelter, the tall girl looked past Jody to the other girls. "The mother grove wishes to speak to she who is called Twylgalit again tomorrow."

"And what are you?" Jody interrupted. "Called, I mean."

"You will not like my name."

"It's too long, yeah, whatever. Don't you have a short form?"

The girl paused a moment. "Call me, Kimeka."

"Kim-ee-ka," Jody tried. "Look, Kim—"

The girl looked sharply at her, the black eyes narrowing, and Jody hastily added, "—eka, doesn't the mother grove want to talk to me, too?"

Wind rustled the leaves overhead and Kimeka tilted her head. Jody wondered if she should ask again when Kimeka abruptly turned. "Not yet. Perhaps later, when you learn to hear." She walked toward the other girls.

"Huh? I hear just fine." Jody looked at the other girls, then turned to look out at the forest again. *Whatever. This is boring.* She missed television. She missed listening to music. It was so *quiet* here. And yet several times Kimeka had seemed to hear something Jody couldn't.

Jody listened. She could hear bugs *cricking* and other weird sounds in the nearby trees and the leaves rustling all around. But that was all. *Boring.*

She let the leafy curtain fall. Ignoring the other girls, she flung herself into a different leafy heap and stared up at the blinking clusters of lights. She hummed softly to herself, waiting for the girls to notice and ask what the song was.

At some point while she was waiting, Jody fell asleep.

*   *   *

Jody dreamed she and Peter were arguing about something. "You don't listen," he said. "You don't listen to anyone anymore."

"That's not true," she replied.

"It is!" Peter shouted. He leaned forward and suddenly his face became all brown and barklike. "Wake up and listen!"

Jody's eyes snapped open. She stared upward, barely able to see the willow's branches stretching above her in the darkness. Leaves rustled softly in the light breeze.

She kept looking upward, listening to the rustle, slowly falling back into sleep. She thought she could hear voices whispering nearby.

"...not a true pren but we can try to help her."

"...will restore some health."

"What about her friend?"

"She's obviously ill as well—that dead yellow color to her hair, those bleached white limbs—I doubt we can save her."

"Poor thing. It's not her fault she's so ugly."

"... and those other deformities..."

Jody's eyes filled with tears as she realized how kind they were to help those ill people—how grateful the sick people would be for the voices' pity and understanding. It was important to fit in, to be normal. She fell back asleep and dreamed that a woman was singing a strange song above her while Jody kept looking for the radio so she could change the station.

CHAPTER 6

JEANNE

She stepped through the shimmering doorway and heard before she felt the squelch of gooey mud underfoot. Rain poured down in sheets from the gray sky. Jeanne huddled inside her jacket and wished it had a hood. She turned up the collar in an attempt to keep water from running down her neck. She could barely see through the downpour. Where were Jody and Twylgalit?

Thunder grumbled overhead and Jeanne glanced nervously skyward. She knew it was dangerous to stand under a tree during a thunderstorm. Even if this one was more than a tree. She'd better find shelter elsewhere.

Jeanne turned back toward the Watcher, expecting to see Peter emerge behind her, and stared in surprise. The tree behind her was not the gnarled oaklike Watcher. This was a large old tree, but of a type she didn't recognize.

Jeanne tried to look around. She couldn't see much through the downpour, but what she could see confirmed that she wasn't in the Watcher's meadow. She didn't know whether to be relieved or irritated. She had expected the Watcher to summon a wizard when they emerged in the Lands, and had planned to ask whatever wizard arrived to send her to Twylgalit's grandmother. *I guess the Watcher had the same idea—and a shortcut. Now all I have to do is find her.*

She tried to calm her thoughts. Twylgalit's grandmother had been ill when the girl had left, and there was no telling how long Twylgalit had been gone. If the evil had attacked again, the grandmother could be near death. Jeanne closed her eyes, shut out the rain from her senses, and closed away her fear that she might be too late. She was looking for the faintest trace of life, of a type similar to Twylgalit.

There. Jeanne turned, her eyes still closed to concentrate completely on that fragile thread. *So slow, so faint.* Stretching out her arms before her, she took one step, and then another. Her fingers brushed a rough surface, and she opened her eyes in surprise to find herself touching the bark of the old tree. She looked upward, making sure there was no one sheltering up in the branches, and then stepped closer to the trunk. "Are...are you Grandmother?"

There was no reply. Jeanne closed her eyes again, intent on finding that thread of life.

It was there, beneath her fingertips. She mentally reached for the faint pulse, reaching until she heard the soft sigh. **So tired, so ill, the life draining away—**

No! Jeanne's eyes snapped open as she fought the urge to let go, to slip away. "You have to hold on," she said softly. "Twylgalit is counting on you to hold on until she returns."

All gone, the sadness whispered. **All alone now.**

"No," Jeanne replied. "You're not alone. I'm here. And I'm going to help you get well again." She reached into herself, to where the power to heal others waited, and began the transfer of energy, looking with another kind of sight to find what ailed her patient.

So tired. So many years holding on, fighting...why?

"You know why. Because you were the only ones who could, the only ones who knew about this. Don't let that thing win now."

Can't...fight.

"Do you truly believe you can't fight it?" Jeanne could feel the blotches of self doubt now. *Just the way I used to feel around Amy and her friends.* Anger grew. She had learned how to handle Amy's bullying, but she could not stand to see anyone else threatened that way. "Or is that what that thing wants you to believe? It is, isn't it? Is that what it told you? Over and over, until you wonder, perhaps it's right. Perhaps nothing can fight it. But you have. You've stood up to it. You and Twylgalit."

Twylgalit. Dear child.

"And if you give up, she'll have to stand alone against it. Without training. Without your help. Which is what that thing wants!"

Twylgalit..safe now.

"Not for long. You know that thing." Jeanne paused. She knew she had to say the rest. "It'll hunt her down. Wherever she goes. She'll never be safe from it."

No. The whisper was slightly stronger now, and Jeanne had the impression of sadness receding. Determination grew. **No, I won't let it hurt my twiglet.**

Jeanne smiled. She still had a lot of work to do, but she knew the most important step had been taken. Her patient wanted to be healed now.

She leaned her forehead against the rough bark and stretched her arms out around the trunk as far as they would reach. "No. We won't let it hurt her," she agreed. She closed her eyes and concentrated on healing.

*   *   *

Jeanne poured her strength and energy into the being until she reached the limit she had set for herself. Then she broke contact and checked her patient. Still ill, but resting and stronger than the being had been when Jeanne had arrived.

Jeanne sighed. Not for the first time did she miss the Ring of Calada. With that magical object, she would have been able to cure Grandmother completely within minutes. Without it, she had to rely on her own strength to provide the energy for healing. That meant she would have to heal in stages, spread out over a few days. Plus she had to figure out what was wrong with the being. She had healed enough humans, cats, dogs, and horses to be able to spot what ailed them within a few seconds of contact. But this was a being new to her. Not truly a dryad, which she had encountered before, but something different.

What had happened to Grandmother? Jeanne had expected battle wounds—from axe or sword—from the impressions she and Peter had had of the armored thing that threatened Twylgalit, but there weren't any large injuries that she could see. Or sense. There was an itchy feeling, like a stubborn mosquito or chigger bite, spread over a large area. Elsewhere was the sensation of an open, bleeding wound, with constant fiery pinpricks. This might be something she'd have to physically look for. The tree core seemed healthy, and the roots held firm and deep. The leaves on some branches were brown and dry, but on others were healthy and green. *I'll have to climb up and have a look there, too.*

Jeanne eased the kinks out of her shoulders from staying too long in one position. She had learned the hard way not to drain herself too far in healing. She would wait, regain her strength, and then begin again.

The rain had stopped sometime while she had been working. She looked around for some place relatively dry to sit and then realized she was already so damp that a little more wouldn't matter. The worn surface of nearby half-buried boulder seemed as if others had used it as a seat. It was more appealing than the muddy ground, and she settled herself there.

Suddenly realizing she was thirsty and very hungry, she unslung her backpack. The energy used in the healing would have to be replaced. She pulled out a granola bar and a bottle of water.

Jeanne studied the tree as she ate. The branches waved slowly in the breeze, the leaves rustling. She smiled. She could almost imagine a face in the trunk, with lined cheeks and smiling eyes, looking very like her Grandmother Tucker. She straightened, suddenly aware that the tree *was* watching her. The imaged face smiled wider, and one "eye" winked.

"Hullo," Jeanne tried. "Are you feeling a bit stronger now?"

The sound of the leaves rustling slowed, a gentle *swishing* that pulsed almost like breathing. Jeanne found herself trying to breathe with the pulse, trying to catch the whisper of the leaves, the whisper beneath leaf-rustle and branch-creak. She listened for the soft voice she had heard before.

Yes, dear, that way. Yes, I feel stronger now. Thank you.

"You're welcome," Jeanne said slowly, surprised at her success. The water bottle, forgotten, almost slipped out of her grasp. She hurriedly recapped it. "I'm not done healing you yet."

Oh, to feel even this much better is wonderful. Where is my twiglet, my Twylgalit?

"I don't know. She and Jody went first through the Watcher. If they didn't come here, they're probably on their way to the Glen."

The Watcher of Gates promised to send her to where she would find help. Did she find you, then, dear?

"After she found Jody."

Who is this Jody? Will she help my twiglet?

"Jody? Help?" Jeanne struggled to turn a reflexive snort into a cough. Grandmother didn't need to know that Jody had come along only to annoy her brother. "Jody is my partner's sister. Wait till you meet Peter. He'll help you against your neighbor."

Is he like you, dear?

"No, he's not a healer. Peter can influence magic. He can believe, or he can disbelieve—very strongly—and magic won't work. He defeated a witch that way."

I should very much like to meet him. Where is Peter?

"I wish I knew," Jeanne said. She closed her eyes and concentrated. She couldn't sense Peter anywhere in the Land, and she always could before—*when you had the Ring of Calada*, she reminded herself. Now she only had her own abilities to rely on, and she was already tired from healing. *I'll check again when I'm stronger*, she cheered herself. She opened her eyes. The image of a face on the trunk seemed concerned, and Jeanne hurried to reassure her. "He's probably with Jody and Twylgalit. He brought a map, so he should be able to find help in no time. And, speaking of help, I should check you some more. Where do you hurt?"

Many places. And many ills. There was a rustling sigh. **We did not realize for far too long that our neighbor had many ways to attack. We had thought our small sicknesses were normal until too late.**

"Germ warfare?" Jeanne asked, straightening with a chill that had nothing to do with the temperature.

Germ?

"Changing bacteria and viruses to something worse," Jeanne explained, hoping she wasn't right. There had been so much on the television about germs and terrorists, and her parents radiated fear with each mention.

Germ warfare, though, could describe what Jeanne was sensing. A sickness that should be little, but changed somehow to be deadly. And if she was right— *What if this is contagious?* Jeanne thought back to the way Twylgalit kept running to trees, touching them—what if Twylgalit had passed on the disease to them as well? To the trees in both her world and the Land? She'd have to check the trees in Wilson's Forest when she returned, but what about the trees here? What about the Watcher? *If the Watcher is contaminated....*

Jeanne finished the last bite of her granola bar, tucked the wrapper inside her backpack and stood up. She definitely needed to check the other side of the trunk.

Bac-teria? I don't understand, dear.

"That's okay," Jeanne reassured Grandmother. She cautiously

approached the tree, putting tight control on her ability. For now she was only to observe and spot where she best needed to concentrate healing when she was stronger. She looked over the surface of the bark, trying to ignore the anxious look in the imaged eyes, then slowly started around the tree.

The trunk was almost as large as the Watcher's, large enough so that if Jeanne and Peter and Jody and Twylgalit had joined hands, they still would have needed four more to completely encircle the tree. Jeanne smiled at that image as she scanned the bark.

She spotted a line of discolored bark and reached upward, stopping just short of touching it. The hot, tight sensation of infection throbbed under her fingertips. Jeanne followed the streaks of heat as they continued around the side of the trunk, then paused in dismay.

The infection had cracked the bark in one place, allowing sap to seep out. Fungi surrounded the foot-long crack and spread like a furry carpet partway up the tree. A short distance away boring beetles had created another oozing crack. Jeanne shuddered, realizing the source of the fiery prickles of pain, and frowned. She'd have to convince the beetles to find another source of food. She looked closer. She thought her Science teacher had said that beetles only attacked dead wood. This stretch was very much alive. *Eaten alive.* She shuddered again, memories of her brothers' favorite horror movies racing through her mind.

Jeanne forced herself to calm. This would take time, but she could heal this. She forced herself to continue on and look for other patches of sickness. *Time enough later, when you're stronger, to come back and fix this.*

It's bad, isn't it. The soft whisper was sad.

Jeanne shook her head, then thought that maybe a tree wouldn't know what a head shake meant. "It's yucky, but we can beat it."

So said we all, once. The voice sounded resigned. **The chestnuts died first. Then the elms...**

"No, I mean it," Jeanne started, then paused. The elms... A memory of her own grandmother talking about elms and chestnuts dying intruded. Jeanne frowned. This had to be a coincidence. She remembered her grandmother's pictures of the town, before Dutch elm disease had struck, and all those big beautiful trees lining the streets had to be cut down. She shook her head firmly. It had to be a coincidence that the same trees were affected here as well as in her world. She continued walking.

...then the laurels and the tanoaks. Now myself.

Finishing her walk around the tree, Jeanne finally stood before the image of a face again. "We can beat this. I know what I'm talking about," she insisted. "You're going to have to believe me." She looked upward past swaying branches at discolored and dead clusters of leaves. She'd have to check those as well. She eyed the lowest branches to see which would be the easiest to climb. "Now just hold still a moment so I can climb up and check your branches."

Jeanne heard a soft sigh, and the branches stopped swaying. She jumped, caught her chosen branch, and pulled herself up onto it. She reached for the next branch and began climbing.

A short time later, she touched the first afflicted branch. Patches of gray and blue lichen fell away, taking clumps of bark as well and revealing the rot underneath. Jeanne nodded to herself as she examined the branch. *Dead, but only from this spot out. I just have to keep the rot from spreading.* She inched back toward the trunk until she could climb to the next diseased spot.

After she had studied all the stricken branches, she glanced toward the top of the tree. Curiosity to see what Twylgalit had described as "the Flood" took hold, and Jeanne grinned and started climbing again. She wondered if she would be able to see any Windkin. *It would be great to see Elin again.*

Soon she had reached the top of the tree. She could see a gray desert stretching out for miles all around. *No, not a desert. There's life in a desert. This looks...dead.* Then, past that was the shimmer of water. A *lot* of water. Jeanne shaded her eyes with one hand, but she couldn't see to the other side of the flood. She'd known from the Windkin that their land was large, but she hadn't realized, even from Peter's map, exactly how large. Seeing it in this way... She shook her head. She supposed healing all of Windgard from the damage caused by the witches' spells would take rather drastic action. But covering the plains with water seemed extremely so. She'd heard from her parents about the damage floods did to farmlands. "I guess the wizards know what they're doing, though." She wondered how long she and Peter had been gone. "It's been five months our time. Wonder how long the water's been there."

The slender branch tips above her waved slowly. **We only learned of it when Twylgalit climbed to where you now stand to see her path. We knew then, that even had she been able to escape detection on the wasteland, that way was blocked.** Leaves stroked her head in a gentle caress. **I wish I could taste that water. Even from here I can sense its magic.**

"Magic!" Jeanne looked again at the sheet of water. *Of course it would be magic! Elves know wood magic; they'd know exactly what the grasslands would need. And what better way to deliver it all!*

She peered at the border between water and desert. *Wonder what's stopping the water from covering the desert as well?*

She slowly began to climb back down, stopping several times to look out and gain more information about Grandmother's home as well as the surrounding wasteland. A long bluff formed one boundary, but there were signs of a recent landslide from there, with boulders as big as cars mixed with the gray soil. Broken branches seeming like reaching fingers protruded from the mixture, and a faint shadow of pain and fear seemed to hover about the mound. Jeanne remembered Twylgalit's grief. She now knew the cause of that sorrow.

The slide had almost reached a stand of skeletal trees around what seemed to be ruins of a house. Perhaps Twylgalit's ancestor had lived there. A small patch of grass grew in its shadow.

Jeanne stopped on a comfortable branch and settled herself. Legs dangling, she placed one hand on Grandmother's trunk in case she needed the extra contact. "Grandmother, I need your help. You feel like a tree, but you also feel...human somehow. And Twylgalit isn't exactly like you either." She took a deep breath. "What *are* you?"

The leaves sighed. **Does it matter?**

"It matters when I'm trying to heal you. It matters because I don't want to hurt you by trying to fix something that is normal to you." She sensed the being's hesitation. "Please?"

**I started life as a seedling, in a forest far from here. Then the wizard came, and asked for help, calling upon the ancient oaths of the Branch and Leaf. Well! To uphold those oaths, to stand on the side of Life against Those who hated Life—what green life would refuse? Many volunteered. I was one.

The wizard's kin had long ago trapped one of Those who hated Life. As long as one of the wizard's kin lived nearby, the Life-hater was forced to stay in its wasteland and not spread its influence elsewhere. But the wizard's kin were no more. He was the last.

Jeanne shared the sadness Grandmother felt. "How could you help?"

The wizard brought us back to his land, this place. And, as he transplanted us, he gave us his lifeforce—his magic, his self. We became his descendents. We held the land for him, after his death, and continued to keep the Life-hater trapped.

Jeanne looked at the ruined house, but she could almost see how the area had looked before, when the house was whole and clusters of tall trees gossiped in the sunlight. "And Twylgalit?"

Although the Life-hater cannot set foot on our land, its influence has spread all around what we hold.

Jeanne nodded. She could see the gray expanse of the wasteland from her perch.

Over the long years, we grew, and spread over our land. We have died, as well, from spell-storms and poison mists—before we learned to defend against those attacks. The magic does not always appear in our seedlings, and many of those died before those of us with magic learned to protect the rest. We waited, and held the land. But our numbers have dwindled. Finally we knew we had to find help, because when we are no more, it will be free to spread its destruction elsewhere. A pren visited the wizard long ago, and those of us who met him remembered his form.

"A pren," Jeanne said slowly, not remembering that word from any fantasy book. "Is that like a dryad?"

Like, yet not. A dryad lives with a tree. A pren will *become* a tree. Leaves rustled in another sigh. **We had to create a form that could go for help. We blended our magics, and several gave up the remainder of their human lifeforce so that our seedling, Twylgalit, the last of us, would be more human than any of us.**

"They died?" Jeanne looked toward the skeletal trees.

A small sacrifice, if in their deaths they save the rest as well as the lands beyond. The leaves rustled a soft laugh. **After all, the wizard thought the same when we replaced his kin.**

CHAPTER 7

TWYLGALIT AND JODY

The notes of the healing song were familiar, although the voice was not. Twylgalit slowly opened her eyes, wondering who was ill. *Gruff Mother has never sung so sweetly before.* The thought stopped as she recalled that her mothers were no more. *Never again to hear them.* The twinge of sorrow faded as she gazed upon the bluish inner leaves of the willow. Beams of sunlight escaping through the leaves sparkled with magic as well as light.

"Who is ill?" she asked, wondering where the three pren were. Had one of them been injured?

You are, small one, the willow rustled gently. **Very ill. Rest, now. You shall be well soon.**

"My friend—" Twylgalit struggled to sit upright. "Jody—"

She, too, will be well soon. Rest, now.

"Nuhhh," came a nearby voice. "Turn off the radiooo. What an awful noise."

Leaves rustled outrage, but the willow fell silent.

Twylgalit climbed to her feet. She did feel better. Had she been ill? "Jody?"

"Nooo," the voice groaned. "Just five more minutes."

Twylgalit looked around the blue-lit shelter until she saw which leaf-heap held the girl. She hurried to the girl, worry filling her as she remembered that the willow had said Jody was ill as well. What had happened?

The yellow-haired girl was curled tightly within the nest of leaves. Her eyes were closed, her breathing slow, but Twylgalit wondered if she saw a faint healthy green beneath the girl's pale complexion. "Jody?"

The girl waved a hand without opening her eyes. "Five more minutes, Mom." Leaves rustled as the hand fell back into the heap.

Jody's eyes snapped open at the sound. "This isn't my room." She turned her head and looked at Twylgalit. "Oh, it's you."

Jody sat up, and her tangled hair swung into her face. "Gross! There's leaves in my hair!" She pulled several leaves out, then leaned over the side of the leaf heap. "Where's my comb? I must look awful!"

Twylgalit thought the leaves looked fine, but she helped Jody search, curious as to what a "comb" was. Jody soon found her carry bag and pulled out an object with spikes on one end. She began stroking her hair with it.

Twylgalit was disappointed. She had expected something with magical powers. But this was another thing made of what Peter called *plastic*.

She went over to the leaf curtain and looked out into sunshine. Birds chirped and sang and she longed to climb and greet the ones overhead. She had always envied the birds who had made their brief homes in her family's branches and had listened with delight as they had gossiped about distant forests and plains.

The trees of the forest rustled and sighed in their discussion, those nearest the willow bowing and waving to her. Twylgalit could hear the murmur of a brook close by, and promised herself to find it.

The wind brought a distant message of leaf-rustle, and soon the willow relayed the summons. **The mother grove awaits.**

"Where are you going?" Jody said behind her.

Twylgalit looked back at the girl. "The mother grove calls."

Jody frowned. "Fine. Whatever. You go ahead. I'm meeting some friends of Kim today."

Twylgalit nodded and continued on her way. The girl seemed angry about something, but Twylgalit had no time to waste. The mother grove was waiting.

The trees gossiped around her as she walked, but she was too nervous to try to catch the undercurrent of their discussion. Had the mother grove found someone else to help? She and Jody needed to return to her grandmother soon. Twylgalit worried that they might already be too late. What if she returned home to find Grandmother dead? What if the evil escaped? The thought was too horrible to bear.

She slowed her pace and calmed herself as she entered the grove. Leaf-rustle stilled as the grove grew aware of her presence.

Bright growing, Twylgalit. Have you rested well?

Twylgalit clasped her hands together to hide their trembling. "Have you—have you found someone to help us?"

The willow has told us that she nursed your ills.

"Thank you, yes," Twylgalit agreed. The clatter of the beaded cords in her hair sounded loud amid the soft rustles and sighs. "But what about my grandmother? I need to bring help back to her, before our neighbor attacks again." She looked at the ground, afraid to say the words. "It will kill her."

There, it was said. She felt tears coming, but ignored that, listening instead to the undercurrent of rustles on the wind.

We have sensed no such evil nearby. You were not well; perhaps you dreamed ill.

"No!" Twylgalit protested. Why would they not believe her? How could they not sense the life-destroyer? "The Watcher of Gates knows what I say is true. He sent me here, to find help!"

Help to heal you. Soon you will be better. And you will see what we say is true.

"No." Twylgalit shook her head, despairing. "I have come so far." She stopped, considering. Was that the problem? She remembered Peter talking about distances, about how far her home was from the Watcher. "Can you sense the waters of the Great Flood?"

A faint taste, nothing more. It is too distant.

"My grandmother and the evil she fights are more distant still," Twylgalit said. "That is why you cannot sense it." She looked around at the watching trees. "Please, if you won't believe me, speak to the Watcher of Gates. This is a threat to all the Lands."

The unified voice of the grove broke apart into several whispering clusters. She felt tingling beneath her feet, as if they spoke by root as well.

There has not been time for an answer from the Watcher.

The birds say there is death past the Great Flood.

"Grandmother?" Twylgalit whispered.

The danger is far away. The wizards will handle it.

If the wizards learn about it in time.

But if they do not?

The oaths of Leaf and Branch bid us to act.

Finally the rustles slowed, merging again into one voice. **We cannot go to her,** the reply came at last. **We will send for help.**

"Thank you," Twylgalit said. She relaxed in relief. She could go home now. "We will leave then."

Stay with us, Twylgalit. Wait with us. You still have ills that must be tended.

"But I feel fine," Twylgalit protested. "And I need to get back to Grandmother."

Wait for help to come, so that it will go with you. Meanwhile, rest and grow well, so you will be an aid for your elder.

*   *   *

Jody plopped onto a leaf heap and glared impatiently at the blue curtain of willow leaves. Where was Kim? After Twylgalit had left, Jody had found leaf trays with fresh fruit left inside the shelter. But she had finished eating long ago and still there was no sign of any of the green-skinned girls. She climbed back to her feet and brushed off her clothes. She pulled out her comb and straightened her hair yet again. She wanted to make a good impression on Kim's friends. But whenever she stepped outside the shelter the wind blew more leaves and sticks into her hair. It almost seemed to be on purpose.

Jody pulled a leafy tendril out of her hair and glared at it. It lazily curled about her finger. "Ick! Let go!" Jody shook her hand, but the tendril hung on. Leaves wrapped around other fingers.

"How sweet," Kim said behind her. "It likes you."

Well, I don't like it, Jody thought. She was about to say so when she turned to face the green-skinned girl, but then she suddenly noticed how similar the tendril in her hand looked to the tendrils making up Kim's dress.

The other girl plucked the tendril from Jody's fingers. "This would look so pretty on you. Here, let me." Before Jody could protest, she wrapped the tendril around Jody's upper left arm.

Jody worriedly looked down at her arm. The tendril disturbingly thickened and lengthened to curl completely around her arm. It spread its leaves and stilled. Jody relaxed when the vine stopped moving. It did look rather pretty, almost like a fancy armband around her sleeve.

"And this," Kim continued, holding up a wreath of leaves and cream-colored flowers, "is for you to wear when you meet my friends."

"But—" Jody protested.

"Isn't it beautiful? They made it especially for you."

"Did they?" Jody felt pleased. The flowers were very pretty, and that shade of cream would look nice against her hair. The open buds had a very pleasant smell as well.

"Let me." Kimeka placed the wreath atop Jody's head. She stepped back and studied the result.

The delicate perfume of the flowers settled around Jody's forehead. She inhaled deeply. "Mm, that smells so good." Jody wished she could take some flowers back with her. Mother couldn't disapprove of this perfume the way she did of the expensive brands. Jody closed her eyes and sniffed again. She didn't care anymore that her clothes were mussed and dirty, that she had a vine wrapped around her arm, or that she had probably missed pulling some leaves out of her hair. Kimeka's friends had made a beautiful wreath especially for her. Amy Evans had never done that.

"Are you ready to meet my friends?" Kimeka asked.

Jody slowly opened her eyes. She was surprised how calm she felt. She should feel excited, but instead she felt as if everything had slowed down around her. She nodded, but Kim waited a moment before turning and leading the way out of the shelter.

Outside, things didn't look the same as what Jody had seen only a few minutes ago. Gone was any bare patch of dirt. Instead, grass stretched like a thick green carpet between the trees. Brightly colored flowers dotted the smooth greenness. The wind gently fluffed Jody's hair, and she smiled as she imagined a trail of the light scent from the cream-white flowers following behind her.

Jody didn't notice how long they walked before Kimeka stopped. The green-skinned girl raised her hands to shoulder height, closed her eyes, and bowed her head. "I have brought the visitor. I present to you, Jody."

Jody quickly copied Kimeka. She could hear whispering all around her and wondered how long she had to keep her eyes closed. The blossoms' perfume was calming.

"Well brought, Kimekasensience," a voice said.

"Bright growing, Jody," another voice said with an undercurrent of laughter.

Jody opened her eyes. She stood before a group of very tall young women with even taller hairstyles. They all wore long elegant gowns of brown or green or gray. Beyond them she could see men with high green hats, who nodded at her and then turned back to their conversations.

"Thank you." Jody bowed her head again. She noticed Kimeka had lowered her hands, and did the same with relief. "It's very nice to meet you. Thank you for the beautiful flowers."

The women at the back of the group whispered softly behind raised hands. Jody decided to ignore them. She kept her attention on the two young women in front. One smiled at her, and Jody thought she seemed friendly. The other, who had cream-colored blossoms within her hair, looked at Jody with a superior expression. "How do you like our grove?"

Grove? Jody looked around at the group of young women. The next stand of trees was a short distance away. And it was just trees. But here... The perfume from the flowers swirled about her on the light breeze, and the green carpet looked soft and inviting. Jody suddenly felt as she had when she had walked into the new store that had just opened in the mall. She had been surrounded by sweet perfume and cool green and light summer pastels. "It's so beautiful," Jody said.

*   *   *

Twylgalit walked slowly through the forest. She tried to summon up her previous delight in its beauty, but something seemed missing. She felt uneasy, but didn't know why. The mother grove was right; she couldn't expect anyone coming to help to know where her home was. But still, she wished she could leave now.

Brittany darted out of the shadows and stopped before her. "There you are."

Clarence dropped out of the branches overhead. "We were waiting."

Twylgalit looked from one pren to the other. Their usually happy expressions seemed solemn. "Why? What is wrong?"

"Not wrong," Clarence said with a head shake that provoked an answering rustle from above. "Right."

"Very right," Brittany agreed, touching her pendant.

The two looked at each other, then Clarence straightened, adjusting the pouches on her belt. "We've come to say 'good wandering.'"

"We're on our way Outside."

"We had planned to leave before now, but Kimeka kept asking us to delay our leaving."

"Don't let her do the same to you."

Twylgalit felt a sudden rush of homesickness. She hadn't wanted to leave her own home, hadn't wanted to leave her grandmother alone.

"Perhaps Kimeka doesn't want to be lonely."

"It's her decision to stay," Brittany said.

"It's ours to leave," Clarence agreed. "Don't let her make her decision be yours as well."

Twylgalit thought of her grandmother, left all alone and waiting for her to bring help. "I won't," she said firmly.

The two smiled. "Will you travel with us for awhile?" Brittany asked. "You have been Outside before."

Twylgalit wished she could say yes. "I cannot leave yet. The mother grove has asked me to wait. Once help has arrived, Jody and I will travel on."

The two pren looked at each other and then back at Twylgalit. "Don't wait too long," Clarence said mysteriously.

CHAPTER 8

PETER

Peter staggered out of the shimmer and bumped into an unyielding surface. "Ow!" Rubbing his forehead with one hand, he put his other hand up and felt a wall before him. It wasn't wood or plastic or glass or any material he recognized. It seemed to extend in a circle all around the Watcher. The light was dim, but as his eyes grew used to it, he found he could see through whatever it was, although it was like looking through dirty glass. "Probably isn't cleaned too often," he muttered. He seemed to be in a grove of large trees. Each tree was enclosed by its own wall.

"What is this?" He turned to glare back at the Watcher. The old oak tree wasn't behind him. The brownish shimmer was still there, though, filling the trunk of a different type of tree, the same type of slender tree as the rest of the grove.

He heard a clatter of metal and stamp of marching feet approaching. He peered through the wall and watched as a troop entered the grove. Their layers of armor reminded him vaguely of that worn by samurai, though there seemed to be large patches of fur added. He backed a step. Maybe it was only their armor and masks, but the soldiers seemed to resemble large armor-clad bears. He backed another step when he noticed they were heading for him! He dashed into the shimmer.

CHAPTER 9

JEANNE

Jeanne snapped awake. It was night, and Grandmother's cradling branches rocked her slowly in the soft wind. Her eyelids drooped, and she forced them open. She was still tired from the healing she had done that day. She needed sleep, but Jeanne resisted the urge to go back to sleep. She felt uneasy, but she wasn't sure why. Something had awakened her. Had it only been a dream? Jeanne tried to remember what she had been dreaming. There had been a presence looming over Grandmother, a huge shadow that towered over both of them.

Jeanne gripped the branches along her arms. She didn't hear or see anything nearby, but she had the feeling that *something* was coming. Something angry. Something that hated with all its being. The hatred and anger were almost overwhelming.

"Grandmother?" she whispered softly.

I sense it also, the soft rustle came. Another branch swung before her to spread its leaves over the girl. **Be very still; do not let it know you are here.**

Jeanne obeyed, hiding deeper under the leaves. *You don't see me,* she projected outward. *You see only what you expect to see. You sense only what you expect.*

If it was indeed their neighbor, it would expect Grandmother to be dead, or nearly so. Would it notice that the being had recovered?

You see only what you expect to see. You sense only what you

56

expect. Jeanne wasn't sure if her ability to control emotions would work on this being. It had to be much older and much more powerful than a witch or an elemental, and she no longer had the Ring of Calada to enhance her ability. But she could try. *You see only what you expect to see. You sense only what you expect. There is nothing new. Nothing to be excited over.*

She sensed a vague puzzlement spreading through the anger. She couldn't place where the faint sensation came from at first, but then something seemed to form on the hill above them, along the rocky border of the wasteland. The being was unsure as to why it felt puzzled. *You see only what you expect to see,* Jeanne projected again. *You sense only what you expect.*

It was pleased. She could sense satisfaction spreading, replacing the puzzlement. It wanted to move closer, to gloat, but it hesitated, caution warring with triumph. Jeanne hurriedly added to the caution. The Life-hater could not cross onto Grandmother's land! She could feel Grandmother's fear and anger rising as the being hesitated. If it came closer, if it crossed the boundary, they couldn't continue to deceive it. *No need to hurry,* Jeanne projected. *You saw what you expected. Best be cautious. This can wait. It will be better if you wait.*

The being agreed. It stood there, radiating a growing mixture of satisfaction, triumph, and pleasure. Then, suddenly, it was gone.

You did something, Grandmother rustled. **What did you do? Why didn't it attack?**

Jeanne sagged back into the support of Grandmother's branches. She felt so incredibly *tired.* "I'm a Sensitive," she explained. "I can control emotions. It saw what it wanted to see." Even so, it had taken so much to influence the being's emotions. But she had done it. They had a bit more time. Time for help to arrive and time for Grandmother to heal. Time for— Her eyes closed, and Jeanne was asleep before she could complete the thought.

*   *   *

When Jeanne opened her eyes again, sunlight was already creating patterns through Grandmother's branches. She stretched. "Morning, Grandmother. How do you feel today?"

Bright growing, Jeanne, the leaves rustled. **I feel stronger.**

"So do I." Jeanne checked her surroundings as far as she could mentally reach. Their neighbor wasn't close by, although she could detect a sullen anger further into its territory. No sign of Peter, but she couldn't detect Jody, either. *Still on my own, then,* she thought. *Back to healing.*

She hurriedly ate a quick breakfast of granola and water, then climbed down to check the infection. She frowned at the moving mass next to it, wings sparkling in the sunlight. *Infection first*, she decided, *then the beetles*.

Jeanne reached out to touch one of the points of infection. She closed her eyes and concentrated on healing.

CHAPTER 10

TWYLGALIT

Wait for help to come, the mother grove said once again.

"I have waited. It's taking too long," Twylgalit argued, looking up at the surrounding treetops. "I have to get back. My grandmother needs me."

Wait. Soon you will have no cause to worry.

But Twylgalit still felt worried. As she left the grove, she decided to find Jody. The human girl had been content to wait. She had even stopped asking about returning home. But Twylgalit thought they needed to talk. Should they continue to wait, or go on? She remembered what Clarence had said before the two pren had left, several days ago. Perhaps they had waited long enough. But first she had to find Jody.

She looked first within the willow shelter. She did not find Jody there, although she did find the girl's carry bag. Twylgalit tried to think of where Jody might be. The first few days they had met each evening in the shelter, and the willow had sung the healing song over them while they slept. Twylgalit looked down at herself, looking for some sign of the illness the mother grove said she had. It was true she felt better than she had before. The paler palms of her hands were more a healthy greenish shade while her arms were her usual brown. She wanted to *leave*. Surely they were well enough now.

Jody had not returned to the shelter last night, but the willow had not been concerned about her missing the healing song. So perhaps Jody was healed. Perhaps it was time to leave.

She had not seen Jody for two days now. Where was the girl? Jody always talked about what she and Kimeka's friends had done. Twylgalit had gone with Jody and Kimeka one day to meet Kimeka's friends. The cluster was beautiful and restful, but all they did was talk—mainly about other trees within the cluster. Twylgalit had not returned with Jody the next day. She had explored the brook behind the willow instead. She had also learned to play a game the squirrels had called "tag." While they played, they had showed her where the best berries grew. The next day she had tried to find birds who knew of the lands past the Great Flood. The ones she had found had talked about mountains or deep forests. Only a few had mentioned a wasteland. But none had been there recently. Twylgalit had climbed many trees and looked out over the vast forest. But Jody had not been interested in that. Perhaps Jody was again visiting Kimeka's friends.

Twylgalit brought Jody's carry bag with her as she left the shelter. Berries grew in many places on the way to Kimeka's friends. She would surprise the human girl with an additional treat.

As she walked, Twylgalit was able to fill Jody's bag as well as herself with sweet berries. She was happy with the wonderful tastes she had found. Now Jody would not worry about being hungry on their journey back to Grandmother.

The trees whispered as Twylgalit approached the cluster of Kimeka's friends. The branches of the outer ring waved greetings, but she could see the nudges given to those trees further in.

The heady fragrances of the blossoms drifted on the wind, as did the insects intent on finding those blossoms. One butterfly lazily hovered before her face, and Twylgalit stopped and waited to see where it would land.

The large green and orange wings fluttered, and delicate black legs reached for her nose. Twylgalit held her breath—the tiny prickly feet tickled!—as the butterfly steadied itself on its perch with slow fans of its wings. It carefully turned and launched itself into the air again.

It drifted and fluttered, its flight winding between the tree trunks, and Twylgalit followed. The perfume intensified as they went deeper into the cluster. The butterfly soared and dipped, but then, as the perfume grew ever stronger, flapped more and more, rising until it reached leaf level. Twylgalit watched as it joined a multitude of others on the flower-laden branches of one of the central trees.

She heard a soft sigh beside her. "Isn't she beautiful?" Jody said.

"Yes. But there are so many of them there that I can no longer see it." Twylgalit gave up trying to locate the green and orange wings she had followed within the brightly colored group. She turned toward Jody and felt surprise strike her like a blow.

"You were looking right at her, silly." Jody looked back up into the tree's branches. "She's so beautiful."

Twylgalit struggled to find her voice. This was not a trick of the light. But how could this be? "Your...hair. It's...green."

"Isn't everyone's?" Jody asked.

Twylgalit couldn't think of a reply. The only way for this to happen was if— She glared up at the tree. "What have you done to her?"

The tree waved the very ends of her branches. **She wished to be one of us. Now she can stay.** The neighboring trees rustled in agreement.

"No! The Watcher of Gates said she would help Grandmother!" Twylgalit turned to Jody. "Tell them! Tell them you can't stay!"

"I can't?" Jody looked puzzled. "But they said I belong."

"You are not one of them!"

"She can still belong." Kimeka stepped from behind the tree. "She wants to stay. She has to stay."

Twylgalit remembered Clarence's warning. Kimeka had wanted the two pren to stay as well. "She has to leave. Now. With me." Twylgalit grabbed Jody's wrist and started out of the group.

"Hey, wait!" Jody protested.

Twylgalit ignored the girl. They had to get out of the cluster quickly, before the trees thought to stop them. Angry rustles followed them and branches began to creak above them.

"No! Come back!" Kimeka shouted.

Twylgalit hurried. Magic such as this would needs be powerful. Powerful magic like this was draining. Those responsible for this transformation would be tired. There was a chance she and Jody could escape the cluster of Kimeka's friends. They had to!

Jody kept trying to free herself, but Twylgalit was stronger. "What would Peter say?" Twylgalit shouted as she ran, pulling Jody after her. She had to remind the girl of her true roots. "What would Amy say? They would talk of your hair, as they did mine. You would never visit the mall again."

"I don't care! They like me here! They said I would be beautiful!"

"You said you did not like 'the green look.'"

"What? No, I didn't!"

Finally they reached the edge of the grouping. Twylgalit hurried, seeing the trees on either side reaching down. She tripped on a root twisting under her foot and fell. Jody crashed on top of her.

Jody pulled her wrist free and climbed to her feet. "What is your *problem*?"

Twylgalit looked up at her. Jody pushed her green hair back out of her face, knocking a wreath of flowers askew. Tiny leaves on threadlike vines dotted her blue jacket.

The nearest tree stretched limbs toward them, and Twylgalit sprang to her feet and knocked the branch-tips away. "Get away from her!" She pushed the girl out of their reach, then grabbed Jody's wrist again. "Look what they have done to my friend!" she shouted to the forest. She heard rustles of shock and horror around them. "We came to you for help!"

"Please stay!" Kimeka emerged from the cluster. "Please! Do not leave me alone!"

Twylgalit turned. "You are not alone. You have many friends right behind you. I only have my Grandmother. Jody is to save us, and you would deprive me of her help. You would change her so that she would have to stay."

Kimeka scowled. "It's no different from what the mother grove has done to you!"

Twylgalit stared at her. She listened to the disturbed whispers of the surrounding trees, remembering how many times the mother grove had told her to wait. "Is that true?" she asked. "Is it?"

We have healed you, the distant rustles of the mother grove answered.

We have healed her, Kimeka's friends replied.

"No! You've changed her!" Twylgalit glared at Kimeka. "Change her back!"

"No!" Jody protested. "You're just jealous they're making me beautiful and not you!"

Twylgalit stared at her. "You let them change you?"

Jody tossed her hair, and the wreath slipped further sideways. "They didn't change me. They're making me beautiful."

"They're making you like them!"

Jody sighed happily. "And they're so beautiful. Such lovely gowns."

Gowns? Twylgalit looked at the cluster of trees. They nodded and whispered softly. "I only see bark."

"And they have such wonderful hair styles. Do you think I'll look as good with my hair up that way?" Jody pushed the back of her hair up, and the wreath slid over her eyes.

"Oh, definitely," Kimeka agreed, stepping forward, her hands reaching toward Jody's head.

"Stay back!" Twylgalit backed away, yanking Jody with her. The wreath tumbled off Jody's head.

"Hey!" Jody protested. She reached for the fallen wreath at the same time Kimeka did, but Twylgalit pulled her back before her fingers could even brush the leaves.

Kimeka held out the wreath of flowers. "Here, Jody, let me put this back on your head."

Twylgalit moved further away, pulling Jody with her. "No. Jody, you don't want that. They do not have gowns. They do not have hair. Your hair is green. You have leaves and vines growing on you. They are changing you."

"Don't be silly. I do not. See?" Jody looked down at herself. She screamed. "Get them off! Get them off!" She brushed at her jacket with her free hand.

"Jody!" Kimeka started forward. "Do not disturb them. Here, put these flowers back in your hair."

Jody looked at her and then at the cluster of trees behind the pren. She pointed. "Where did they go? Why are there trees there? What happened? Shimmerillience!"

I am still here, came the reply from within the cluster. **Calm yourself. Breathe deeply. Do you smell the perfume?**

Twylgalit could smell the perfume as well. She stared as the blossoms on the battered wreath in Kimeka's hands stirred and opened wider, pouring more of the scent into the air.

Jody took a deep breath. "Yes, it smells wonderful." Her eyes slowly closed. A bud on the vine around her arm opened, adding its fragrance as well. Jody's eyes fluttered open and she looked at the group of trees. "There you are!"

Come back to us, Jody, the cluster called.

"Back," Jody repeated slowly.

"Back to your friends," Kimeka said.

"No!" Twylgalit grabbed the vine around Jody's arm and pulled. It clung stubbornly.

"What are you doing?" Jody protested. Kimeka started toward her with the wreath.

Twylgalit backed away, pulling Jody with her. The vine ripped loose and Twylgalit flung it at Kimeka.

"Hey!" Jody protested. "Don't you like flowers?"

"Not those." Twylgalit glared at Kimeka. "You would trick her. Change her against her will just to keep you company. You are no true friend." She turned toward the mother grove. "Did you mislead me as well?" she shouted. "Have you summoned help?"

We healed you, the mother grove whispered in reply.

Twylgalit turned away. "We are leaving."

Jody tried to pull her wrist free. "No, we're not! Let go!"

Twylgalit kept walking. Once they were out of the perfume's influence, Jody would thank her. She knew now that Jody did not want to become a tree.

"Don't leave me," Kimeka pleaded behind them.

Twylgalit kept a tight grip on Jody's wrist and kept walking.

She is nothing to us. Let them go, Kimekasensience.

Yes, you're right, came other whispers from the cluster. **Nothing.**

"No! Shimmerillience!" Jody protested. "You can't mean that! Twyl, let me go!"

Less than nothing. Better that they leave.

"No," Jody sobbed. "You don't mean that." But she stopped struggling against Twylgalit's hold.

"Please!" Kimeka shouted.

Twylgalit stopped. She looked back at the pren. *Why does she think she'll be alone? She won't be alone with Shimmerillience and the others.* "You could come with us," Twylgalit said.

Kimeka's eyes opened wide. She backed a step, one hand closing about her pendant, then she turned and ran back into the cluster.

"Let me go, too," Jody pleaded. "Let me go back to my friends."

Not wise, commented a nearby hackberry tree. **Spiteful bunch.**

"They are not your friends," Twylgalit said firmly. She began walking again.

"They are too! They gave me those beautiful flowers. They said they would make me beautiful. They said it didn't matter that I couldn't rustle my hair. They said I could stay!"

"Listen to yourself!" Twylgalit wanted to say aloud. *"'They said, they said!'"* Why was that so important? *It's the spell*, she reminded

herself. *You believed what the mother grove said.* She tried again. "You don't want to go home?"

"Home?" Jody sounded puzzled. "Of course I want to go home. Shimmerillience said my home is with them. Where are we going?"

Away, Twylgalit thought to herself. *Far away from the mother grove.* The direction she had chosen headed away from the Watcher of Gates as well, but Jody could not leave until Grandmother was safe. "Toward the Great Flood. The birds say there were wizards along its edge. We will find help there."

"What if we don't?"

"We will. The Watcher of Gates said we would."

"That nasty old tree also said we would find help in these woods, but you don't want to stay with them."

"They were not the help we needed." Twylgalit felt cheered by a sudden thought. The Watcher *had* pointed them in this direction. The mother grove was not the help they needed, but perhaps those who would truly help her Grandmother were only a short distance farther. "We will find the right ones."

CHAPTER 11

JEANNE

"Dad's right." Jeanne sighed. "He always says we should pay more attention to plant diseases." She tried to remember what her father looked for in the crops as she studied the dead branches she'd removed from Grandmother. "This lichen seems similar to something back home, but I think I've only seen this on rocks there."

Our neighbor could not create life, being so against it, but it could modify what was at hand, Grandmother rustled.

Jeanne nodded. "Just like it did with the beetles. And what was changed once, could be so again." She studied the beetles swarming over the stack of dead branches. Now that their compulsion to devour living plants had been removed, they didn't seem as creepy. And they *were* pretty, in their own way. She turned her attention back to the patch of lichen on the branch she held. "Back to rockivorous rather than herbivorous."

Rock-ivorous?

"Rock-eating, then. And I can think of some ways to turn lichen like this back against a wasteland covered with all sizes of rocks. Especially since we have volunteers willing to carry every scrap with them as they go." With a whirr of wings, a beetle alighted on the tip of the dead branch. It waved its black and white striped antenna at her, and Jeanne smiled in return.

She looked back at the patch of gray and brown lichen. Now that she had all the lichen gathered in one spot, she could be sure of returning them all to what they had been. It should be easy enough. She could see the modification with her healing sight, a slight *twist* in one spot deep within. She would place some lichen on the rocky borders within Grandmother's land and see how they did here, protected from the neighbor's attention. Then the beetles would carry the rest out to the wasteland and hide minute patches on rocks and boulders. *And then hope those escape its notice, being so tiny and so many.* Jeanne frowned thoughtfully. *It's a slow process, and unlike that thing, I don't have years to wait.* She tucked her hair back behind an ear and sighed.

Why, whatever is wrong?

"It's going to take so *long*."

Grandmother chuckled. **Oh, now that I'm stronger, I can help. And with the two of us together**—Jeanne had a brief mental image of her own grandmother rolling up her sleeves—**there isn't anything we can't accomplish. Just you wait and see.**

The tree suddenly shuddered from her roots to her branch-tips, dislodging more bits of the dying fungi mat. Several of the birds industriously digging for beetle larvae fluttered up a short distance from the trunk with scolding cries before returning to work. **I still feel... itchy.**

"They haven't finished yet," Jeanne said. "And neither have I."

The birds had appeared suddenly, one by one, while Jeanne had been trying to convince the more stubborn beetles to change their ways. One moment she had been arguing with a beetle, the next a blue blur snatched it from the trunk. Jeanne looked up. "Hey, I was talking to that!"

The blue jay swallowed and wiped its beak on the branch it was perched on. The bird eyed her and fluttered its wings like a baby chick begging for food. Jeanne could almost hear it pleading, *More?* It spotted the mass of beetles before Jeanne and swooped into the midst of them to begin picking them off the trunk. Beetles began fluttering frantically out of danger.

Grandmother had thanked her for summoning the bird, but Jeanne didn't think she had. Still, the arrival of more and more woodpeckers, nuthatches, flickers, and other winged insect-eaters she didn't recognize, all intent on digging out larvae from beneath Grandmother's bark, had meant she could turn her attention to other problems. Such as healing the wounds caused by those beetle larvae and the scavenging birds. And turning lichen back into rock-eaters. Jeanne re-focused her attention on the patch of gray and brown.

*   *   *

Jeanne was exhausted when she climbed into Grandmother's branches that evening after another healing session. Once she had finished changing all the lichen, she had placed selected bits and pieces in a rocky area near one border. The pieces were so small, and the area so large, that she didn't think their neighbor would notice anything different if it came by again that night.

She looked up at the stars through the leaves, listening to the sleepy chirps of the birds settling into their roosts higher in Grandmother's branches. "It seems to me that it would be easier to deal with this life-destroyer if we knew who or what it is. Do you know, Grandmother?"

Grandmother rustled so softly Jeanne could barely understand her. **We do not speak its name. Speaking the name summons it.**

Jeanne frowned. "Maybe, but I have to be able to name it to understand it."

Ah...to gain control over it? Yes, I see.

Jeanne blinked. She hadn't been thinking along those lines, but Grandmother was right. Vana had used a name spell to control Graylod and had tried to take Jeanne's name from her as well. She shuddered at the memory. Fortunately, her own powers as a Sensitive worked in a different direction. "Um, I need to know more *what* it is. What are its powers, what are its weaknesses—"

The wizard tried seeking its name, but it is older than most magics.

Jeanne thought about that. The being did have a more primitive, single focused, pattern than others she had encountered. *It's definitely more like the Dark One, the shadow elemental, than the flame elemental. And they were bound to Vana. So that's one weakness. But how* did *this thing get bound?*

*   *   *

Jeanne's dreams that night seemed to be filled with voices. In one, Grandmother was talking to a class of bouncy little sprouts. Whenever she paused, the class all sang out loudly, "Grow, grow!" in squeaky excited voices.

In another, Peter was in the midst of a large flock of birds. The birds were all chirping, "Go! Go! This way food!" More and more birds swirled around him until she could no longer see him.

The class of sprouts returned, and they were hopping down from their desks and spilling out of the classroom. Out of the doors, out of the windows, all the while singing, "Grow, grow, grow! Up and over! Under and around! Grow, grow, grow!"

They were so happy and bouncy that Jeanne found herself singing along as well. "Grow, grow, grow!" she said, and woke herself up.

She opened her eyes and stared at the leaves over her head. The hammock of branches rocked gently in the early morning breeze. "Something happened," she said slowly, sensing an aftertaste of magic around her. "Did you do something?"

Something, Grandmother agreed. **Come down and see.**

Jeanne didn't see anything different at the base of Grandmother's trunk. Prompted by her dreams, she walked over to the rocky area where she had placed lichen pieces the evening before. She stared.

That did not take so long, Grandmother murmured smugly.

"I'll say!" Jeanne surveyed one lichen-covered boulder with both pride and amazement. She raised her gaze to include the next boulder and the next cluster of rocks and the next beyond them, all with their accompanying patches of gray or blue or brown. The lichens were spreading toward the wasteland much faster than she had expected, even with Grandmother's magical help. "I thought this would take months, not overnight!"

The oaths of the Branch and Leaf holds even to the smallest plant. They were most eager to help. And the chewing pests as well, once the birds made their promise.

Reminded of that, Jeanne could now see the small flickers of sunlight off insect wings, as beetles launched from rock tops or scurried toward the wasteland, each with a scrap of lichen to deposit. Birds watched from Grandmother's branches, their raucous comments speeding any slowpokes. Those beetles were safe for now from bird attack, but any beetle or larva still on Grandmother was not. Jeanne watched the departing beetles and smiled. "Our neighbor won't know what hit it."

The dark spots on the white boulders resembled Appaloosa patterning. Jeanne sighed. She missed her horse. *I should have exercised Robin before I left, and Starbolt needs a workout as well. Wonder if I'll get back in time for evening chores.*

What is wrong? Is this not what you planned?

Oh no! I sound so ungrateful! Jeanne thought. She hurriedly explained, "No, this is much better than I ever hoped! It's just...I was just thinking of home."

Grandmother was silent a moment. **I miss my twiglet, too.**

Jeanne wondered where Twylgalit and Jody and Peter were. Had they found the wizards yet? Were they on their way to the wasteland? She tried once again to sense her partner, but there was only silence along their link.

She studied the horizon. She missed Peter's way of analyzing a situation. He always had a plan. Jeanne frowned thoughtfully. Perhaps he was still too far away. Or perhaps... She remembered her dream about Peter and birds. It was only a dream, but something about it bothered her. She glanced back at Grandmother's branches and the feathered occupants. "Do you know where Peter is?" she asked softly.

She didn't expect a reply, but a blue jay wiped its beak on the branch beneath it and tilted its head to study her out of one black eye. It fluttered its wings and looked at her through the other eye. "Jay! Jay!" it called. It was excited—*no*, Jeanne thought, reading the emotions deeper, *impatient. With me! What am I missing?* "Where is he?" she asked aloud.

The blue jay squawked. It rapped its beak on the branch below its black feet and looked at her.

Jeanne stared. *It's not just looking for food. It's actually trying to answer me. But I don't know what it means.*

The blue jay rapped on the branch again and looked at her. It squawked impatiently and rapped yet again.

"Grandmother," Jeanne said slowly, hoping she was guessing correctly, "are you like the Watcher?"

The Watcher of Gates is far older and wiser than I, dear.

"But I came through you."

The Watcher of Gates controls all the portals and passages. It opened one for Twylgalit to escape and for you to arrive.

"Can you talk to it?"

I can try.

"Please. Try telling it what I send you." Jeanne looked at the blue jay. It spread its wings and squawked encouragingly. She pictured the Watcher in her mind and thought at it. *I need Peter's help. Where is he?*

She sensed a faint reluctance. *Please?* she pushed.

She somehow heard a distant sigh in her mind. *Oh, very well...* It definitely sounded cranky.

"Jay! Jay!" the blue jay cried excitedly.

CHAPTER 12

PETER

Peter stumbled forward and tripped over the uneven floor. *Floor?* Recovering his balance, he turned, intending to complain. But there was no Watcher behind him. Only the remains of a stone wall with a tall panel of silver-gray wood. "Oh, great. Now what?"

He turned slowly, studying his surroundings. There was the ruined wall behind him and tumbled stone blocks that could be the remains of a matching wall off to his right. The ground fell away to his left, and he walked over to look out over the edge. "You have got to be kidding me!"

The hillside sloped down to the edge of a big lake. Was it a lake or a sea? He tried to spy the other side, but water stretched as far as he could see, muddy and still. He looked at the water's edge, wondering how deep it was.

Walking around the ruins took only seconds. There was just the one partial wall, part of a floor, and a jumble of stones. The small hillside the ruins stood on was the only patch of dry land he could see. The hill was completely surrounded by water.

Peter sighed. The Watcher really had it in for him. What did it expect him to do here? What *could* he do here? "Where is here, anyway?" he muttered. He didn't remember any large seas on his map.

He unslung his backpack and pulled out his homemade map of the Lands. Spreading it out on the floor, he looked from the map to his surroundings.

He was right. There was no large lake or sea on it. But all he had learned about the Lands had come from elves or Windkin. Perhaps this was in an area where neither had explored? Or outside the Free Lands entirely?

Peter shook his head at that thought. He had to be somewhere in the Lands. Somehow he was sure of that. But where? He couldn't even be sure he was in the same time period as Jody and Jeanne. "I thought it would be so easy," he complained. "Just head east of Windgard and—"

He paused and looked again at the map. He looked out at the water. "You dumped me in the middle of the Great Flood?" he shouted at the wall.

Peter rolled his eyes and turned back to the map. This ruin had to be somewhere in Windgard. Maybe not the actual middle, but he would find out soon enough. All he had to do was head east.

He looked up at the sky. From the sun's position, it could either be midmorning or mid-afternoon. He only needed to wait a bit, note the change in its position and then he would be able to figure out which direction was east.

A distant speck in the sky caught his attention. A faint memory came to him of being surrounded by birds, of being immersed in their calls, touched by wingtips on their way to—where?

Peter shook his head. "Weird," he decided.

*   *   *

An hour later, Peter stood at the edge of the water. The ruins had nothing he could use to build a raft, except perhaps the panel in the wall. He really wasn't tempted to try prying that loose. Even if he could remove it from the wall, standing on the wood might be dangerous. If the Watcher decided to open the portal again, who knew where he might end up next?

He eyed the muddy floodwaters. The question was, how deep was it? Would he have to swim? *Won't know until I try*, he thought. He took off his shoes and socks and tucked them into the backpack.

He balanced again on the edge. There was no point in delaying further. He had already determined which direction was east and he could use the sun to navigate during the day. He took a deep breath and waded into the water.

Surprisingly, the water was warm. He could feel the ground continue to slope downward under his feet, and the water rose higher up his legs. Finally, when the water was just above his knees, the ground leveled off.

Peter released his breath in a sigh. At least he wouldn't have to swim to the Gray Hills. He slogged eastward.

After he had walked for awhile, he began to notice something odd about the Great Flood. The water never rose higher than above his knees. Yet the ground itself wasn't level. There were times when the bottom should have dropped out from under him and times when submerged hills should have broken the surface of the water. He glanced back down into a submerged gully and shook his head. *It's almost as if there's a coating of water over everything,* he thought. *But that's*— He stopped that line of thought. Magic was at work here. He could worry about the impossibility of things once he was away from the Great Flood. Far, far away.

The sun was directly overhead when he came to dry land.

Peter stood in the flood and studied the wasteland. *If anything deserves to be underwater, it's that,* he thought. There was nothing living that he could see, only a wide stretch of sand and rocks. He couldn't see anything that stopped the flood from sweeping over this land as well. *Invisible forcefield? Maybe the wizards set up a barrier to contain the flood. But why?*

His stomach rumbled, and he decided he could study whatever barrier there was just as easily on dry land. He waded forward.

His legs and feet tingled slightly as they passed through whatever was keeping the water from the wasteland. Peter looked around the wasteland, wondering if he had set off any alarms. He wiggled his wet toes in the sand. They didn't look any different from before, other than wrinkled and pruney from being soaked too long. His stomach growled again, and he unslung his backpack and pulled out a packet of trail mix to munch.

When he examined the barrier from this side, it was almost as if he was looking into an aquarium. The water just stopped at some invisible boundary. He bent down and tried to tap on the "glass," but his fingers just passed through the barrier. He waggled his fingers in the water, then pulled his hand out again. "Hmm."

Peter straightened. Interesting as this was, he needed to find Jeanne and Jody. He turned toward the east. There were hills not too far distant. He'd find out soon enough if they were the Gray Hills. He put the sunflower and pumpkin seed mix in one of his pockets, picked up his backpack, and started walking again.

Gray, gray, and more gray. Peter wondered if walking on the moon was this boring. There was nothing around but gray sand, gray rocks, and gray ground so dry it was cracked. *Spirit* and *Opportunity* probably found more exciting things on Mars than he was finding here. It resembled the area around a volcanic eruption, all coated with gray dust. The very air smelled dry and dusty. Peter was also strongly reminded of the war-torn hillsides in the television news, where the land looked so damaged and blown up and destroyed that he could never think of why they were all fighting over *that.*

His bare feet protested about the rocks, and Peter sat down to put his shoes back on. His legs and feet had dried as he had walked, but the legs of his jeans were still damp. He wrung out some water as he unrolled them.

He was about to climb to his feet and move on when he noticed the ground below him. Where the water had fallen didn't look so...dead anymore. He pulled a water bottle from his pack and sprinkled a few drops on the ground. The water vanished without a trace, and the ground remained dry and gray. "Regular water, no effect," he muttered. He squeezed a few more drops from his jeans. The ground darkened, turning from gray to almost dirt-colored.

Peter looked back the way he had come. *Must be something special about the flood. And I'll bet it wasn't the wizards who put up that barrier. Maybe I've found Twyl's neighbor.* He looked about the wasteland and grinned thoughtfully.

CHAPTER 13

ELIN

Elin could see the worry in Salanoa's eyes as she straightened his mane. "Think about it, Elin. You and I are the only ones sensing this. The Winds haven't reported anything unusual to the Windrunner." She glanced over to where the tall black stallion was conversing with Graylod and the green-cloaked Guardian. "The Green knows they've reported everything else our spell has done so far."

Elin stamped his hoof. "There's something *wrong*." He looked out at the Great Flood. "Out there. Somewhere." He lowered his voice and edged closer to whisper, "I can't help but feel whatever it is somehow related to what we found when we tracked the srikes."

The brown wizard looked at him quizzically. Elin tilted his head to indicate a browsing Windkin whose path had begun to wander their way. The old one was supposedly watching the flood, but his ears were canted toward them.

Salanoa nodded. He knew she would understand that the topic of magic was still frowned upon by the herd. Even though magic was being used to restore the land damaged by the witches, some of the herd had decided that the wizards needed to be watched. Elin, being both an outcast Windkin and a new wizard-in-training, was even more suspect.

Salanoa casually began to walk away from the forest's edge, and Elin followed.

Once they were out of earshot, she resumed their conversation. "The Windlords' Gate? But it was sealed by the Council long ago. And still sealed when we came across it, despite the srikes' efforts." She touched the brown stone of her pendant. "I wonder if Vana planned to use it to escape the Lands."

Shaking her head, Salanoa looked out across the Great Flood. "There's...something to the east of Windgard. Somewhere in the Gray Hills. There's a need..."

She released her pendant with a sigh. "But that's all I can sense now. All my magic is tied into restoring Windgard." She turned back to Elin. "We have to discover what this disturbance could be. No offense, my friend, but I for one would like you out of my dreams."

Elin flicked his ears. "But I—"

The wizard gazed thoughtfully back at the flood. "You were telling us something and we weren't listening."

"We?"

"For some reason I thought the Watcher was with us."

"But we weren't in the Watcher's meadow," Elin said, confused. "We were in Windgard."

"I know. It was a dream, not a vision." Salanoa shook her head slightly and smiled at him. "Now, much as we would both like to charge across the flood, you know we can't risk disturbing the spells yet. You feel whatever this is is related to our trip. You must have seen something back then. What better test of your new powers than solving this riddle? You have the Ring of Calada. I'm sure it will help you relive that time."

"Jeanne hated the visions it kept sending her," Elin grumbled.

"But this is your memory. You, a Windkin! Windkin never forget anything!" Salanoa studied him with mischief in her smile. "Aren't you the least bit curious?"

Elin sighed deeply. He was *very* curious. So many things had happened right before the witches invaded the Land and cast the curse. Had the curse affected his memory? Had he seen something then that still needed resolving? He closed his eyes and lowered his head to touch the gold ring on a light chain around his neck. *Very well,* he thought to the ring, *show me what I've forgotten.*

*   *   *

Kelan the wizard slammed the massive book of spells shut with a bang. Black brows lowered as he glared at his student. "I taught you to read so that you could study lore on your own, not dip your nose into spellbooks!"

Elin of the Windkin shuffled his hooves and studied the pattern of the carpet, keeping one eye on the hem of the black robe before him. "I'm sorry, sir. But in the tale I was reading, the leprechaun used a spell that was so—I mean, he stopped a witch with it! I had to read it for myself. And then, I, uh, saw another spell from a different tale and, uh..." He risked a glance upward and saw a faint smile twinkle in the wizard's dark eyes.

Kelan frowned sternly at him, but his eyes still smiled. "I suppose you're no different from any other apprentice I've had. But I had expected better behavior." The wizard settled himself on the only corner of the long table free of stacked books and manuscripts. "Did it work?" he snapped abruptly.

Elin backed a step. "T-the spell? I-I didn't try it," he stammered. "My people can't do magic."

"So they say." Kelan frowned thoughtfully, smoothing his small black mustache. "Very well, then, show me what you've learned. Recite some of the spells."

The gray-and-white spotted colt raised his head, worriedly glancing at the massive spellbook. "I...can't, sir."

Kelan's black brows lifted. "Can't? What do you mean, can't? You couldn't have forgotten them. A Windkin never forgets anything."

Elin's ears lowered and his long tail twitched. "No, I haven't forgotten them. It's just that I...uh..."

"Yes?" The Lore-Master waited as Elin's head sank lower and lower. "By the Green, Elin, what stops you?"

"I don't want the spell to happen," Elin said miserably.

"I thought your people couldn't do magic."

"They can't!" Remembering that he was speaking to a wizard, Elin refrained from stamping a hoof. "Some spells don't require magical ability."

"Ah, so you discovered those spells as well. Just how thoroughly did you read this book?"

Elin's ears flickered. He had hoped the wizard wouldn't ask that.

Kelan smoothed his mustache again. "Recite the water-seeking spell; that's an easy enough one."

Elin squirmed uncomfortably. He didn't want to disobey his master, but the idea of actually saying a magic spell aloud went too strongly against the ways of his people. What if the Windrunner heard?

"Look at me, colt," Kelan said firmly. Elin lifted his head. The wizard snapped his fingers. "Elin, do you know the name-spell used to bind Vana the Immortal?"

Elin found himself unable to hedge or lie. "Yes, sir."

"I thought that was your hair I found." Kelan nodded. "Recite it."

To his horror, Elin felt his mouth open, his tongue beginning to form the words. He fought against the compulsion. "I...can't!"

Kelan snapped his fingers again, and Elin's mouth closed so quickly that he almost bit his tongue. One brow lifted as the wizard studied his apprentice. "I think you've been dabbling more than a little in my spellbooks, Elin."

Elin hung his head. "I remembered that queen's name from the tales of our Memory-Keepers and when I came across it, I couldn't resist reading—"

"I wasn't referring to the name-spell. Although how you just *happened* to come across it in a book hidden by both a false panel and an illusion, I'll inquire into some other time." Elin tried to look blankly innocent, and the wizard's eyes smiled.

"No, Elin, I was referring to what you did a moment ago. Not many beings can resist the truth-compulsion I set on you. A small one, true, but not one easy to break." The wizard retrieved a small crystal globe from the clutter atop the table and studied it idly. "Elin, why did you come here?"

"To study lore," Elin said, puzzled. "You're the Lore-Master; you know more about the Lands than anyone."

"To study lore," Kelan repeated. "But not to learn magic?"

Elin's mane rippled as he shook his head.

"Which, I suppose, is why I found your long nose deep in my spellbook today." Kelan smiled wryly. "If you can read the spells without any twinges from your Windkin conscience, why won't you repeat them back to me, so that I can test your memory of them like any other bit of lore?"

Elin laid his ears back. "I don't want the spell to happen."

Kelan sighed in exasperation. "If you don't want the spell to happen, you simply make the hand gesture while..." His voice died as his gaze fell upon his pupil's four hooves.

Elin resisted the urge to ask "what hands?" and instead said helpfully, "I could always wiggle my ears."

The Lore-Master chuckled and shook his head. "If you wouldn't insist on poking your nose where it doesn't belong..." He smoothed his mustache thoughtfully, glancing at the shelves of books and stacked manuscripts lining the walls. "I seem to recall..." He set the small crystal on the table beside him and rose to his feet, starting toward the nearer shelves.

Elin turned away, hoping the Lore-Master would not find whatever it was that he was seeking. He glanced nervously at the window and was relieved to find it shut. If it had been open when Kelan had found him reading that spell, Elin knew the Winds would have carried their conversation to the Windrunner. Elin shuddered at the thought. He was outcast from the herd already for just talking with wizards. If the Windrunner learned he was reading magic as well, any hopes he had of ever re-joining the herd would be permanently trampled.

He stifled a sigh as he watched the wizard. It had been such fun finding the Lore-Master's hidden spellbooks. He had almost located the last of them, too. The elaborate illusions, concealed panels, and such probably would have been baffling to a sense-dulled human, but not to a Son of the Wind.

Elin raised his head, whuffling the air. He glanced at the wizard still staring thoughtfully at the shelves, then studied the room. Magic was being used here and if not by Kelan, then by whom? The scent was very familiar.

He followed his nose to the table and backed a step when he saw the cause. "Kelan! The crystal is glowing!"

The light about the small globe brightened as the clear crystal suddenly began to fill with brown. Elin pricked his ears. "That's Salanoa's color! Kelan!"

"Yes? What is it?" the Lore-Master said absently. He replaced one volume and pulled down another, rapidly scanning the pages.

"Salanoa's contacting you through the crystal! May I stay? I'll be very quiet."

Kelan lowered black brows and looked at him with a mock-fierce expression. "Quiet? Colt, you don't know the meaning of the word." He returned to his study of the book he held, but—to Elin's relief—started walking slowly toward the table. "Salanoa, shall I let him stay? I warn you, though, his word can't be trusted. I found him looking through my spellbooks."

At the Lore-Master's acknowledgment of the spell-caster, light shimmered above the globe and reformed into a small faint image of the brown wizard.

Elin flicked his ears at the seeming of his friend. With its small size and apparent ability to hover in midair, Salanoa's image bore a slight resemblance to the fairies of the Great Woods. But only from a distance. As he moved closer, he could see that the wizard's travel attire of earth-colored tunic and loose trous was not the fairies' scalelike garb, nor was her long brown hair their feathery down.

Salanoa shook her heard, her long braid swinging. "Poor Kelan. And when could any apprentice resist a look through your spellbooks? You had ample warning of this one's arrival."

She turned back to Elin with a friendly grin. "Did he tell you that he foresaw having an apprentice again before you were even born? Of course, he thought at the time that you would be either an elf or a dwarf."

"So much the better that he's not," Kelan grumbled. "You know how much elves and dwarfs dislike studying other people's histories. But they at least stay out of spellbooks when they're told."

"Oh, they do?" Salanoa asked in an amused tone of voice. "How about when—"

"That was my own fault," Kelan said hastily. "I left the book open."

Salanoa's grin widened. "And then I heard about the time when Nee—"

Kelan slammed the book closed. "That pesky dwarf was never my apprentice! And when I—"

He stopped at Salanoa's merry peal of laughter. "I thought that would get your attention! I refuse to pass on important messages to you when you're reading, Kelan; you forget them as soon as they're spoken."

"Salanoa—" the Lore-Master began in a dangerous tone.

"Don't look so disappointed, Elin," Salanoa continued blithely. "I'll tell you about your predecessors some other time."

"Promise?"

Kelan laughed. "Don't give him ideas, Salanoa!" He put the book down and raised his hands so that she could see them. "You mentioned a message?"

Salanoa nodded, all amusement gone. "More of a request, actually. Srikes have recently been seen flying into the Windgard, and Graylod and I believe that the Shadows seek something here in the Lands."

"You and Graylod. Not those on the Council?"

The brown wizard sighed. "Seemingly not. They reminded us that nothing happened after the elves first reported srikes entering the Lands."

"Nothing other than that the Watch Tower was opened once again and guards placed on the borders of the Shadow Lands," Kelan disagreed. "Don't tell me that they plan to change that! We can't turn our backs on evil just because we once managed to exile a few of the Shadows' minions."

"According to the Council of the Wise, we should do exactly that!" Salanoa scowled.

"What did you do this time, Salanoa?" Kelan prodded when the silence seemed to lengthen.

She grinned twistedly. "Me? Kelan, you know I am a model of discretion, ever resorting to diplomacy to make my point."

Elin snorted.

"Yes, I know," the Lore-Master said dryly. "What did you do this time? And why do you need my help? Surely Graylod—no, that's right, he's worse than you when it comes to dealing with the Council. If such is possible." He sighed in exasperation. "What did you do and why do you need my help?"

Salanoa fingered the pendant around her neck. "I've had reports that srikes have been flying over Windgard and along the Silvergreen Hills. I don't know if the Windkin have noticed anything, since I'm looking at the only one who would talk to me." She smiled at Elin.

"Windgard along the Silvergreen Hills," Kelan mused. "That was once human lands."

"It was the Children of the Winds' before them," Elin inserted. Kelan looked at him, and Elin lowered his ears and kept quiet.

"And after the Windlords," the Lore-Master continued, watching his apprentice, "at least four kingdoms occupied that land before the humans withdrew to the Last Kingdom." He shook his head. "There could be any number of ruins or objects buried in that area. What would interest the Shadows after all this time?"

"I was hoping you would know." Salanoa sighed. "I plan to follow the srikes and attempt to discover just what it is that they seek. And, just to prove to the Council that there is danger in srikes entering the Lands, I've challenged Telynalle to come with me."

"Telynalle?" Kelan smoothed his mustache. "Good choice. For an elf, she's more open-minded than most of the Council."

"But not by much." She scowled. "I grow weary of beating against the closed wall of their minds! Have they forgotten the past so quickly?"

"And how many times have I asked that same question?" Kelan

studied the image of the brown wizard. "Very well, I shall search my records to see what could attract the srikes."

"Actually, Kelan, I was hoping you would come with us."

Kelan drew himself up. "Wizard of the Brown, it is impossible for me to be searching my records *and* wandering all over the Lands at the same time! However..." A delighted grin spread across his face. "If you need someone with instant recall of lore, you can take my apprentice."

Elin perked up his ears. Had he heard that correctly? "Me? I can go?" He pranced excitedly.

Salanoa grinned. "Just the person! But, Elin, you're outcast, and we'll be crossing Windgard. Are you certain you wish to come?"

Elin stopped and looked at his master. "The Windrunner knows I'm your apprentice. The Winds would have told him long ago. So long as I don't attempt to rejoin the herd, they'll probably just ignore me."

Kelan nodded. "I don't think that's what Salanoa meant, though."

"Elin—" Salanoa started.

Elin snorted in amusement. "Can I endure being ignored? Salanoa, in the eyes of some of the herd, I've been outcast since the day I first spoke to Kelan—and I was just a season-old foal when he last visited Windgard! I'm not of the herd anymore. I don't care what they think of me."

Salanoa looked at him as if she could see into his heart, and Elin tried not to squirm under that gaze. Then she nodded. "Very well. Kelan, could you send him to me? I'm at—"

"If you're about to suggest that I waste a perfectly good place-shift spell on this lazy apprentice, don't. He can use the exercise."

Elin shuddered. "No spell. You know how fast I can run, Salanoa."

Salanoa held out her hands in the peace gesture. "No insult intended, Elin. I'll wait for you by the Ea below the Highlands. Kelan, you will contact me if you find word of anything the Shadows might seek?" At his nod, she touched her pendant, and her image vanished.

"I see I'll have to wait to hear what spells you've learned," Kelan commented. He picked up the small crystal and stood looking into it for a brief moment. "A long time," he said absently, "but perhaps I will, before.." He closed his eyes and set the crystal down.

"Kelan?" Elin asked uneasily. "Shall I leave now?"

"Hmm?" Kelan's dark eyes opened. "Leave? Without—" He stopped and smiled, studying the Windkin. "It seems odd not to have to prepare food and clothing for my apprentice to take on his journey." He shook his head. "Now, apprentice, so that we may coordinate our searches, I'm going to establish a mindlink with you. I know you don't want to do magic, but I'll be controlling the spell, and it will only be for communication. You can talk to me at anytime and I will be able to pass on to you whatever I've found."

Elin glanced at the closed windows. "Only for talking?"

"Nothing else. I would have given you a crystal, but without hands..."

Elin braced himself. "Very well."

Kelan chuckled. "Stop acting as if you're about to be executed. And bring your head down to where I can reach it, young giant."

Elin obeyed, closing his eyes as the wizard neared him. He felt the touch of the wizard's hand between his eyes.

There. Can you hear me?

"Of course I can hear you. There's nothing wrong with my ears."

You aren't hearing me through your ears.

Elin opened one eye. "I'm not?" He decided to try the mindlink himself. *Can you hear me?*

"Excellent!" Kelan beamed proudly at him. "Now, you'd best be off. Don't stop to talk to everyone along the way, and stay out of the Highlands."

*   *   *

Elin stopped atop the sun-baked ridge and glanced back at the white castle nestled in the green valley. It seemed tiny, compared with the elf halls and dwarf caverns and human castles that filled the tales he had studied, but Kelan had wanted a still smaller dwelling to house his many books and only one tower for his star-scanner. The wizard had not reckoned on the dwarfs from the nearby Healic Ranges, however. Objecting to the "hovel" he had planned, the dwarfs had built instead the three-towered white-stoned castle, with doorways and stairs designed to accommodate any of the Free Folk who might visit. Elin twitched his tail at the memory of some tight squeezes and amended that to "almost any."

"Still, I feel more at home there than I ever did in Windgard," he said aloud. A light breeze whispered around him, tugging at his mane, and Elin tossed his head defiantly. "And you can tell the Windrunner that I said so!" he added, glaring at the empty air about him.

Turning his back on Llyfrgell Castle, he scrambled down the faint path. In the distance the magical Ea sparkled in the sunlight. He would follow the stream south out of Dewin Heights, then detour west around the Highlands before rejoining and crossing it at the northwestern border of Windgard, home of the Windkin. He tried not to think of what his welcome would be like.

*   *   *

Elin stood fetlock deep in the cool water and looked wistfully at the wide expanse of plain before him. The long grasses dipped and swayed with the playful winds, beckoning him home. Windgard. The most beautiful spot in the Free Lands. The breeze tugged at his mane, swirled about him with the scent of sweet grass and flowers. His hooves itched to race, but Elin held himself back from following the insistent breeze.

The apprentice studied the far bank, hoping to locate Salanoa before crossing the Ea into Windgard. Despite his brave words to the wizards, Elin was still worried. The only outcast in Windkin lore that had returned to the herd had challenged the then Windrunner and been killed. Elin didn't plan anything so foolish, but he still felt as if he would be marked for death the moment he crossed the border. A gust of wind struck him, and the outcast looked about apprehensively. Where were the sweeprunners? He hadn't expected to see them, but he should at least have heard their warnings to the herd.

"Elin!"

The outcast groaned inwardly at the sight of the blue-black youngling racing toward him. This was going to be worse than he had thought. Resignedly, he crossed the stream and waited for Hahle.

The young sweeprunner slid to a halt before him. "You're back!" He play-lunged, then spun away and galloped excitedly around his friend. "You're back! I told Renw you'd come back! I told him!"

"Hahle—" Elin tried uselessly. Why couldn't Renw have been patrolling this area?

Hahle reared slightly. "Race you to the herd!"

Elin shook his mane. "I'm not going back to the herd."

Hahle turned and came back to him. "It might be rough at first, but Renw and I will be there. And I'm sure that once you explain to the Windrunner you've changed your ways, he'll let you back into—"

"I haven't changed my ways and I don't plan to rejoin the herd." Elin stamped a hoof. "Hahle, I'm apprentice to the Lore-Master now. He sent—"

"That black-robed wizard?" Hahle's ears flickered uneasily. "The one whose castle Renw and I trailed you to? Then you were serious, what you said then? About studying…magic?" He spat the word as if it was an ill-tasting weed.

"Lore," Elin corrected gently, but not without an inward twinge. "I'm studying lore, not magic. Like our Memory-Keepers. Hahle, I'm learning to keep the memories of the Free Lands! It's important to me."

"More important than friends, huh?" The blue-black ears lowered.

"Hahle—"

"First you, then Renw. I don't have any friends left."

Elin flicked his ears in puzzlement. What had Renw done? He shook his head. "Hahle, I'm still your friend. I'll always be your friend." He glanced along the border. "And as your friend, sweeprunner, I think you'd better warn the herd that I'm here before you get into trouble."

Hahle lowered his head. "I don't care. Why do they have to know, anyhow?"

"Hahle, it's your duty—"

"Elin, if you're not rejoining the herd, you're still outcast. And an outcast can't—the herd will— What are you *doing* here?"

Elin butted his head gently against Hahle's side. "Crossing Windgard, like any other traveler. Go on, sweeprunner. Warn them. I don't mind. The Winds have already told the Windrunner, anyway. You don't want to get into trouble." He caught a familiar scent, but did not let that distract him. "If you don't, Hahle, I will."

Hahle looked at him rebelliously, then opened his mouth.

"And make sure you announce us correctly, Hahle," Salanoa said from behind the black.

Hahle turned so quickly that he bumped into Elin. His eyes showed white as he stared at the brown-garbed wizard.

Salanoa grinned mischievously at him as she leaned forward on her staff. "The last time, you announced me as a dwarf. So much for the famed Windkin eyesight. Now, we are two wizards and one apprentice."

Hahle slowly backed up into Elin. "H-how—"

"Illusion." Elin moved out of his friend's way, wondering how Hahle could have missed the scent of the approaching spell. "She's a wizard, remember?"

Hahle shook his head as if to clear it. "She knows the signals!"

The wizard studied the end of her waist-length braid and flicked it back over her shoulder. "How could I not learn the signals, as many times as I cross Windgard?"

Hahle opened his mouth, shut it, then tried again. "*Two* wizards? But I see only—"

Salanoa frowned at the horizon. "She was supposed to meet me right— Ah, there she is."

The air *rippled* before her. Elin had the brief impression of feathers, of a wing raised and settled, and suddenly the scent of magic filled his nostrils.

An elf stood before them.

With a squeal, Hahle startle-jumped and bolted.

Elin stood quietly, studying Telynalle. The elf-wizard was taller than Salanoa, almost his height. White and blue feathers were braided into her long light brown hair and dangled from her blue and white robes. More white feathers made up the panels running down from her shoulders. Her loose hair flowed over her shoulders to just below her knees, and down her back into an elaborate construction from midwaist down.

The large blue eyes studied him in turn, the pale eyebrows rising slightly as he sniffed to catch and fix all of her scent—a curious mixture of magic and birds—in his memory.

"You are a bold one, sweeprunner," she commented.

"You frightened away the sweeprunner," Salanoa chided. "This youngling is Elin, Kelan's new apprentice." Elin bowed to the wizard as deeply as he would to the Windrunner. "Elin, this is Telynalle of the High Council."

The elf looked surprised and somehow pleased. "Kelan's apprentice? A Fleogen has left the herd? Has the spirit of Helundar returned?"

Elin started slightly as a cluster of white feathers on the elf's shoulder suddenly moved. A black beak emerged from her hair, followed by a crest of blue feathers. Black beady eyes set in a band of black feathers blinked sleepily, then suddenly pinned. Snapping fully awake, a fledgling blue jay flapped its stubby wings and squawked at him.

Elin snorted in reply and Salanoa smiled. "A new apprentice?" she asked.

The fledgling shrieked alarm at her as well, and the elf winced at the loud cry next to her ear. "An apprentice would be less trouble." She ran a finger along the white breast feathers, calming the young bird. "I but convey it, since it has only begun gliding. Its parents will join us shortly."

Elin could hear Hahle at a distance give the warning calls for the herd. Salanoa cocked her head and smiled. "Sounds as if he's recovered from his fright. At least he has the calls right—I was expecting a warning about evil bird-creatures."

The elf ignored her and looked across Windgard. "We have a distance to travel. Shall we begin?"

Salanoa grinned ruefully behind the elf's back at Elin, and he shook his head at her. Teasing a wizard was dangerous enough, and when the wizard was an elf as well... Elin stopped that thought and flicked his ears, remembering elves he had met that had a stranger sense of humor than Salanoa.

"I still do not understand why we could not have gathered by the northern Silvergreen Hills and begun our search there," the elf complained as they walked.

Salanoa shrugged. "Other than having so many place-shift spells risk alerting whomever sent the srikes that wizards were nearby. You and I were at the Council, Elin was at Kelan's in Dewin Heights, this was the closest location." She patted Elin's shoulder and added softly, "And I would not have you cross Windgard alone."

Elin murmured an equally soft "thank you," but the elf glanced at them curiously and he was certain she had heard. Elfin hearing was very sensitive. But she did not comment further.

They had not traveled too far when shrill *jays* sounded overhead. Wings whirred as an adult blue jay descended, landing before the elf. It hopped forward on its black feet and cawed at her.

Telynalle glanced skyward, where another blue jay circled off to their right. "There's a Fleogen paralleling us. It's not the same one as was at the border."

Elin shook his mane. "No, Hahle had to stay on sweeprun. The Windrunner would have sent someone else to run escort."

Salanoa shrugged as the elf glanced at her. "Fleogende custom. One gets used to being followed." The brown wizard looked over at the circling jay. "That's not nice," she called to it. "He's supposed to stay out of our sight. Just act as if he's not there." The jay shrilled its raucous call, then swooped down.

Elin winced as the jay dropped waste as it finished its dive and climbed upward again. He only hoped the escort wasn't someone he knew.

The elf walked onward and the blue jay at her feet fluttered up to join its fledgling on her shoulder. "Birds don't pretend."

Salanoa and Elin exchanged glances behind her, and Elin shook his mane. This was going to be a long trip.

CHAPTER 14

JODY

"I'm tired," Jody complained. They'd been walking for *hours*! Jody still couldn't see why they had to leave Kimeka and her friends. All because they were going to make her beautiful. It wasn't fair!

Twyl tilted her head as if listening to something. "We should be safe here." She handed Jody a familiar bag.

"That's mine!"

"I know. You left it at the willow. I filled it with berries for you."

Jody had started to open it, then stopped, horrified. Everything inside was probably all sticky now with berry juice. It would never be the same again.

Twyl was still talking. "You can probably save those for later. I see more berries over here." She walked over to the orange spotted bush.

Jody sat down on the ground. "I'm not hungry," she said. Her bag was ruined. How could she think about food? She watched as Twyl picked berries from the bush and began eating. *She's not even offering me any*! Her stomach rumbled.

Suddenly Jody felt warmth beneath her right hand from where it rested on the ground. The warmth spread, from the ground to her hand, from her hand up her arm. Jody quickly pulled her hand away, but the warmth lingered. She shook her hand. Her fingertips tingled.

Her jacket *rustled*. Jody looked down, and sprang to her feet. "Get them off! Get them off!" There were leaves on her jacket, and they were moving!

She tried to pull off her jacket, but it seemed to be stuck to her! "Twyl! Help me!"

Twyl hurried to her side. "What did you do?"

"What do you mean, what did *I* do? I didn't stick leaves all over myself! Get them off! They're moving!"

"Stand still, or this may hurt." Twyl cautiously plucked a leaf. Jody shuddered as she saw tiny rootlets come loose with it. Out of *her* jacket! "Shimmerillience controlled them before," Twyl said as she reached for another leaf. "Her cluster doesn't want you now. You must have done something."

Jody shook her head. "I didn't do anything!" She thought back. "Well, the ground got warm and then my hand got warm, but I didn't do it."

Twyl's eyes grew wide. "They changed you that much!" She caught up both of Jody's hands and examined the palms.

"What?" Jody demanded. She looked at her hands. Were they that dirty? Her left palm did look grass-stained, and she remembered that she had been leaning on that hand. She rubbed at the stain. It almost looked as if the green stain was below the skin.

"We have to find someone to help us," Twyl said.

Jody was so tired of hearing that. She opened her mouth to say so, just as Twyl added, "Before it's too late for you."

Jody froze, her mouth still open. *What* had Twyl said? What did she mean by that?

Twyl glanced up at the sky. "Can you move your feet?"

"What's *that* supposed to mean?"

Twyl hurried back to the bush, snatched a few more berries, then looked back at her.

"Walk. Can you walk? We need to keep moving."

"Now? But we just stopped! And what about these leaves on me?"

"Pull them out as we go. They're not too deep—"

A coughing roar from overhead startled them both.

CHAPTER 15

JEANNE

Grandmother's "something" had energized more than just the lichen. Jeanne spotted more and more patches of green as she explored Twylgalit's home. Moss now ringed her favorite boulder near Grandmother. Other tiny sprouts had appeared beneath the shadow of Grandmother's branches, but Jeanne didn't know yet what those might be. *Weeds? Flowers? I should be able to recognize these, but I don't.* She looked upward and realized she was almost directly below the roosts. *The seeds could come from anywhere in the Lands.* Jeanne wondered how far Grandmother's magic had spread. She remembered the patch of grass she had seen near the ruined house and turned her steps in that direction.

She was cheered to see how much the grass had spread around the ruins. *Much more than before*, she decided. And among the green she could see spots of color. *Flowers? Wildflowers? Didn't Mr. Ludwigson say in Science class that seeds could stay dormant for a long time? And only start growing when conditions were right?*

She suddenly remembered how her father had to pull up stumps in the fields because trees would grow back. She turned toward the skeletal trees near the ruins. After a close examination, she found several shoots of new leaves near the base of each. She checked if any were affected by the fungus that had sickened Grandmother. *None, so far. Now if you all just stay healthy...* She was sad to see that all the new growths were pure tree, without a trace of the *humanness* that Grandmother and Twylgalit had. *Still, I guess that—*

She stopped when she saw a figure alongside the ruins. It beckoned to her to follow.

What is that? I can see it, but I can see through *it.* The emotions she could sense from it felt like a distant echo. There was sadness, but a faint happiness as well. The shape flickered suddenly, and although she could now see a smiling man, he was even more transparent than before.

"Are...are you the wizard who lived here?" she asked.

He didn't look like a wizard. He had no beard, and, rather than a long robe, he appeared to be wearing a loose shirt and breeches.

The figure smiled and nodded, then gestured again for her to follow. *I wonder if Grandmother knows she has a ghost,* Jeanne thought. She was about to ask, but the figure held a finger to his lips.

The spirit floated over to the landslide and hovered near where broken branches emerged from the debris. Then, still smiling, it slowly faded away.

Jeanne eyed the unsteady mound of dirt, rock slabs, and broken trees. Climbing carefully, she found a level place to stand, close to one of the branches, and then concentrated, searching for any trace of life. She reached deeper and deeper. She could barely detect a faint...

Suddenly her eyes snapped open. Something angry had touched her awareness! She looked up and saw an armor-clad figure atop the bluff. Behind her, the blue jay shrieked an alarm cry. She could hear the rush of wings as birds swarmed into the protection of Grandmother's branches.

Jeanne kept her attention on the being above her. Anger grew within it as it looked beyond her. Its gaze returned to her.

"How dare you." The voice was cold. The being raised a hand, and a spinning ball of violet shot from the palm to hurtle toward her.

Leaves suddenly swirled around her, forming a protective bubble, and the ball vanished against it with small explosion of light. The being roared and started forward, then stopped as abruptly as if it had run into a wall.

The binding still holds, Grandmother remarked. **You cannot enter here.**

The armored being lowered the hand testing the invisible barrier. "So you still live, tree." Its hatred and anger grew as it realized it had been deceived. The helmet turned to regard Jeanne. "You are on a fool's errand," it said to Jeanne. "You cannot hope to stop me."

"We already have," Jeanne said. She hoped she was able to hide how badly she was trembling inside. *If Grandmother hadn't protected me just now...*

"But not for long." The helmet was still turned in her direction and Jeanne wondered how it could see without eye slits in the armor. "You are not of the blood. Where is the last?"

Out of your reach, Grandmother retorted.

"Where is it?" the being repeated, ignoring Grandmother and still looking at Jeanne.

Jeanne was irritated at its rudeness. "She said, 'out of your reach.'"

It can't hear me, dear. It doesn't have the patience to listen.

"Oh, my reach is very long, as the binder's kin discovered." The helmet turned to look back across the wasteland. "So it is gone. And a human in its place. You think to replace it? You are not of the binder's kin. You would be wise not to interfere."

What would Salanoa say? "Wiser still to follow the way of the Wise. And they so often interfere, don't they?" Jeanne replied, trying to sound cryptic. She remembered the brown wizard's teachings. *Act as if you know what you are doing and your enemy may believe it. So I keep it uneasy and it may misstep.*

The helmet swung back to regard her again. *It's definitely wondering about me now.* Suspicion and uncertainty radiated from the being. Impatience and anger rose again. It turned away.

"I will find the last of your blood, tree. It cannot hide from me. It is outside your protection now. Once I've dealt with the last, then I will come back for you." The armored creature started to step away.

The blue jay shrieked a warning as the being turned back and shot another ball at Jeanne.

The leaf swirling bubble was still in place, however, and the violet ball exploded harmlessly. **So very predictable,** Grandmother commented.

The being roared in fury and raised both hands. Then, just as Jeanne braced herself for the attack, the armored figure suddenly hesitated.

Jeanne was startled. The being was afraid. Something had happened, something that the being feared. *I can add to that fear*, she thought, spotting an opening. The increased fear triggered paranoia, and she added to that as well.

The being backed a step.

What is wrong with it? Grandmother asked.

"I don't know yet," Jeanne whispered back.

She couldn't detect anything near it. Jeanne shut down her link to the armored figure before it could become aware of her influence and scanned outward from Grandmother's land. *Peter!* She could detect Peter out on the wasteland! *He must have done something. But what?* She hid her excitement as the being lowered its hands. "The tree can't protect you forever," it said coldly. It turned and strode away.

I've got to warn Peter! Jeanne thought. She concentrated, finding the link to her partner.

What happened? Why is it leaving? Grandmother rustled.

"I don't know," Jeanne said, trying to send her message to Peter at the same time. He seemed pleased with himself. "I think Peter did something that frightened it."

Peter? Your friend? Then Twylgalit returns? Fear and worry rose in the tree being. **We must warn her!**

Jeanne paused. She didn't sense anyone near Peter. *Where are Jody and Twylgalit?* "I don't think Twylgalit is with him. She might still be safe."

But not for long. Grandmother sighed with a rustle of leaves, and Jeanne could feel the tree being's concern and resolve. **I'm healed now. I can protect myself, hold this spot against it. You heard it—it's going after Twylgalit now. As long as I live, it's trapped in the wasteland. But Twylgalit cannot return. If she tries to cross the wasteland, it will kill her. Please, protect my grandchild.**

"I will. And so will Peter. But you're not completely healed yet, and I'm not leaving until you are." Jeanne turned back to study the mound at her feet. *And not until I find out what that ghost was trying to show me.*

CHAPTER 16

PETER

The flood surged through the large break in the barrier and spilled out across the gray land. *That ought to get someone's attention,* Peter thought happily. With luck, one of the wizards, without—well, the thing needed to be distracted from Twyl's grandmother. *Might as well do something useful while I'm at it.*

He felt a familiar touch against his mind. Jeanne! He felt relieved. She was here and okay! The deeply buried worry that he was in the wrong place and time dissolved at the contact with his partner.

Jeanne seemed pleased he was here. A sense of danger came along their link, and he realized it was a warning. He looked across the wasteland for signs of movement. *I must have gotten the neighbor's attention and it's coming this way. Jeanne wouldn't be that worried otherwise.*

He left the barrier and headed across the wasteland, looking for someplace to hide. As he walked, he set up defenses in his mind. *If I believe strongly enough that it can't detect me, then it can't use magic to find me.* He had been able to influence magic in that way before. *I just have to remember how to do it again.*

The flood waters had spread out far enough across the gray land that finding a dry spot in which to hide was also important. Peter found a small rocky rise he could crouch behind just as he heard a roar coming from further within the wasteland. He ducked down out of

95

sight.

The roar was repeated. It sounded much closer, and much angrier.

Peter risked a peek over the rocks.

An armored figure stood in the path of the encroaching flood. It flung both hands out and pushed against the empty air. The flood directly in front of the figure stopped. The figure kept one hand palm out, but used the other to gesture at the barrier. Water stopped flowing in through the break Peter had made. *Huh, guess that answers the question of whether the water is being kept in or out,* Peter thought.

The figure pushed at the air before it with both hands. The flood started to retreat, but then the waters stopped. The level dropped as if the water was soaking down through the dry soil. The figure roared again, but none of its gestures stopped the water this time. Within minutes, the water had vanished, leaving behind rich dark soil. The being's howls this time sounded very frustrated.

Peter ducked back behind the rise and clapped both hands over his mouth to muffle any laughter. *I don't think it counted on that!*

He peeked back over the rocks.

The armored being fell silent. The helmet face seemed to be looking across the Great Flood. Then the face lowered to look along the barrier.

Peter was struck by a sudden worry. *I hope it's not looking for footprints. I hope all of mine got washed away.* He frowned and reinforced his belief that the being would not be able to detect him by magic. *You can't find me.*

The being stood still for several moments. Then it turned and began walking back into the wasteland.

Peter watched and waited until he was sure the being had gone. Then he cautiously went to the edge of the previously flooded area. He crouched down to study the ground. The dark soil definitely looked like something that plants might like to grow in. He looked at the Great Flood. *The wizards* are *trying to turn a desert back into Windgard*, he reminded himself.

He looked back at the wasteland. Maybe it might help Twyl's grandmother if her neighbor was worried about this border. He grinned and moved to another section of the barrier holding back the floodwater.

CHAPTER 17

JODY AND TWYLGALIT

Jody froze as she heard the strange roar overhead. Twyl pushed her to the ground and followed right behind. Jody looked back at her indignantly. "Will you stop pushing me?"

A brown winged shape passed over their heads and crashed into the thick undergrowth beyond them.

Jody screamed. She had had a brief impression of big wings and sharp claws in the rush of wind as the thing had flown overhead. And now it was on the ground near them!

Twyl climbed to her feet, watching the waving brush.

The bushes growled. The growl turned into whimpers. "Ow, ow, ow, ow."

Jody stopped screaming. That sounded like a boy. "Ow," said the bushes again. A cute boy, Jody decided. She pushed herself up and hurried toward the bushes.

"We've got to help him," Jody said, although she wasn't sure what they could do against that winged thing. She wondered where the cute boy had been hiding—had he been following them?

Twyl followed her as they eased through the broken tree limbs and crushed vegetation. Jody stopped and stared. Tangled in fallen branches were a giant eagle and a mountain lion, but it was only one animal! The front half looked like a white eagle. It struggled against the branches pinning its brown dappled wings. The sharp yellow beak opened.

"Ow," it said in the cute boy's voice.

"Oh." Jody didn't think this big cat-bird-thing would have had time to eat the cute boy.

Twyl glanced at her, then approached the tangle. "Are you all right?" Twyl asked.

"No—ow!—I'm caught—ow!" The bird head frowned at one huge outstretched wing pinned at a point out of reach of its talons.

"Here, let me help," Twyl said. She started to move some of the branches.

The cat back half of the creature awkwardly sat, its long spotted tail lashing among the leaves.

"What are you?" Jody asked. "Some kind of cat-bird...eagle-cheetah?" The markings on the back legs did almost resemble those skinny cheetahs she'd seen on television.

The bird head looked at her. Pointed ears emerged from its feathers as the hooked beak opened. "I'm a gryphon," he said, the ears vanishing again. "What are you two?"

Twyl freed the trapped wing, and the gryphon retracted it with a pleased sound. He stretched it out again to straighten some feathers with his beak. "I'm Twylgalit," the girl said with a nod that made the beaded cords in her green hair rattle.

"Thank you, Twylgalit," the gryphon said politely. "I'm Rafi."

"And I'm Jody." Jody was relieved to finally find someone with a short name. Even if that someone did look kinda weird.

The gryphon sniffed at her and the ears pricked up through the golden-edged white feathers. "I've never smelled anything like you before."

"Thank you." Jody tried to remember which perfume she was wearing today then realized she wasn't. "Excuse me?" she asked frostily.

"You smell...green." Rafi's golden eyes widened. "Of magic." The gryphon sneezed explosively and backed away. "Sorry." He sneezed again. "Sorry. Magic affects me this way sometimes." He backed into a bush and batted at his beak with one birdlike foot. "It twists my sister's tail when I interrupt her spells."

"Your sister?" Twyl asked.

"She's powerful enough to be a wizard, but Poppa won't test her." He looked at them and his ears lowered. "You...you haven't seen her, have you? She's much bigger than me—almost full grown."

"Bigger?" Jody squeaked. Rafi looked pretty big to her. *He's* my *height,* she realized. The thought of a bigger gryphon around somewhere was enough to make her skin creep.

"Oh yes. I'm only six years old—Momma says I'm still growing into my feet. She says I'll be as big as her in another couple of years." His head lowered. "But Soraya will still be bigger."

Jody glanced at Twyl, but the other girl only looked thoughtful. "We saw a gryphon several days ago. It might have been she."

"That?" Jody turned on Rafi. "That was your sister? Why did she chase us into the forest?"

He cringed. "I don't know. She was looking for wizards. Maybe she wanted to ask you directions."

"Yeah, right." Jody couldn't see anything that big needing help with directions. "If she already knows magic, what's she looking for wizards for?"

"Poppa's too busy to train her. Momma said wait, but Soraya doesn't want to wait. So she flew away from home." Rafi studied his front feet. "She wouldn't let me come with, but I followed her."

Jody was surprised when Twyl clapped her hands together. "Maybe she is the one!"

"The one what?"

"The one to help us!" Twyl turned to Rafi. "We need a wizard to help us!"

"I could help," Rafi said shyly. "I don't know as much as Soraya, but I'm going to learn magic."

"You sneeze when you're around magic," Jody commented.

His ears drooped, but he didn't reply to that. He turned to Twyl. "What do you need help with?"

His politeness irritated Jody. "There's a big mean monster threatening her grandmother," she said before Twyl had a chance.

"M-monster?" Rafi repeated. His skinny back half crouched.

"It is not a monster," Twyl said sternly. She turned to Rafi. "It is one of the Old Ones. One which hates all life."

"Sure sounds like a monster to me," Jody commented as Rafi's yellow eyes grew wide and his feathers flattened.

"And you want to fight one of *those*?" Rafi hunched within his wings.

"We must," Twyl said simply. "Otherwise it will destroy all the Lands."

Jody felt a chill suddenly. It was almost as if something was watching them. She looked at Twyl, who had also become very still.

Goosebumps ran up her arms.

Rafi sneezed explosively. He sneezed again and again, and his wings almost lifted him off the ground. "Sorry." He sniffled.

Jody and Twyl looked at each other. Jody giggled. How silly. She had almost scared herself. It was nonsense to think that anyone was watching them.

Twyl still looked worried. "I did no magic," she whispered, "and neither did you. So why is Rafi sneezing?"

"Hay fever?"

Rafi's tail lashed. "I have no fever." He padded past them and sniffed the air deeply. Then he shook his head. "It is gone now."

Twyl looked even more worried. "We must go as well," she said to Jody.

"Hey, we barely had a break!" Jody protested. She followed Twyl out of the tangled vegetation to the open spot where the gryphon waited. "Well, it was nice to meet you, Rafi."

Rafi watched them wistfully. "May I accompany you?"

Twyl bobbed her head. "You would be most welcome. Do you agree, Jody?"

Jody looked at Twyl, but Twyl was looking at her. "What, it's my decision for a change?" Jody asked. Twyl wordlessly shrugged one shoulder, and Jody looked back at Rafi. Although the gryphon was clumsy, he did have claws and a sharp beak. *He could protect us.* "What about your sister?"

Rafi hung his head. "I can't find her. But if you're looking for wizards as well, she may find us."

Jody wasn't sure she liked that idea. *But Rafi would be with us. And he has such a cute voice.* "Sure, you can come with us, Rafi."

The gryphon's ears perked up, and there was a bounce to his step as he trotted beside her. As they passed the berry bush, he slowed enough to have several mouthfuls before quickly dashing after them.

"You're a vegetarian?" Jody asked, feeling faintly relieved. At least she wouldn't have to worry about their new friend munching on them.

Rafi looked wide-eyed at her and finished swallowing the berries. "What's that?" He looked back at the bush. "I love sweets. Those are the best."

Jody sighed and held out her bag. "Here, there's more inside. Just don't eat my comb."

Rafi's ears perked up as he reached out to take her bag. Then he sneezed suddenly and pulled back. "You need to preen yourself," he said, shaking his head. "It can't be good for you to have those growths in your pelt."

Jody looked at her outstretched arm and shuddered. There were more leaves on her sleeve.

"That is the other reason we need to find a wizard," Twyl said. "Or perhaps a healer."

Rafi looked from one to the other as he walked between them. "This is a spell?" He sneezed. "Oh. Yes, it's a spell. I thought it was a disguise—you mean you don't want to look alike?"

"Of course not!" Jody was indignant. "We don't look alike! For one thing, her hair is green and mine is blonde." She pulled a portion forward to show him.

Rafi tilted his head to one side. "Looks green to me."

Jody looked at the hair she held. "It's green! My hair isn't supposed to be green! What happened? Why is it green?"

Twyl sighed. "They were going to make you beautiful."

"Well, yeah. But they didn't say anything about turning my hair green."

Twyl looked as if she was about to say something, then she turned to Rafi. "Is there anything you could do?"

Rafi's ears flicked back and forth as he studied Jody. His beak reached out and gently plucked a leaf from her sleeve. He held it on his black tongue for a moment or two. Then he swallowed. "Hmm."

"Well?" Jody asked.

"Hmm." Rafi plucked a few more leaves. "These taste good."

"That's it?" Jody pulled her sleeve away. "I should just prune myself? What about my hair? What about"—she looked at her green stained palm and held it in front of his beak—"that?"

Rafi sneezed. "That is serious," he said, pushing her hand away with one taloned foot. "Do not call upon that magic again."

"What magic?"

"I will help you with your preening when we next rest. Those growths will be a nice snack."

"Hey!" Jody stopped and glared at him. "I am *not* some type of…salad bar!"

Rafi cringed, and his ears laid flat. "I'm sorry. Did I offend?" He looked back and forth between Jody and Twyl. "Oh. I'm a stranger. Only family members preen together. I'm sorry."

Jody looked at Twyl, then suddenly realized what the gryphon meant. "We're not family." And if Peter were here, somehow she couldn't see him offering to pull the leaves off her. She'd have to do it herself. She looked down at her jacket and grimaced. This would take *forever*! "Okay, Rafi, you can help, if you want."

Rafi clicked his beak. Then he bounded away from them. "Berries!" he cried.

This time Jody joined Twyl and Rafi in gathering and eating dark purple berries from a short tree. She was surprised that she actually recognized it as a mulberry. She didn't think she had come across the name before, except perhaps in a nursery rhyme.

She looked around them. It was odd; she knew the names of most of the trees around them. *When did I learn this?* Before, one tree had always looked like another. Now she could detect differences. And she could *hear* the differences as well. The rush of an elm, the chatter of a birch, the delicate chimes of a llarwydden—*I don't remember learning that in Science class.* She could almost hear faint whispers around her.

Jody shook her head and returned to her berry-picking.

*   *   *

She's not like you, is she?

Twylgalit smiled at the llarwydden's question. Not far from her, Jody stopped in her berry picking and looked around. "She is a hero," Twylgalit replied softly. "She will save my grandmother."

She thought on this while they walked, with the gryphon bouncing around them when space allowed, or taking to the air to scout out their trail. Actually, she and Jody were more alike than before. She was part human because of her ancestor, while Jody was now part tree because of Kimeka's friends. *But I still don't understand her*, Twylgalit thought sadly.

"I don't understand him," Jody remarked. She watched as the gryphon circled overhead. "Did you notice how he apologizes all the time? I'll bet his sister is a big bully." Jody frowned. "And probably a know-it-all, too. So why is he following her? So she didn't want him to come. So? He's better off without her around."

Twylgalit looked up at Rafi. He looked happy in the sky. "I wish I had a sister. Or a brother. Perhaps he follows her for the same reason your brother followed you."

Jody looked surprised. "No, I—" She stopped and shook her head. "It doesn't matter." She looked down and plucked a few leaves Rafi had missed from her sleeve.

"Do you miss your brother?"

"Miss Peter? As if!"

Twylgalit thought Jody's voice and expression said something different from her words. She looked upward again. "I miss my grandmother. I hope she's all right." She stared. Rafi was swooping downward directly at them.

"Danger!" he screamed. "Behind you!"

Twylgalit started to run, but saw that Jody had frozen in place. She grabbed the girl's arm as she passed her and pulled her along. Twylgalit risked a look behind.

A large brownish gray cloud rolled into the clearing where they had been. Rafi flew through it and crashed into the bushes behind them. He struggled to his feet and lifted his wings. He sneezed, then started beating his wings at the miasma.

"What is that?" Jody shrieked.

Twylgalit stared at the cloud in horror. It looked exactly like the cloud that had swept over the border when she was very small. "It's found me."

CHAPTER 18

JEANNE

"Found it!" Jeanne sat back on her heels. Before her, the center of a muddy puddle bubbled, and the circle of water slowly began widening.

What is it?

"It's a spring, I think." Jeanne looked around for the ghost. *Is this what it wanted me to find? No wonder I couldn't detect any life.* Her hands and arms ached from digging, but she knew that soreness would soon go away. "Did you know you had a spring here?"

There was one, long ago. It dried up when the wasteland began to grow.

"Well, it's going strong now." Jeanne backed up as the puddle widened again. There was a whir of wings, and the blue jay alighted atop the edge of the trench Jeanne had dug into the landslide. They eyed each other. "Don't tell me you knew about it," she said to the jay.

The blue jay fluttered down to the puddle's edge and regarded it with first one eye, then the other. Then it hopped into the puddle, fluffed out its feathers and began splashing water into its feathers and under its wings.

There's thanks for you, Jeanne thought. "You're welcome," she said aloud. She rose to her feet to avoid the splashes.

The energetic splashing made Jeanne realize she was thirsty herself. Leaving the blue jay to its bath, she walked back to the boulder where she had left her backpack. She eyed the level of water in one bottle, and then finished it off. *Good thing I packed more.*

The sopping wet blue jay hopped, stalked, and fluttered past her. It scrambled up Grandmother's trunk and clung to a patch of bark. Then it shook itself, sending water flying everywhere.

"Hey!" Jeanne protested.

Grandmother's leaves froze, then whipped as wildly as if by a windstorm. **What is this? The moisture tastes...of magic!**

"What?" Jeanne stared at the jay. The bird began preening its feathers, radiating smugness. *Obviously good magic, not poison, or it wouldn't be so pleased with itself.* "You could have said something," she told it.

The jay fanned its tail, shook it, and cawed at her. It chortled and muttered softly as it went back to its preening.

She stared at it for a moment. *That bird is* so *much smarter than average.* She knew on Earth blue jays were often considered as smart as crows, but there was something more about this bird.

Jeanne ran back to the spring with the empty bottle. The flow had carved out a bowl-like hollow to one side of the spring. She slowly dipped a finger in the water, trying to sense what magic Grandmother had detected. A gentle wave of well-being swept through her. She could almost feel her aches dwindling. "Whoa, that's strong stuff." *Definitely magic. Why didn't I sense it before?* She thought back to how she first found the muddy trickle. *Maybe it was too muddy.*

She held the bottle in the deeper part of the hollow, where the water was clear. While waiting for the bottle to fill, she noticed that the spring's bubbling had slowed. *Don't stop,* she thought at it. She hurried back with the filled bottle to stand by Grandmother's trunk. "Do you want this evenly poured around you or just in one place?"

All around would be best.

Jeanne slowly walked around the tree, carefully doling out the water. Small sprouts splashed by water droplets stirred and grew before her eyes. She went back to the spring twice more for refills, each time anxiously checking to see if the spring's flow had stopped. Could the spring water be similar to the flood waters? If so, did Peter have something to do with this?

As she worked, she reached along their link. Her partner was pleased with himself again. *He's going to need help eventually. If he doesn't start heading this way, I need to get out there. And we need the wizards' help. I wish there was some way to contact Salanoa or Elin.*

She glanced at her ring. If she still had the Ring of Calada, she might have been able to reach Salanoa. *Elin has the ring now. He was learning how to speak mind-to-mind, but I'll have to wait for him to contact me. If he even knows I'm here.*

CHAPTER 19

ELIN

Elin waited and remembered. He was confident the visions of the past the ring showed him had some significance to the present disturbance. He was sure eventually he would discover it. *The ring always had a purpose when it showed visions to Jeanne.*

*   *   *

As they traveled, a steady parade of birds began appearing. They headed straight for Telynalle—wrens and finches, gemwings and crows—fluttering before her, landing at her feet, chirping and squawking.

Elin looked bemusedly at the small visitors. "What—?"

Salanoa smiled. "They talk to Telynalle. She sent a call out to report to her anything new within their territories."

Elin flicked his ears in amazement. "All have seen something?"

Telynalle sighed. "Not all. Unless you count us. Some are curious and just want to gossip, some have comments and suggestions about the best way to raise a blue jay—which I will *not* follow. 'Feed him to an owl,' indeed. What would your mother say? Oh, you are his mother? Madam, your son is far too bloodthirsty."

Salanoa chuckled as the elf walked on, still chiding the unrepentant sparrow. "Mind your feet later," she warned him. "I've sent a similar call out to the furred folk."

Elin resigned himself to being considered a mobile perch by some of the feathered visitors. They chattered to each other and preened his mane as they awaited Telynalle's attention.

The elf glanced sharply at him when he sighed. Suddenly she smiled and waved her free hand, and his nose caught the subtle puff of magic drifting over himself and Salanoa. "A small charm to repel droppings," she said at his startled look. "The wild ones cannot be expected to know civilized manners. The ground will appreciate the extra nutrients more than us."

He bowed his head in thanks for the kindness and hoped their watcher would not notice this use of magic.

Soon Salanoa had visitors as well, furred ones ranging from rabbits and squirrels to foxes and pronghorns. Her reporters were far fewer than Telynalle's. "It's because their territory is on the ground," Salanoa explained when he asked. "Most pay little attention to what flies above."

The piercing cry of a hawk sounded from overhead. The rabbit at Salanoa's feet and the flock attending Telynalle scattered in panic. Salanoa cast a weary eye skyward and sighed. Elin looked as well and saw no high-wheeling shape, only the adult jays overhead. "Mimics," Salanoa muttered. The fledgling on Elin's back shrieked at her. "I suppose you think it's funny, too," she scolded it, before turning back to Elin. "Some of the furred folk watch for hawks and owls, but srikes don't resemble those."

Wings swooped past Elin's ear, and one of the blue jays landed on his back to stuff an insect into its chick's peeping maw. It launched itself back into the sky.

Salanoa watched as the jay flew off to their right to scold and harass their watching escort. "I'm beginning to wonder if some srikes had been illusion-cloaked against our watchers. The furred ones say that srikes have been searching up and down along the border of Windgard and the Silvergreen Hills. But the Council had no reports of their appearances."

"If indeed they were searching," Telynalle commented. "Maybe there were no reports because there was nothing *to* report."

Salanoa pressed her lips together and shook her head. Elin flicked his ears, wondering what else the furred ones had told the brown wizard.

Elin stopped and looked about his homeland. What *could* interest the Shadows about this place? Not the flowers or the wide expanse of prairie grass, not the groves or streams. What, then?

He shook himself and trotted to catch up with the wizards, still thinking. Back in the days when he had run escort duty, whenever Salanoa crossed Windgard Elin spent the time asking her about past kingdoms. He knew, from those talks with the wizard and from his own delving into Kelan's books, that Windgard's boundaries had not always stretched this wide. Once human kingdoms stood where they now walked, cities and farms where now prairie and scattered groves dominated.

The herd's Memory-Keepers did not remember the past kingdoms—their kings, their peoples, their wars and treaties were not important—only those humans who had touched the herd's lives. That was one of the reasons Elin had not thought to study with them; he had been more interested in the wider knowledge held by the Lore-Master.

As if his thought summoned him, he heard the distant Kelan ask, *Elin, have you joined Salanoa and Telynalle yet?*

Elin nodded, then remembered his master couldn't see him. *Yes. We're in Windgard now.*

No problems so far?

Elin grimaced. No problems, other than frightening off a friend. *Everything is well. Have you found anything for me to tell Salanoa?*

Not a thing yet. I begin to wonder if my histories are too limited. Could you speak with your Memory-Keepers? Perhaps they may hold knowledge of what the srikes seek.

Elin shook his head violently. *Me? They won't talk to an outcast.*

"Elin?" Salanoa looked at him. "Is something wrong?"

He sighed. "Kelan asked me to speak to the Memory-Keepers."

"Kelan? How clever, he set up a mindlink with you? Excellent idea. And why are you shaking your head?"

Elin lowered his head as the elf turned toward them. "I'm outcast. They won't talk to me."

"Nonsense," Telynalle disagreed. "Summon them."

Salanoa leaned on her staff. "No, he's right. They won't speak to him. And they probably won't speak to us either—talking to wizards is the reason they cast him out of the herd," she said hurriedly as Telynalle scowled.

"Of all the—" The elf looked skyward to where one jay still circled. She pointed to the area below the betraying bird. "You there! Summon your Elder, the Windrunner. Now!"

"You can't—" Elin protested.

Can't what? Elin, what is happening there?

Telynalle demands the Windrunner's presence! Elin looked about wildly, for a moment feeling as if he was a young foal about to be punished with his worse nightmare. Even at his top speed, he could never reach the safety of the border before the Winds caught him.

"Telynalle, think about this," Salanoa said. "The Windkin are not members of the Council; they have their own laws, and we are on their land." She paused. "And they're not going to understand commands shouted in Elvish."

Elin calmed. Salanoa was right. In his panic he hadn't noticed the language shift. The escort wouldn't have understood Telynalle's order. In fact, depending on the Windkin running escort, even a command in the Common Tongue might not be understood. He was safe for now.

Telynalle scowled. She pointed at Elin. "He understood."

"Elin is a scholar and speaks several languages," Salanoa said. "As I said before, the herd outcast him for that."

"Then *you* summon your Elder," Telynalle ordered him.

Elin backed a step, the legend of the Outcast flooding his mind and filling him with horror. Was this how it started? He laid back his ears and glared at her. "No!"

"Courtesy, Telynalle," Salanoa said softly.

"He knows we're here," Elin said angrily. "If he wishes to speak to you, he will come. But to summon him, to demand his presence as if he is your slave—"

"She did not mean it that way," Salanoa soothed. She eyed the elf. "Did you, Telynalle?" Without waiting for a reply, the brown wizard raised a hand, curling it as if for a bird to perch thereon. Elin could almost see the light breeze brushing against her fingers. "The wizards Salanoa and Telynalle bid greetings to the Windrunner," she said formally, "and would speak with him on a matter that may concern Windgard." The breeze ruffled her hair as it drifted away.

Relieved, Elin bobbed his head at her. "Thank you."

Salanoa nodded back.

"The High Council speaks to the safety of the Lands," Telynalle retorted. "If there's something here in Windgard that is a danger—"

There was a tale. In his growing anger at the elf's arrogance, Elin remembered a tale he had read for his mentor. Of one time when the High Council interfered with his people. No, not his people—the *ancestors* of his people! "The Windlords' Gate," Elin said.

Salanoa and Telynalle turned to look at him. "The Windlords'

Gate," Elin repeated. *Could that be it, Kelan?* "The High Council sealed it long ago, but it's still here." *In the Windgard that is. Ignored during all the kingdoms' existences, which is why Kelan can't find it in the histories.* Somehow he knew he was right.

You could be right, Elin, Kelan replied. *Where did I leave that elven tale of the Children of the Wind? I'll start from there.*

"It sounds like a good place to start," Salanoa agreed.

Telynalle shook her head. "Why would be the Shadows be interested in a sealed Gate?"

"We won't know until we examine it. Elin, can you lead us there?"

Elin hung his head. "It's forbidden to the herd."

Salanoa studied him with a twinkle in her eye. "Knowing you, that means you know *exactly* where it is. Lead the way, apprentice."

*   *   *

A familiar scent distracted Elin. It did not fit with his memory of that time. *He did not arrive until later,* Elin thought. He struggled to free himself from the visions. Something had to have happened. *Ring, release me from the vision for now.*

Elin opened his eyes. He was reassured to find Salanoa still beside him. Next to the brown wizard stood the Windrunner, studying the younger Windkin with a regard that once would have panicked Elin. "Windrunner, I—"

The black stallion interrupted him. "The Winds have brought me an interesting scent." He eyed both Salanoa and Elin before continuing. "Peter has returned to Windgard."

CHAPTER 20

PETER

The flood spilled through the break in the barrier. Peter sprinted in front of the rushing waters, heading for the spot where he planned to hide and wait for the armored figure. He had walked ten minutes down along the barrier from where he had broken it before. He was interested to see how long the being would take to respond this time.

He scrambled up the small hill and settled himself into his hiding place. *I should try breaking the barrier from a distance next time,* he thought. Maybe he could break it at more than one spot at a time that way. He grinned. *That would be sweet.*

He slowly noticed a faint rasping drone. It seemed to be coming closer. Peter looked around just as a dark beetle with black and white striped antenna landed near his hiding place.

It crawled between two rocks, then emerged after a few seconds and flew off, heading toward the flood. Peter stared after it. *So there is some life in this place!*

There was movement down along the edge of the flooded wasteland, and Peter flattened himself back into hiding. He waited a few moments. Just because the neighbor couldn't detect him magically didn't mean he could risk being seen physically. Or however that thing "saw" without eye slits. He slowly and very cautiously peeked around the edge.

The armored figure held back the flood with one hand. The other hand, having resealed the barrier, moved back beside the first, then scooped downward and up as if lifting empty air.

The leading edge of the flood water suddenly *peeled* away from the ground! Rising slowly into the air, it began to roll back upon itself like a carpet of water.

Peter's jaw dropped. How did it do that? He caught himself. He could almost hear Jeanne's voice scolding him again for believing what he saw. He braced himself. The being wasn't going to have its way. "That is impossible," he muttered firmly, disbelieving the spell.

The roll of water suddenly splashed down as if it was a pricked water balloon.

The being hastily backed out of range as the freed water surged forward. The creature flung up both hands. The flood stopped, lapping against the new invisible barrier. The armored being gestured with first one hand and then with both. The only effect Peter could see was that the water had begun sinking into the ground again.

The face of the helmet looked out across the flooded Windgard for several long moments. Peter hurriedly ducked back out of sight as the being turned and strode back into the wasteland. Peter waited, wanting to give the being time enough to get a good distance away. Then he emerged from hiding and looked in the direction the being had gone. No sign of it.

Skirting the new dark soil, Peter jogged back to the barrier. He had a couple of ideas he wanted to try, but first he had to prepare. He had one empty water bottle, so he filled that with flood water by reaching over the barrier. He sorted through his backpack and found two empty plastic bags, which he filled with water as well. He fingered the waterproof lining of the backpack, but decided to save that for later. Now for his experiments.

He studied the flood water held back and supported by the invisible barrier, wondering how far down the barrier went. He thought back to the way the water had disappeared into the soil. He remembered one of the presentations for the science fair at school. Madelaine had had a cross section diagram of soil layers. He tried to picture it. He had been interested in the exhibit at the time, and now he was glad he had studied the diagram. First were humus and topsoil, then the leaching layer, then the subsoil, then the regolith layer containing the water table, and finally bedrock. He nodded to himself, the mental diagram complete. Wouldn't it be great if the water that had vanished earlier had soaked down to the water table? The magic-charged water could be anywhere under the wasteland now and Helmet Face could never stop it. He smiled at the thought.

"The barrier is only at the surface," he said slowly, believing every word. "There's nothing stopping the water from getting through the other layers."

He looked at the flood water. Was it his imagination or was the water level dropping? "Go on," he said. "Soak through and under. Spread out under the wasteland."

Peter walked along the barrier, grinning as he noticed that the water level *did* seem to be dropping. He looked inland. For his next experiment, he needed a good vantage point. Spotting a likely hill, he headed for it.

He skirted a patch of dark soil from a previous soaking. By leapfrogging back and forth along the barrier, he hoped that the being wouldn't be able to predict where the next break would come.

Peter climbed the small hill, constantly watchful for any sudden appearance of the armored figure. *Good thing I wore the gray sweatshirt; it's good camouflage.* He remembered his favorite TV hero and the time when the bad guys had been hunting him in the desert. *At least I don't have to worry about helicopters.* Peter glanced around the hillside, remembering other parts of the show. *He rigged up alarms and traps. Wish I'd brought some fishing line; I could have done that as well.* He thought about the armor on the being. Would it withstand falling rocks? Big falling rocks? *Wonder why it wears armor?*

Peter located a spot where he could hide quickly and stashed his backpack there to mark it. He continued up the hill and looked out over the wasteland toward the barrier. *Might as well start with the most distant,* he decided. He concentrated on one spot. *There's no barrier there.*

A short time later, he watched as the armored figure stamped back and forth repairing breaks in the barrier. It had taken longer to respond to the flood waters' invasion this time; Peter had broken the barrier in four different places before the figure had arrived to fix the first. *Maybe it was in the middle of something else. Maybe it will get tired of responding and will let the wasteland be returned to normal.* Not that he thought that the being would give up that easily. *But I can hope.*

This time the being wasn't attempting any fancy spells to pull the water away from the area it had flooded. With four breaks, the figure only stopped at each one long enough to stop the inrush and reseal the barrier before stamping on to the next one. Behind it, the trapped floodwater was left to soak into the ground.

Peter toyed with the idea of opening a few more breaks while the being was there, but decided against it as too risky. He decided to snack while he waited for the being to leave. Reaching into his backpack without looking, he located the open bag of the pumpkin and sunflower seed mix and started to grab some seeds. He froze in amazement. There was water inside the bag. He carefully pulled out the bag. As soon as he saw its contents, he felt his jaw drop. Not only was there water inside the bag, but the seeds inside had all sprouted. "Those were salted and roasted," he said slowly. "That's—" He clamped his mouth shut and looked out at the Great Flood. *The wizards are restoring a desert,* he reminded himself. *Obviously they're putting some powerful magic into that spell.*

He sorted through his backpack and found that one of the small bags containing flood water was leaking. *Right into this bag,* he thought, looking again at the bag of sprouts. "I'll find a safe place to plant you," he promised, then mentally sighed at himself. *Now I'm talking to plants.*

Peter glanced over the edge of his hiding place to see if the being was still glaring at the flood. It was, and Peter could understand the being's frustration now. *No wonder it's trying to block out the water. Super Grow for plants!*

A light breeze touched him, and he spotted a tiny movement at his eye level just inches away. Reaching out carefully, he picked up the object. It was a fluffy white down feather. He held it between his fingertips, recalling again the brief impression of a multitude of birds. He looked around the dusty and rocky area, thinking as the breeze ruffled the tiny feather. Birds and insects were probably the only safe travelers in this area. *Hard to track a flyer—there's no trail to follow. So, move light and fast and try not to be spotted.*

He ducked back down as the armored being turned. He heard the heavy thuds as it began to stride back inland, and raised his head to watch the figure until it was out of sight. *I'd better get moving myself.*

Before leaving his hiding place, he closed his eyes and touched his link with Jeanne. She felt tired, but pleased about something. Since she didn't seem worried, he might have time to annoy their neighbor further. He opened his eyes, struck with an idea for another experiment. *If I could only find a dried up streambed.*

On his way down the hill, he emptied the remaining bags of water onto a rock-free patch of ground and watched as the dust turned into dark soil. He planted the sprouts there and turned the bags inside out to make sure that the former seeds had the full benefit of any remaining moisture. "Grow big and strong," he said in parting. He imagined the tiny leaves waved at him as he left. *I just hope that thing doesn't find them.*

CHAPTER 21

JODY AND TWYLGALIT

"What do you mean, 'it's found you'?" Jody asked. "That's just smog!" It was odd that there was such a small patch of it, but there was no reason for Twyl and Rafi to act as if it was something serious. They had made her frightened of it, too, but that was only at first, before she realized what it was.

Twyl stared in horror at the swirling brownish gray mist. "The life-destroyer. This is what it used before."

Jody looked from the small cloud to Twyl. Did she really think a *cloud* was going around looking for her?

"Run!" Rafi ordered. He sneezed, but continued to flap at the cloud with powerful strokes. Jody blinked. The cloud actually seemed to be held in place by the flapping. And it seemed to be shrinking as well.

Twyl tugged at Jody's arm. "He said run!"

Jody pulled away. She was tired of being dragged all over the place. Anyone could see this wasn't dangerous. It was just a patch of smoke. "Don't be so worried. Rafi is blowing it away."

The smoke thinned to mere wisps. Suddenly one wisp darted past Rafi straight at Jody.

Jody opened her mouth in surprise. The tendril of smoke clamped over her mouth and nose. Startled, she tried to take a breath, but couldn't. She tried to pull whatever it was off, but her fingers slipped through the mist. There was nothing there, but she couldn't breathe!

116

She could see Twyl and Rafi staring at her as, struggling to breathe, she fell to her knees. Rafi pushed Twyl behind him. He reared up and began fanning his wings at her. Her vision turned red, then black.

*   *   *

Twylgalit stared in horror as Jody fell to her knees, choking on the fog. The brownish gray tendril resembled the poison fog that had killed two of her cousins. Rafi shoved her behind him and began flapping at the killer mist.

She had to do something before it killed Jody! What had Grandmother done? She remembered the feel of the spell, the sound of the spell. Twylgalit dug her toes into the ground in case she needed its power. She concentrated on the feel of the spell Grandmother had used. One hand raised on its own. Her hair began to rustle, creating the sound as the spell began.

Jody fell forward, and both hands, palms down, hit the ground. Suddenly her head jerked up and her green hair swept upward as if lifted by a stronger wind than that Rafi produced. Her blue eyes flashed green. Green light poured out of her mouth, blasting the fog into nothingness. Then her hair tumbled down, her eyes closed and she collapsed.

"What?" Rafi lowered his wings. "What happened?"

"I did it." Twylgalit looked at the green palm of her raised hand. "I think I did it. Maybe Jody did it." She suddenly flung her arms around his neck. "You were wonderful! Thank you for saving us!"

"Aww." Rafi clicked his beak softly. As she released him she saw his ears were flicking back and forth but his spotted tail was up. He looked away. "I still missed a piece. Will she be all right?"

Twylgalit pulled her feet from the earth and hurried to the fallen girl. "She seems to be breathing," she said. Jody's eyes were closed. She checked Jody's hands. In the center of each palm was a green splotch. She hoped the spell hadn't worsened Jody's condition. She looked at the girl's back in dismay. There were more leaves than before all over Jody's jacket. There was hardly any blue visible.

"Yum, more snacks!" Rafi dipped his beak, then stopped. "Do you think she'd mind if I start preening? All that magic and flapping makes me hungry."

"I don't think she'd mind." Twylgalit feared Jody would be most upset at the appearance of even more leaves. If only Rafi could remove them all before the girl woke up. Twylgalit reflected a moment. There was something missing. "You're not sneezing."

"Nope." Rafi delicately plucked several leaves. "I'm used to your scents now. It's only new magic I sneeze at." He swallowed and went back for more. "My sister was always trying new stuff. If she only stuck to one type I'd be fine. But she keeps switching and never lets me get used to it."

Twylgalit thought as he continued to preen. She gestured at Jody's back. "But it isn't this new magic?"

He flicked his ears at her. "Not according to my nose. It smells like you two." He plucked a few more leaves. "Why didn't you say you had magic?"

"I don't." Twylgalit sat on the ground next to Jody and began pulling leaves as well. "My grandmother has the power."

Rafi eyed her. "And so do you."

"No." Twylgalit shook her head. The beads clicking in her hair comforted her. Beads from her mothers. "No, not me. Grandmother offered to teach me, but my mothers always said it was too soon. And then it was too late." She pulled her knees up to her chest. "It said I didn't have power. It said I would never stop it." She caught her breath on a sob.

Rafi reached over and nibbled gently on her shoulder. "I'd say you did stop it. With your magic."

Twylgalit brushed at her tears and smiled up at him. "I did, didn't I." She held out the handful of leaves she had gathered, and he carefully took them into his beak with his dry tongue.

Rafi swallowed and sat down beside her, his tail coiling elegantly about his feet. He reached for more leaves off Jody's back. "If your grandmother offered to teach you, then she thought you could do magic. So why don't you believe her? Did she ever lie to you?"

Twylgalit was indignant at the thought. "No!"

He considered. "Is she a minor spell user?"

Twylgalit shook her head again. "She is the most powerful of us all. She knew the wizard."

"Yet you believe a monster over your grandmother?" He ruffled his feathers, shook them into place, and reached for another leaf.

Twylgalit blinked. Put that way, why had she listened to the life-destroyer? She looked at her green palm again. She *could* do magic.

"I'm all right," Jody said groggily. She slowly sat up. "Not that anyone seems to care."

"We care," Rafi protested. "We've been waiting for you."

"How do you feel?" Twylgalit asked.

"Fine." Jody began to brush at her jacket, but stopped as her fingertips touched the leaves. She looked down at her jacket front. "Oh my gosh, I look like one of those Plant Pets!"

Rafi flicked his ears at her. "Is that like a salad bar?"

Jody examined her arms and then tried to look over her shoulder. "Not funny." She tugged at her jacket. "And I still can't take this off." She waved her hands. "This is too creepy."

Rafi clicked his beak. "We'll soon have those off."

"We'll find a healer," Twylgalit soothed her, "and if we don't, my grandmother will know what to do." She only hoped her grandmother was all right. Their neighbor must have discovered that she was gone. Yet it only sent its killer mist, so it was not freed yet. *Grandmother must still be alive*, she told herself. Still, she worried. How had it found her?

Jody looked around. "Did that cloud blow away?"

"Blasted to nothing." Rafi bounced. "What a spell! Green light just came out of your eyes and mouth, and *pffft!* no more cloud."

Jody clamped her hands over her mouth. "Euuww," she said from behind her hands. "That's awful!"

Rafi and Twylgalit looked at each other. "I thought it was awesome," Rafi said. He turned back to Jody and swiveled his head almost upside-down as he stared at her face. "I wonder why light didn't come out of your nose as well?"

"Euuuwww!" Jody hunched her shoulders. "So, is it in me now?" she asked faintly.

"No, no," Rafi assured her, "it's destroyed. You should have seen it. Your hair shot straight up—"

"My hair?" She grabbed the ends of her hair. "Oh no, my hair gets all frizzy when it's foggy!"

"And then this light came pouring out of you—"

While looking at her hair, Jody noticed her hand. She looked from one hand to the other. "My palms are green!" She showed them to Twylgalit. "You said this was dangerous! Ohhh," she moaned, "I don't feel well."

Twylgalit felt guilty. Why had it attacked Jody rather than herself? She looked for a possible resting place. She knew they should move on. After that attack, it would not be safe to stay in one place too long. But if Jody was not well… "Can you walk?" she asked. "Just a short way?"

Rafi was of the same mind. "I can carry her. Poppa said I should build up my muscles by carrying weights."

"Hey!" Jody protested.

"And Jody can preen me as we go," Rafi continued happily. "There's some pin feathers I haven't been able to reach lately and they're very itchy!"

Twylgalit looked at his feathered half. "Pin feathers?"

"New feathers. They're called pin feathers because, when they first come in, they're encased in a sheath that's very sharp at the end. The ones I need help with just need to have their casings loosened." He pointed to a sheathed feather among his chest feathers. "Like this. Avoid the blood feathers—you can see the red in those—and look for the hard dry white ones where the casing is starting to flake off. You just need to rub the casing off." He demonstrated. "All right?"

Twylgalit nodded.

"I can walk," Jody said.

He stretched out beside them. "Are you sure? Can you run if another mist appears?"

"Okay, okay." She looked at his wings. "Where am I supposed to sit?"

Rafi turned his head. "Let's try next to my neck. Don't block my wings."

Jody gingerly eased onto his back and settled herself. She seemed to sink into his feathers.

"Hang on to my neck. I'm going to stand up."

Jody leaned forward and wrapped her arms about his neck as first his front half, then his back half stood up. Twylgalit hadn't realized before how thick his feathers were—Jody's arms just seemed to vanish into his neck feathers. *His front half must be as skinny as his back half,* she thought.

"Not so tight!" he gasped. The black-furred tip of his tail lashed wildly.

"You said to hang on," Jody complained.

Rafi coughed, then snapped his beak. Glancing aside at Twylgalit, he flicked his ears and started forward, his tail twitching. Twylgalit walked beside him, watching to make sure Jody stayed on his back.

"This is all Peter's fault," Jody muttered into Rafi's feathers.

CHAPTER 22

ELIN

"Peter's here?" Elin asked. "What about Jeanne?"

"If he's here—" Salanoa paused a moment in thought. "How could he have traveled to Windgard without any word?"

"There was word as well." The Windrunner laughed. "Winds, let them hear."

A small breeze swirled around them. "You dumped me in the middle of the Great Flood?" Peter's voice shouted.

Salanoa turned to Elin. "The Windlords' Gate," she said. "Somehow it's been unsealed."

"But where's Jeanne?" Elin repeated.

"So Peter is the disturbance you sensed." The Windrunner chuckled again.

"Maybe—" Salanoa looked thoughtful, then shook her head. "Maybe not. Does Graylod know of this?"

"Graylod knows," the gray wizard said, joining them. "The Windrunner was talking to us when the Winds brought him the news. The Guardian is examining the restorative spell. She's convinced Peter's presence could do a great deal of damage to it."

"He could aid it as well," Salanoa argued.

"He could," the Windrunner agreed. "He could also pass through it without affecting it, if he so choose."

"If he so choose." Graylod paused suddenly. His head turned as if he heard something and he looked out at the Flood.

Elin saw that Salanoa had the same absent look in her eyes. "There is something..." she began.

Elin suddenly realized he felt something as well. It was almost as if something tugged at the magic he had put into spells now across Windgard.

"Someone is attempting to tamper with the spells," Graylod agreed.

"Peter?" Elin asked. Whatever he felt didn't remind him of the human boy.

Salanoa shivered. "It's gone now."

"But will it return?" Graylod frowned. "Too much of our powers are in those spells. I must speak to the Guardian."

"I will accompany you," Salanoa agreed.

"But what about Jeanne?" Elin asked.

Salanoa paused. "Try contacting her mind to mind. You have the Ring to aid you."

Elin blinked. It was possible. He had been able to speak mind to mind with the human girl when she had the Ring to aid her. And if she was with Peter, the distance from the edge of the Great Woods across Windgard would not be greater than when Kelan and he had used a mindlink to communicate from Dewin Heights across Windgard.

The Windrunner studied him as the two wizards hurried away. "Did the Winds say anything of Jeanne?" Elin asked.

The black stallion shook his head, his mane rippling. "Nary a sound. But she can be quiet. A good Sensitive can blend into her surroundings, and she is very powerful. Do you think they are not together?"

"I don't know." Elin sighed.

"And what of yourself?" his Elder asked, looking after the wizards. "Shouldn't you be with them? Didn't you put your magic into the spells restoring Windgard as well?"

"Yes, but not as much as theirs." Elin lowered his head. "I'm still learning, and right now the Ring boosts my powers."

The Windrunner nodded with a faint snort. "Then you provide strength for them to draw upon if needed. Well run. You do well, young wizard. Let no one say otherwise."

Elin raised his head in surprise. The Windrunner fixed him with a stern gaze. "No one," the Elder repeated. He wheeled about and trotted back among the trees.

Elin stared after him, embarrassment warring with pride. The

Windrunner had helped train Peter, so Elin knew his Elder was more accepting of magic than the rest of the herd. But to hear it from his own mouth was a marvel to be prized as much as when Jeanne had given him the Ring of Calada. "Jeanne," he reminded himself.

Dropping his head to touch the ring, he pictured the dark-haired human girl as he last saw her and held the image in his mind. *Jeanne?* he called. A flash of rainbow-colored light from the ring filled his physical eyes.

The reply came swiftly. *Elin! It's so good to hear you!* Jeanne sounded as if she stood beside him. He looked around to be sure. He stood still on the edge of the Great Woods, with no one nearby.

Where are you? he asked.

We're in the wasteland. Past the Great Flood. He suddenly could see in his mind a picture of the land as if seen from high up. There was a desert with water along one side. *We need help.* Her mental voice faded. *There's a danger...*

Jeanne! he called, but the link was gone.

Elin sighed deeply. His legs trembled beneath him as if he had just run a great distance. *I feel as if I did run all the way to the Gray Hills and back.* He started walking unsteadily toward the group of wizards. He needed to talk to them. He needed to find a Memory-Keeper. The witches had created several wastelands and deserts during the years of their rule. But there had been one area even before the invasion that all young Windkin had been warned to avoid. Some stories he vividly remembered hearing, told as late night scare tales among the foals. But he needed to hear more. He needed to hear the truth behind the stories.

He shook his head in frustration. He missed his mentor, Kelan. It was hard to see the wizard again in memory, knowing that the Lore-Master had been killed in the Battle of the Seven and the Nine, when the witches had invaded. Kelan would have known most of the human and elfin tales and known where in his library to find more. But now, without him and without the knowledge contained in Llyfrgell Castle, the Lands could be in serious danger.

He pondered the memories the ring had shown him. While Vana had ruled, Renw and Leereho had found an elf wizard in the Gray Hills. She had been near death and had forgotten both her magic and her name. He wondered suddenly who that wizard was. Was she Telynalle? Had she recovered with the breaking of the curse? Had she even survived Vana's purge of the wizards? He searched his memory. Had Renw said where in the Gray Hills she had been found? They had thought her affliction had been due to the spells laid to weaken any of the Wise who came near the witches' castle. But what if there had been another cause?

He was so intent on his questions that he almost walked past the small gathering of wizards.

"I don't feel anything different," a massive wizard grunted.

"Only a small portion is affected," the Guardian pointed out. She pulled her green cloak tighter about herself as if she felt chilled. Elin suddenly realized that, as the one coordinating all the wizards' spells, she would be the one most affected by any changes. She was looking unwell to Elin's eyes. "It is difficult to plot the shifts of the spell. It seems to be covering a larger area suddenly—no, that has changed again." She raised a hand to her head and closed her eyes. Elin felt a faint queasiness as well and saw similar unease among the other wizards involved with the spell.

"Can we locate this disturbance?" Salanoa asked. "Is it near the Gray Hills or—"

"The Silvergreen Hills," the Guardian corrected, her eyes still closed. "Now that the curse is broken, the plant life returns. The old name should be theirs once again."

"The Silvergreen Hills, then," Graylod agreed. He looked at Salanoa. "Do you think this is related to what you and Elin sensed earlier?"

"It could. Elin, do you think so as well?" Salanoa gestured him to join her.

Elin tried to put any shyness aside. He was one of them now, hard as it sometimes was for him to think that way. "Are there any wastelands remaining?" he asked. "Jeanne said they were in a wasteland past the Great Flood."

"Are you certain?" the Guardian asked. She glanced among them. "We extended the spell so that even the Wasted Land, where our last army was destroyed by the witches, would be healed."

"There are no wastelands this side of the Flood," Graylod said. "And none within Silent Forest. Perhaps past Gimstan Mountain."

"Jeanne showed me," Elin said. He touched his lower jaw to the Ring and concentrated. The image of the desert edged on one side by water hovered in the center of the group.

"That is the Flood," Salanoa agreed.

"I don't see any hills, though," someone argued.

"There is a story of my people," Elin said, "of a desert that has been slowly spreading out from one of the valleys of the Gray— Silvergreen Hills into Windgard."

"A story?" The Guardian studied him. "How old is this story?"

Elin paused, thinking. He had heard it from oldsters who had been told it as younglings by oldsters. Did it come from still earlier times?

"Would not our spell heal this as well?" a soft voice murmured.

"How soon will this spell be done?" the massive wizard asked. "There are other parts of the Lands to heal. No offense to your people, young wizard. I am sure they would like to return to their home soon as well."

"If the spell is damaged—"

"Then we should finish it and be done before this tamperer has time to damage it further."

The discussing voices dwindled into background noise as Elin tried to remember where he had first heard the story. Or was it only a story? Someone had complained about it. He *remembered*.

*　　*　　*

Elin remembered the whisper of the breeze through the long grass as the black stallion trotted toward the two wizards. "Greetings, Salanoa," the Windrunner said. "The Winds told me that a bird-creature had arrived, so I must see if Telynalle indeed graced our lands once again."

Telynalle seemed amused. "Well said, youngster. Have we met?"

"Not I. But my granddam told tales of her talks with you on the plains of the Watcher."

Elin stared in amazement. The Windrunner's ancestor spoke with elves? The Windrunner eyed him, and Elin quickly lowered his gaze.

"So, has the Council at last decided to stop the spread of the wasteland? It has grown since the days of the humans. Or will you allow it to continue to invade Windgard?"

Salanoa shook her head. "I have not heard of this. We"—she glanced at Telynalle and corrected herself—"I will be happy to speak with you further on this. For now, we are on another quest. Srikes have been seen in Windgard and the Silvergreen Hills. We wish to find what they seek."

"The lands change over time," Telynalle said. "This area"—she spread out her arms—"was forested long ago. A wasteland is nothing unusual." Elin heard a faint sound from Salanoa, but the brown wizard's features were composed when he glanced in her direction.

"Have the Winds spoken of srikes?" Salanoa asked politely. "Do you know what they might seek here?"

"The Winds have brought the scents of ill magic, but the sweeprunners have not seen the cause." The Windrunner eyed Elin. "Perhaps this one may have done better, but his path went in another direction."

Elin dropped his head. He had disappointed his Elder. But the Elin that remembered did not hear disappointment this time.

"As to what they may seek..." the Windrunner sighed. "Human kingdoms spread across that part of Windgard in the past. The earth sometimes reveals one ruin and buries another."

"What of the Windlords' Gate?" Telynalle pressed.

Elin kept his head down as the Windrunner's silence lengthened. "The cause of much resentment and ill will," the stallion said at last. "Does the Council regret its interference now? Or do you fear the bindings have loosened over time?" He blew out an angry breath and shook himself. He nodded at Elin. "This young one can guide you there. I will tell your escort to let you pass." He reared slightly, spun on his back hooves, and dashed away. Elin watched as the Windrunner stopped briefly at a distance to confer with their escort. Then he was gone.

Salanoa sighed. "That could have gone better."

CHAPTER 23

JEANNE

Grandmother stretched her branches with several loud creaks and swishes. **That feels so much better.** Birds flew circles about the tree, scolding or chirping with each loop.

Perched on her boulder, Jeanne smiled as she watched the aerial display. The spring water had greatly helped to complete Grandmother's healing. Any remaining scars in the bark from larval burrowing or beak chipping were gone, and the ends of broken branches were sealed and sprouting new growth. She could almost see the being glowing with health and energy.

Three birds left the loop at its highest peak to wing their way westward. Jeanne hoped they were high enough to escape the neighbor's notice. Now that most of the beetles had left, and their larvae removed from Grandmother, there was little food to hold the flock here.

I should leave as well, the thought came. Jeanne watched five more birds depart, her thoughts scattering with them. Why did she feel she had to leave? Wasn't her main reason for coming here to help Grandmother? *You've done that*, the stubborn thought came. *You don't need to stay here now.*

Jeanne shook her head. What else could she do? Grandmother had asked her to protect Twylgalit, but Jeanne couldn't do that here. *What could I do, anyway? Grandmother had to protect me from the Life-*

destroyer. The little voice was stubborn. *If you had the Ring of Calada still, would you hesitate?* She couldn't lie to herself. She knew she wouldn't.

She closed her eyes and lightly scanned the area nearby. The sullen anger of their neighbor was moving, heading almost directly for where she sensed Peter to be. But Peter didn't seem frightened or even worried. His strongest emotions could be summed up as expectant, watchful, but excited at the same time. *Just like in Science class.* But maybe he wasn't aware of its approach. *I hope it's not sneaking up on him.* She reached along their contact to warn him.

Jeanne could tell Peter already knew of the being's approach. His "reply" was excitement, an almost "wait 'til you see this!" bounciness. Peter seemed to be doing well on his own—whatever he was doing out in the wasteland. He didn't need her help. There was a slight curiosity directed at her, along with a faint impatience. Was he expecting her to join him? She shook her head. She had expected him to join her with Grandmother! But perhaps that was no longer necessary. *Grandmother is healed now. We can take the fight to the life-destroyer. If Elin is able to bring other wizards, we can choose where to fight it, rather than wait for it to come to us.*

She wondered where Jody and Twylgalit were. *And that's another reason to find Peter. If Twylgalit tries to return home, that thing will be waiting for her at the border. We've got to protect her.*

Another line of birds departed, calling and chattering to each other as they flew. Jeanne watched as they soared to distant dots, still nagged by one question. How was the neighbor bound to the wasteland? Grandmother didn't know. The wizard had never told the trees. Jeanne had tried summoning the ghost, both at the spring and at the ruined house, to ask, but with no response. She again tried to see if she could sense the spirit. *I could really use your help.*

She waited, but saw no sign of the wizard's ghost. Perhaps he hadn't known himself how his ancestor had done it. *If I could find out how or why, we might have a way of stopping it completely.*

She suddenly realized Grandmother was watching her. **Will you be leaving me as well?** the being rustled sadly.

"Yes," Jeanne said, surprised she no longer doubted the need. Now that she had said it, she suddenly felt a sense of urgency. "Maybe tomorrow." She looked up as another line of birds left, bright colors flashing in the sunlight. She felt the urgency increase. *I feel as if I should leave* now!

She reached along her contact with Peter. Was he calling her?

But Peter didn't seem troubled, and the sullen anger that was the neighbor was walking away from her partner again. *What is Peter doing to get it so angry?*

Jeanne had learned to trust her feelings. Sundown would be soon. It probably would be safer to rest and prepare herself in the safety of Grandmother's protection, but somehow she thought that was no longer an option. She felt she had to leave *now.* "I gotta go," she said, throwing things back into her backpack. She stopped by the spring and filled empty bottles, scratching the labels so she could tell which contained the magical water. "I'll be back if I can."

Now? The imaged face looked worried.

Jeanne hugged the tree being. "I know, it's sudden. I just have a feeling...." She stepped back and shook her finger at Grandmother. "Now you take care of yourself. I'm counting on you."

She shrugged on her backpack, turned in the direction her sense of *Peterness* was strongest and began walking.

CHAPTER 24

PETER

Peter walked along the filling stream. He was pleased at how successful this attempt had been. After finding a dried up streambed, he had dug a canal from it to the flood's edge. Once the barrier was broken, the water gushed along the canal and poured into the course of the vanished stream.

The renewed stream soon outpaced him, rushing along its banks as it plunged toward the interior of the wasteland. Peter kept walking, glancing ahead along the stream, off to the sides and back the way he had come every few minutes. He didn't know in which direction the armored being appear this time.

As he walked, Peter was startled to notice spots of lichen on rocks. Those patches splashed by the stream seemed to spread wider as he watched. He smiled, thinking that the wasteland had a chance for recovery now.

Peter had walked away from the break and the barrier for eight minutes when he decided, *Time to start looking for a hiding place.* He jogged away from the stream toward a likely looking spot. The being had been taking longer each time to respond to breaks in the barrier. Peter still should have plenty of time before the being appeared, but he wanted a good view of how it attempted to handle a stream. Would it seal the break in the barrier first, or would it obstruct the stream from going further into the wasteland?

He glanced at the sun slowly approaching the horizon. *Hard to believe it's only been a day—less than half, actually.* He wondered how much time Jeanne would need to heal Twyl's grandmother. *Only seconds if she still had the ring—but then she'd be passed out for awhile. Maybe I should keep Armored Guy busy out here tomorrow as well and give Jeanne more time.*

Peter started up a small rise, then hurriedly dropped into cover behind it when he spotted a familiar shape. *You can't see me,* he thought as strongly as he could. He cautiously peeked over the edge.

The armored being was not facing in Peter's direction. It was slowly heading toward the stream, but the helmet face turned from side to side as it walked. The being was obviously searching for something, and Peter wondered if he was its target. *But how would it know to look for me here?*

Peter ducked back out of sight as the figure passed below his location. He cautiously raised his head and looked over the rise.

The neighbor continued to walk toward the stream. Peter frowned as he noticed something. There was a change in the way the being moved. It almost seemed as if it was an effort for the figure to walk. Its whole body was canted as if it was pushing against some great force attempting to hold it back. *I wonder if Jeanne is doing something to cause that,* Peter thought.

The being finally reached the stream's edge. It gestured at the stream, and the flow right before it was bisected as if a barrier had been placed across the stream bed.

Peter waited and watched. The water behind the barrier piled up and up until it began to spill over the stream's banks and around the blockage.

The armored figure gestured several times, but Peter didn't see any change in the situation. The being backed up as the pooling water headed for its feet. It abruptly turned and began striding toward the border of the wasteland.

Peter waited until the being was almost out of sight, then climbed over the rise. He walked back in the direction the figure had come, trying to see what the neighbor had been searching for.

He had checked several ravines and other possible hiding places when he finally noticed one that did not look right. He stared at the spot, wondering what it was about it that was wrong. The drift of sand wavered like an unsteady television picture and he heard a gasp from somewhere within it. A hand reached out, grabbed his shoulder, and pulled him forward until his shoulder hit gray earth.

"Hey!" Peter protested.

Pressure on his other shoulder kept him trapped. "Do not destroy the illusion," the owner of the hand hissed at him.

Peter blinked. The tall thin woman stared into his eyes, and he recognized the young-old look of an elf in hers, as well as suspicion and determination. She nodded abruptly and released him. She raised her head to glance past the concealing illusion, and Peter studied her in turn. She wore a loose shirt and trousers that might once have been a shade of bluish-gray but were now splattered and smeared with gray dirt. *Homemade camouflage*, he thought. Her short boots were coated with dust as well. Rolled up on the ground near his feet was a gray cloak, similar to those the elves had once given to himself and Jeanne. Her pale brown hair was coiled around her head, but stray strands drifted beside her dust-streaked face. She turned back to face him, and Peter was surprised to see anger on her face.

"At what do you play? Do you not realize what danger lurks here?"

Peter tried to hold back his own anger. "If you mean that big suit of armor stomping around out there, then yes, I know it's dangerous. What are you doing here?"

She made a sour face and glanced outside their shelter again. "Looking to find what I lost." She released him and settled back against a boulder to study him.

Peter saw how carefully she moved and realized that a dark splotch against her right side wasn't dirt. "You're hurt."

She grimaced. "The Old One has tracked me from the Gray Hills. It is relentless, and I have little enough protection as it is. I have no time for a healing trance, though it had helped to conceal me before." She tilted her head. "You are human."

"Are you a wizard?" Peter felt a spurt of hope. Maybe the wizards were actually doing something about the neighbor.

The elf spread her hands and looked sadly at them. "I was. Something happened. I…was injured. Scouts found me in the Gray Hills, my powers and my memory gone. But…this land is familiar. I remember…" She looked across the wasteland, but Peter wondered if she was seeing something else. She sighed. "When the Lands were freed, I regained some of my memory. But not enough to recall what had happened to me."

"But you still have some magic," Peter said. "That illusion—"

"A simple spell," she said, waving her hand as if dismissing his words. "One any elf could perform."

Peter wasn't so sure of that. His elf friend Leereho hadn't used illusions.

The elf lifted her head. "The murmur of water has ceased. Your doing?"

Peter looked outside their hiding place, then realized he couldn't see the stream from there even if it was still filled with water. "Not the stopping," he said, slipping back under the illusion. "Our buddy has probably sealed the break at the barrier." He glanced around their hiding place. "Do we want to stay here? It was looking for you before; it will probably be back."

"How well do you see in the dark?" the elf countered with a faint smile.

"Oh." Peter hadn't considered that. He glanced at the setting sun. "Not very," he agreed ruefully.

"The eve approaches, and the Old One will have the advantage of familiar territory. We shall stay here, then." She wearily slid to a sitting position and rested her arms atop her knees.

"If you need a healing trance, I can keep lookout," Peter said. "I can help hide us, too." Reminded of that, Peter quickly expanded his can't-find-me bubble of disbelief around their shelter, careful not to disturb her illusion.

The elf eyed him. "A human. You can do this?"

"Already have. And," Peter added, thinking back to how he had helped Salanoa remember a name spell, "I might be able to help you with your memory problem. Do you know the wizard Salanoa?"

CHAPTER 25

ELIN

Memories of their journey swept by Elin's internal eye at an increasing rate.

*   *   *

"The Gate should be right *here*." Elin trotted back and forth, then began a widening circle, studying the landmarks. The stream curled just so, the taste of the long grass was right, but where was the small hill? The scent that he had always associated with the Gate, the mixture of old magic and the overlapping layers of the seal was here, but it was faint, only a trace here and there.

"It does not appear as if anything had been here," Telynalle argued. "Are you certain this is the spot, apprentice?"

Salanoa grasped her pendant. "It's not been hidden by any spell I can detect. And if the earth had swallowed it, the ground would still show signs of disturbance."

Elin stopped pacing and considered what his senses told him. He knew the various scents and tastes of concealing spells. Those were not here. Had the Gate been destroyed there would have been fragments of the magic all around. The scent he could detect was only in one direction... Elin whirled. "The Gate—It-it's been *moved*."

Salanoa's eyes widened in surprise. "How do you move a Gate?"

Elin shook his head. "I don't know. But I can smell traces of it—

like a drag trail." He sniffed again, more confident now. "Heading this way." He started forward, following the scent.

The scent trail led toward the Gray Hills. Before long the parent jays, flying ahead, came winging back to greet them, cawing at Telynalle. The fledgling shrieked back, flapping as if it wished to join them. The elf wizard winced and reached up a hand to protect her ear. "They have found a ruin," she said.

The tumbled stones that hid the Windlords' Gate were soon visible. As they approached, Salanoa studied the ground around the small hillside. "The earth is not disturbed."

"Perhaps the young one only thought he remembered the location," Telynalle commented. "Easy enough to lose direction in these plains."

Elin snorted. His people knew the exact location of every spring and tree throughout Windgard, as well as the most succulent bushes and the sweetest patches of grass. And he knew that the Windlords' Gate had not stood here before. Salanoa glanced at him worriedly, and he shook his head at her. "No. It's been moved to here." *During the time I've been studying with Kelan*, he thought. *It could have been done slowly enough so that perhaps the Windrunner did not notice, but it* has *been moved.* The lingering magical scent of its passage was obvious to his nose.

A distant shriek came to his ears. Elin had learned to tell a false hawk cry from a real one. But this sound was unfamiliar. He suddenly realized the chilling call came from above, not from one of the two mimics on his back. His ears flattened as he glanced skyward. "Salanoa!" he warned.

*   *   *

Elin pulled himself from the memory. He did not need to recall the battle they had fought with the srikes or its aftermath. He knew now what had been forgotten, and what Salanoa's dreams had tried to remind her. He went looking for the brown wizard.

He finally found her standing at the edge of the Great Woods, looking out over the Flood as the setting sun colored its waters. "Someone wants the Windlords' Gate," Elin said.

Salanoa nodded, still gazing out over the waters. "And sent the srikes."

"No."

Something in his voice must have alerted her, for she turned to look at him. "You remembered?"

"I remembered finding the Gate moved. You and Telynalle didn't believe me, but the scent was clear in my memory. The srikes didn't know where the Gate was. If they did, they would have flown straight to it and we might never have been aware of their passage." Elin stamped a hoof. "No. The srikes did not locate the Gate until we found it. Someone else had already attempted to move it. That someone is still out there. And it still wants the Gate."

CHAPTER 26

JODY

The shadows were deepening under the trees as Rafi carefully lowered himself down in a small clearing before a large sweet gum tree. "I'm tired." He sighed, stretching his head forward to rest it atop his front feet.

Jody glared at the back of his head. Was he implying that she was too heavy? She climbed off his back and leaned against the sweet gum's trunk. She looked up at the nearby trees. This was still so weird. She was used to seeing tall buildings and traffic. And then her family had moved to a town were the tallest building was a grain elevator and the traffic jams only took place at railroad crossings. But these trees were taller than any grain elevator. She could almost be in a city of tall green and brown buildings.

Rafi turned his head back and straightened a few feathers where she had sat. "I'm so sleepy," he murmured into his feathers.

"This looks like a good place to stop," Twyl agreed. "I'll climb up and see how near we are to the Flood." She patted the tree and started to pull herself up onto a low branch.

"My tree!" an angry voice shouted.

Jody looked around. Who had said that?

Twyl dropped back to the ground, looking around as well.

"This is my tree!"

Jody started as a girl stepped out of the gray trunk only inches away. She had dark brown skin and long greenish hair that floated behind her. Her short dress was patterned black and white like birch bark. She glared at them. "You can't have him! Go away!"

What a snob. Jody scowled and lifted her chin. "As if."

"What?" Twyl and the girl both asked. Twyl looked puzzled and the girl's scowl deepened.

"As if we'd want your old tree," Jody repeated. "C'mon, Twyl, over there's a better tree to climb than *this*."

The girl's dark eyes narrowed. "There are many dryads who would want this tree. My Donunay is special." The tree's star-shaped leaves rustled softly.

"He is beautiful," Twyl agreed. The leaves rustled again, and the girl seemed slightly pleased.

Jody rolled her eyes. She didn't see what was so great about it. The tree did smell nice and the leaves were pretty, dark on the star-shaped top and pale on the bottom, but nothing she would call *special*. She glanced over at Rafi, intending to ask him. The gryphon was curled in a tight circle, fast asleep.

She sat down nearby. "Sorreeee," Jody said with a shrug as the girl glared at her again. "We're not leaving until he wakes up."

The girl seemed surprised to see the sleeping gryphon. She backed a step toward her tree, one hand at her belt. When Rafi did not move, she edged forward again, studying him.

"Go ahead and wake him if you want," Jody said. "I'm not stopping you."

"We have walked a very long way," Twyl apologized. She sat down as well. "Tell us about how your tree is special."

The girl looked from one to the other, her gaze lingering on the gryphon. "You are not dryads here to steal my Donunay?"

"Do we *look* like dryads?" Jody asked.

The girl shrugged. "In form and appearance, yes."

Jody opened her mouth to protest, then reached up and pulled her hair forward to check. It was still green. She sighed.

The dryad looked back and forth between them. "In speech and behavior, no." She sank gracefully down beside them. "Why are you here, then?"

Jody indicated Twyl. "She's looking for help for her grandmother."

Twyl nodded. "We need to find a healer as well." She pulled Jody's arm forward to show the leaves. "For these." She stared at Jody's sleeve. "Jody, when did these thorns appear?"

"Thorns?" Jody looked closely at her sleeve. The leaves were gone. Instead, there were numerous tight curls of thorny tendrils. Panic choked her throat. She looked down at her jacket. Long thin vines with sharp thorns crisscrossed each other. Buttons had sprouted numerous spikes like small porcupines. She looked up at Twyl. She wanted to scream, but all that came out was a faint whimper.

The girl leaned forward to study the sleeve and the rest of Jody's jacket. "What are these?"

Twyl shook her head. "I had thought only a mischief. But now—"

Overhead the leaves rustled and Jody thought she heard a voice whispering. The dryad nodded. "The spell has gone awry. You'd best remove them before they harm you."

Jody gaped at her. Her voice returned. "I've been *trying*."

"You have not tried enough. Donunay says you have been allowing them to feed on you."

"What? I have not!" She tugged at the front of her jacket. The spiny buttons stabbed her fingers as she attempted to unbutton the jacket.

"You cling to them as tightly as they cling to you," the girl said.

"I do not! Stop saying that!" Angered, Jody grabbed the bottom of her jacket and attempted to pull it up over her head. She grew frightened when the vines and underlying cloth clung to her body. "I can't!"

The girl was firm. "Take back your life. Will you allow those to rule you?"

Jody felt like screaming. She was *not* going to be taken over by a bunch of spiky plants!

"Kimeka had clothing of woven vines," Twyl observed. "Did you still wish to look like her?"

Jody scowled. How could Twyl say that? She had never wanted to look like *Kimeka*! "Get this off me!"

"Only you can free yourself." The dryad drew a knife from her belt and handed it to Jody hilt first. Jody looked at it, unsure what she should do with it. It looked at first like a knife, but it was made of wood, with no sharp edge or point. It seemed more like a spatula than a knife.

She slid the flat blade into the front opening of the jacket, expecting it to snag on the button threads. Much to her surprise, the blade moved easily behind the front panel, parting the opening as if the buttons no longer held it closed. She peeled back a section and shuddered at the sight of the root ends protruding from the inside of the jacket. The light was dim, but she could see that her apricot shirt underneath was dotted with numerous tiny brown spots. *My good shirt!* Jody went to the other front panel and continued sliding the blade along the inside of her jacket, slowly peeling it away from her shirt. She could feel a slight prickling along her skin as the blade passed. The sleeves were awkward, but she was able to fit the knife into the openings near her wrists as well as those near her arms.

The jacket abruptly writhed in her hands as she pulled it off. She flung it away from them and stared at it in horror. The jacket *moved!* It slithered toward her. Jody screamed and scrambled to her feet.

Rafi's head shot up. "What?"

Twyl and the dryad were on their feet as well by now, but the jacket headed only toward one.

Jody backed away from the jacket. Her hand shook as she pointed the knife at it. The writhing vines on the jacket twisted and curled, reaching for her. "Get away from me!" She flung the knife at it, but the wooden blade fell short. Circling around the object, the jacket continued toward her.

Jody turned to run, but tripped. She screamed as the jacket inched closer.

Rafi roared and pounced on the plant-covered jacket, anchoring it to the ground. He yelled as vines wrapped around his talons, stabbing him with spikes and thorns. Twylgalit pulled Jody to her feet and they backed against Donunay and the girl. The girl turned and vanished into the trunk. "Hey!" Jody yelled. She pounded her fist against the trunk, glancing back at Rafi and the jacket.

Rafi's beak stabbed downward, and he slashed at the vines. He shifted his stance on the cloth and methodically began to shred the jacket into quivering pieces.

Jody stopped pounding on the tree when the gryphon dropped the last scrap from a sleeve. Rafi eyed what was left while his beak opened and closed as if trying to remove a bad taste. With a last shake of his head, he sat down and slowly began to pluck thorns from his feet. Twyl lowered her hands.

Jody stared at the tatters of blue fabric. "That was my best jacket," she mourned.

"You were wonderful, Rafi," Twylgalit said. She nudged Jody. "Wasn't he, Jody?"

"Yes, thank you for saving me, Rafi," Jody responded. *My best jacket—I'll never find another one that looked as good.*

Twylgalit studied Rafi. "You didn't sneeze once."

Rafi studied a talon, then delicately closed his beak on a remaining spike. "Tho?" he muttered unclearly. "Id wathn'd new magic."

"It wasn't new magic?" Twyl repeated slowly. She looked at Jody.

"I didn't do anything!" Jody protested. "Maybe that girl did—she totally ran away fast enough."

"Smelled the same, tasted the same." Rafi felt around his beak with one taloned foot. He yawned. "I can't believe it gets exciting just when I fall asleep."

The tree rustled overhead and Jody glared up at it, stepping hurriedly away from its trunk. She could hear someone whispering.

Twyl looked puzzled. "You were put to sleep?"

Rafi's talons stopped in mid-stroke. "I was?" He thought a moment, and the talons resumed probing into the feathers around his beak.

"That is what Donunay says," Twyl said.

Jody looked at Twyl, then glanced back at the tree. It talked?

Rafi's ears flicked and he gave a faint groan. "Probably the plants I ate. Soraya always warns me about eating magic stuff." He sighed. "But they tasted so *good*." He lowered his head to his front legs. "And now I'm hungry again."

Jody eyed the deepening shadows. It was getting too dark to look for berries. She remembered her bag and the berries Twyl had put inside it. Jody braced herself and cautiously opened it.

Rafi's head shot up. "I hear frogs!" He sprang to his feet and bounded past Donunay.

Jody watched him disappear into the growing shadows. *What is it with boys and frogs?* she thought with a shudder. She looked down into her bag, hoping to see some unsquashed berries. She carefully reached inside. Some berries felt mushy, but others appeared to be intact. She ate two, then asked, "Twyl? Do you want some berries?"

Twyl nodded. As she left Donunay, Jody saw the dryad emerge from the trunk behind her. The tree girl looked at the scattered bits around the clearing.

"What do you want now?" Jody asked, giving Twyl her bag. "Why did you leave? Why didn't you help us?"

"I did what I could," the dryad said, retrieving her wooden knife and hanging it from her belt. "I could not stand by and watch you kill it."

Twyl pulled a berry from the bag as she looked back and forth between the two.

"It was after me!" Jody protested.

The girl glared at her. "You did not have to destroy it! Now I know you are not a dryad! Plant killer!"

"Did someone say berries?" Rafi galloped back out of the shadows, bringing a damp, muddy smell with him. Water dripped from his legs and underbelly, and a frog leg stuck out of one corner of his beak. Jody shuddered as he gulped and the frog leg disappeared. He looked from one to the other. "What? I was hungry." He wiped his beak on a bush. "Did you want one? I could catch another."

Eww, Jody thought. "No, that's okay," she said aloud. "I have some berries, unless we're going to be called plant-killers for eating *those*."

Twyl looked puzzled. "The berries were freely offered."

Rafi studied the dryad; the gold around his eyes widening, then narrowing. "If you had another way to stop it, you should have done so." Jody was proud of him; he wasn't apologizing for once.

"It only wanted to be with her!"

"And take her over," Twyl said firmly. "You know the dangers as well as I."

The tree rustled overhead and the girl looked down and sighed. "Yes. I am sorry." She looked up at Jody. "You had no choice."

Jody gaped at her, chills washing down her spine. What were they saying? She had been wearing that jacket for days and it had been dangerous all along?

"Thank for your help in removing it," Twyl said. "We will go now."

Jody frowned at Twyl. "No way. It's getting dark."

"Please stay," the girl said, and the tree behind her rustled wildly.

Rafi plopped onto the ground at Jody's feet. "Sounds like an invitation to me." He nudged Jody's arm with his beak. "Didn't you say you had some berries?"

Twyl passed the bag back to Jody, who handed it to Rafi. He looked at the bag's small opening, then upended the bag and dumped its contents onto the grass.

"Hey!" Jody knelt as Rafi's beak sorted through scrunchies and hair ties, gobbling up berries. Twyl quickly joined her.

Rafi held up Jody's brush in his talons and delicately removed the remains of a punctured berry from between its bristles with his tongue. "What's the dryad doing?"

The berries were all gone. Jody checked to make sure all the sticky remains were out of her bag and began putting her belongings back inside. Twyl tried to help, handing her gum and hair ties as well as an occasional stick or leaf. The two looked up.

The dryad held the wooden knife against Donunay's bark. Sap oozed out above it, collecting on the flat blade. "Donunay is a sweet gum tree," Twyl said, as if that explained it.

Jody looked down at the gum in her bag and shook her head. Not the same.

Rafi clicked his beak. "So that's where sweet gum comes from. Momma says it's wonderful for aches and small ills."

The dryad headed their way, carefully holding the wooden knife. "Donunay's is special, even among sweet gum trees." She held the knife and the small glob of sap out to Jody. "Donunay says this will help you."

"I can't eat that!" Jody recoiled. Tree sap? They expected her to eat tree sap now?

"You don't eat it," the girl said patiently. "Just chew it until you feel better."

"I feel fine now," Jody protested.

Rafi nudged her shoulder. "This is an honor," he whispered loudly. "Do you know how much my Momma has to barter for a much smaller piece of sweet gum for us?" He poked one of the brown spots on her shirt. "These don't hurt?"

"Ow! It does when you peck at it!"

"She must be in pain," Twyl told the dryad. "She's not usually this grumpy."

Jody opened her mouth to deny this, then frowned at Twyl. She was *not* grumpy!

Rafi eyed the sap. "My back aches. Could we split it?"

"Are you saying I'm heavy?"

The tree rustled overhead, and the dryad tilted her head. "Donunay's gum helps to cure magical ills, but he says a little will aid you."

Rafi's ears pricked up. "Thank you!" He bit off a small piece.

The girl held the remainder of the sap out to Jody.

"Please, Jody," Twyl said. "You will sleep better tonight as well."

Jody felt ready to cry. Why were they all picking on her? She wasn't grumpy; she was still hungry—those few berries had not been enough. She was also tired and her muscles ached from riding the very skinny gryphon. Maybe the sap would help that.

I promise that it will help you feel better, a deep voice whispered.

143

Jody's attention was on the golden lump of sap. "Oh, all right." She cautiously picked up the glob. It was soft and sticky like a caramel. She sniffed, trying to place its faint sweet smell. It didn't smell like the piney drips she sometimes found on the family room's paneling. Jody cautiously put it in her mouth. The sap tasted bland, like a sugarless gum. *Sweet gum, riiight.* She chewed slowly, hoping the sap wouldn't stick her teeth together.

Rafi clicked his beak and stretched—first his front and back legs, and then his wings. "Oh yes, that helps." He sneezed, and his feathers fluffed out.

Twyl and Jody both looked at him. Jody froze in midchew.

Rafi shook his feathers back into place. "Good magic," he said, adding several beak clicks. "Tastes yummy."

"That's what you said about the plants," Jody said worriedly. She kept mentally checking herself, waiting to notice any effect. The gum had slowly changed from bland to somewhat sweet in her mouth, but she hadn't noticed anything else. She cautiously resumed chewing.

The tree rustled softly overhead, and Twyl smiled up at the branches. "We would be happy to tell of our adventures. But we have not done much."

"Just a lot of walking," Jody sighed.

CHAPTER 27

JEANNE AND PETER

As she walked, Jeanne almost wished she had the power to heal the gray land. Once she had left the borders of Grandmother's sanctuary, the wasteland was as dead as the Gray Hills had been under the witches' curse. There was no small life, no plants, no sign that there had ever been life. *Not only dead, but long dead.*

She didn't think she could sense the small patches of lichen that the beetles had planted, but she still kept watching for them, hoping some had survived.

Jeanne slowly began to realize why she had felt the urgent need to leave Grandmother. Now that she was focusing on detecting any life in the land around her, she could sense someone was hurt. A great hurt. Someone else was in the wasteland besides Peter. Someone besides the neighbor.

She could sense the neighbor's presence as well. Its constant sullen anger was easy to locate in the otherwise empty land, and the occasional spikes of fear mixed with irritation and frustration told her Peter was keeping the being busy.

That reminded her that she had to look to her own defenses. She remembered how Salanoa had taught her illusion-casting. *"You can do elaborate ones with the Ring,"* the wizard had said, pointing at the Ring of Calada that Jeanne had worn. *"It has power to spare. But you can cast illusions without it as well. And emotion illusions are particularly easy for a Sensitive."*

Jeanne practiced as she walked, concentrating on a very simple illusion. *You don't see me. You don't sense me. There is nothing here.* The more she did it, the easier it became and the faster the illusion formed.

She searched for the other presence in the wasteland. How serious were its injuries? She suddenly realized she had drawn close enough within the wasteland to sense other things about the being. *Feels like an elf. Why would an elf be here? The hurt I sensed before is an old pain, something that hasn't healed. But there's a newer pain now. What happened?*

She quickened her pace as she noticed the neighbor seemed to be following the elf. Not long after that, she noticed that her awareness of Peter seemed to be intersecting the paths of the other two. She began to feel that she was watching a show with the sound turned off. First the neighbor grew irritated and moved away from the elf and Peter. Then Peter and the elf met, with an interesting clash of emotions. *At least now I can find them both at once.*

Twilight deepened around her. Jeanne knew she would soon need to decide whether to find a place to hide and rest or to continue on, guided by senses other than eyesight in the growing darkness. *Walking has been bad enough in the daylight when I can see the loose rocks. Those two can protect each other, and the elf's injuries don't seem to be life-threatening. I could rest tonight and look for them tomorrow.*

She felt a presence nearing her from overhead and whirled, activating her illusion. *You don't see me. You don't sense me. There is nothing here.*

"Jay!" A familiar blue jay alighted near her, radiating confusion. It hopped a few steps, looked past her, then looked all around. "Jay!" it squawked unhappily.

"You?" Jeanne dropped her illusion, and the jay shook its wings excitedly at her. "What are you doing here?"

The blue jay was happy about something. *It's happy about finding me? Why?* "Did Grandmother send you?" Jeanne asked.

"Jay!" Much to her surprise, the blue jay launched itself into the air and landed on her shoulder. She felt its weight shift, heard claws scrabbling and cautiously turned her head to see the bird attempting to perch atop her backpack. It settled its wings and looked smugly back at her. "Jay!"

Jeanne was surprised at first, but then it seemed both funny—the bird was so pleased with itself—and odd. This blue jay had already proved to know things that she hadn't. Maybe it had some purpose in following her. "So, you want to come with me? It's pretty dangerous out here."

The jay chortled softly.

"Glad to hear one of us is confident," Jeanne replied. She turned and resumed walking toward Peter.

Before too long she had found a safe place to stop. She looked around approvingly in the limited light. The warmth of a fire would be nice, but she didn't want to risk one. She didn't need it for cooking, and there was natural protection from the wind if she wanted to stay the night here.

The jay complained as she unslung her backpack. It fluttered to a landing nearby and studied her out of first one black eye and then the other. Jeanne pulled out a granola bar and a water bottle and settled herself on the ground next to her backpack. She broke off a piece of the granola bar and held it out to the bird. "Want some?"

The jay fluttered its wings, begging for a piece. Jeanne tossed it, and the bird snapped it out of the air. She took a bite out of the bar and stared into the night. Her awareness of Peter and the elf's position had not changed. She leaned against her backpack as she took a sip of water.

Radiating impatience, the jay paced back and forth. It would walk a short distance away, turn and stalk back toward her, then walk away again. As she capped the water bottle, it stalked up to her, tugged at the bottom of her jean leg, then walked away again.

"What's the big deal?" she asked. "I can't see in the dark, and neither can you. I need sleep! Can't we stay here tonight?"

The jay walked back to her and tugged strongly at her jeans. "Jay!" it demanded.

Beneath its impatience, she could detect its fear as well. *It's frightened, but it wants me out there. Why? Wish I could talk to animals like Salanoa.*

She mentally scanned the wasteland. There was sullen anger near Peter and the elf, but it didn't seem aware of the two. *For now.* She remembered its late night appearance on Grandmother's border and wondered if the neighbor ever slept. *That might be why the jay wants to keep moving.* She sighed and put the water bottle and the rest of the bar back into the backpack.

The jay waited as she stood and slung the backpack straps over her shoulders. Then it launched itself up to perch atop the backpack. It cawed softly in her ear.

"All set?" Jeanne asked. "Hang on." She walked cautiously into the darkness, using her awareness of Peter as her guide.

*   *   *

The star-filled sky still held a few lingering streaks of crimson and lavender over the western horizon. *The Great Woods are west of here,* Peter thought, remembering his map, *past the Great Flood.* He wondered if anyone in the Watch Tower ever scanned in this direction. *Why hasn't anyone noticed this wasteland?*

He glanced over to the cloaked figure of the elf, deep in her healing trance. As eager as Telynalle had been to regain her lost memories, she had not been able to ignore her injuries any longer. Peter shook his head, remembering what Leereho had once told him. *When an elf is badly hurt, he goes into a trance and wakes up healed. Nice trick, unless you're being chased by something!*

As the light faded, he stared out into the night, watching for the faintest movement. There was no plant life to sway in the wind, no animals to create any misleading sounds. The only thing moving out in the wasteland would be the neighbor, and it was probably still hunting the elf.

Peter was so intent on looking for movement that he almost missed seeing a still figure a short distance away. The shape was unmistakable. It was the armored being!

He edged slowly over to the elf. He reached out to alert her and felt fingertips brush his hand. Telynalle was awake and knew of the danger. He didn't waste time wondering how she could have known while in a trance. He waited, trusting in her superior sight.

The figure stood motionless. Peter wondered how it had managed to come so close to their hiding place without him seeing it. *You can't see us,* he thought, as strongly as he could.

The figure turned. "Do you think to hide from me, elf?" it boomed. "Your blood betrays you."

The elf glanced down and Peter looked at the cloak hiding her blood-stained side as well. The being hadn't used magic to track her! Peter knew his disbelief couldn't block a sense of smell. The elf pulled her cloak tighter with one hand while gesturing with the other. Peter wished that Telynalle had her full memory and powers back.

The elf blinked. Her eyes widened as she looked at him.

The armored figure stepped closer. "I have but to reach out and—"
The being stopped.

Peter and the elf exchanged glances. Peter shrugged; he hadn't done anything. The elf gave the briefest of head shakes. *She didn't do anything either?* Peter thought. *Then what's happened? Is it trying to scare us? To make us betray ourselves?*

The silence grew longer as the bulky figure stood in place.

Peter took advantage of the being's distraction. He visualized one of his memorized portions of the barrier, and then pictured water pouring through it and *believed.* He hoped the being was still intent on protecting the wasteland from the flood.

The figure stirred. It backed a step, turned, and began walking toward the barrier. Peter released his breath as the being disappeared into the night. He turned toward the elf, but she lifted a hand as he was about to speak.

"Something still watches," she said softly.

Peter waited, watching the shadows. There was a faint scrabbling sound at ground level, and he looked down just as a bird stalked past his feet. It carefully stepped up to Telynalle, then grabbed the bottom of her cloak with its beak and tugged. It looked up at the elf.

"You?" The elf crouched and held out an arm to the bird, which chortled and hopped on.

"However did you find me?"

"I'm not sure which is more stubborn," a familiar voice said out of the darkness, "that blue jay or the neighbor."

"Jeanne!" Peter said. "So you're what stopped it."

"Barely." Jeanne sighed. She unslung her backpack and sat beside it on the ground. "It's so stubborn! I couldn't turn it away." She pushed her dark hair out of her face and glanced at Peter. "You did something, didn't you? That's why it finally left. What did you do?"

Peter shrugged. "Same thing I've been doing all afternoon." He turned to the elf, who was removing the jay from her hair. "Telynalle, this is Jeanne. She and I broke the curse. Jeanne, this is Telynalle, a wizard."

"A wizard! You can help us, then!" Jeanne paused. "But I think I should help you first."

Telynalle was incredulous. "You? How—"

"Oh, she's a Sensitive," Peter explained.

The elf looked from one to the other.

"Your trance started to heal that burn," Jeanne said. "I'll just finish

149

that and then we'll talk."

"We've got time," Peter agreed cheerfully. It was *so* good to be working with his partner again.

Telynalle's voice reflected her confusion. "A Sensitive? I do not need—"

Jeanne was firm. "You do. That's a nasty burn and it's still bleeding as well. Sit."

Telynalle pulled herself upright. "I shall stand."

The jay squawked and pecked at the elf's hair. Telynalle winced.

"Suit yourself," Jeanne said, climbing to her feet and going over to the elf. "Just hold still." She stopped in front of the elf. "Open your cloak, please."

The elf sighed but obeyed. Peter looked away, but he stayed in earshot as he stood watch.

Jeanne *tsked.* "Barely started healing. Did a violet forceball do this? Or does the neighbor have other weapons?"

The elf sounded surprised. "How did you know?"

"A. I'm a Sensitive. B. It tried that on me, too."

Peter was shocked. "Jeanne!"

"I'm fine, Peter. Grandmother protected me." She was silent for a few moments. When she spoke again, Peter could hear exhaustion in her voice. "There. That's all I can do for now. It should heal completely the next time you do a healing trance."

"I thank you," the elf said softly. Peter heard the rustle of cloth and waited a few moments before turning to join them.

Jeanne opened her backpack. "So, where are you heading, Telynalle?" She pulled out a water bottle, felt the label, then returned it and pulled out another, which she opened and sipped.

"I had hoped to reach the Great Flood." Telynalle looked down. "I was a wizard. I am no longer."

Jeanne stopped in midsip. "Omigosh, it did it to you, too."

"Did what?"

"Made you doubt yourself. Big time."

The elf shook her head. "No, I lost my powers."

"No way. There's magic around you. I can tell. So that's where that blob of doubt came from! It's the same as I sensed around Grandmother." She paused and muttered softly, "I'll bet it tried to do it to me, too."

Telynalle raised her hand. "I may still have the magic all elves have, but I am no longer a wizard. I lost my powers long before I came here. I—" She paused.

"You said you thought you remembered being here before," Peter said. "Back when you lost your memory."

Jeanne nodded. "Peter, if the neighbor ever starts talking to you, don't believe a word it says. I mean it. It's a bigger liar than Vana."

The elf shook her head. "No, I have lost my powers."

"You haven't lost your powers," Jeanne said. She grabbed Peter's hand. "Listen to me," she said to the elf. "*Believe* in yourself."

Peter didn't understand completely what was going on, but he recognized a cue when he was given one. "You're still a wizard," he said, believing it.

"You still have your powers," Jeanne insisted. Peter could sense she was doing something else as well as talking. "Remember what they felt like. Reach for that. They're still there."

"You can remember," Peter said firmly.

"I... remember," Telynalle said slowly. "I used a...place-shift spell to bypass the witches' guards around the Gray Hills. Someone pulled me away. Something—" She looked at them, and the jay hunched down on her shoulder. "It was the Old One! It talked to me..."

"Thought so," Jeanne muttered.

"It said..." The elf closed her mouth, and through the link with Jeanne Peter could feel the elf's anger rise. "Lies! All lies!" Blue light shimmered around her right hand and grew as she closed it into a fist.

The jay began flapping its wings, though it remained perched on the elf's shoulder.

The elf stared at her glowing fist. Peter was glad her anger wasn't directed at them!

Slowly the blue light began to fade.

"So," Peter asked, "what do you plan to do once you reach the Great Flood? Wade across it?"

The elf still watched the faint light around her hand. "If I can reach the Flood, I can send a message to those wizards maintaining it."

"That thing is at the Flood," Peter argued. "Wait, I have some floodwater with me. Would that work?" He rummaged in his backpack and pulled out a bottle.

Telynalle looked doubtful, but Peter noticed she used her nonglowing hand to take the bottle. "They will not be pleased with me."

"Why?" Peter was surprised. "Because you're asking for help?"

"Because I needs must draw upon their spells. It might make

them…upset."

"Upset as in 'angry' or upset as in 'queasy'?" Jeanne asked.

"Queasy. Perhaps even nauseous." The elf handed back the bottle and Peter had a sudden attack of worry about his experiments with the floodwaters. "The spells are there, but this is cut off from the wizards. I shall have to continue on."

"It's too dangerous for you to try to reach the Flood," Jeanne argued. "That thing is between us and the border. There's a better place, and one that needs your help. You can see in the dark. And I'll bet this jay can help you locate Grandmother."

The blue jay fluttered its wings and chortled.

"Grandmother?" the elf asked.

"Long story. It's because of her and her people that thing is still trapped on the wasteland."

Telynalle was amazed. "She holds it here?"

"And protects her land. You'd be safe there."

"But what of you two?"

Peter and Jeanne exchanged glances. "It hasn't spotted me so far," Peter said.

"It's seen me," Jeanne admitted. "But only on Grandmother's land. I think I can keep hidden."

"You think?" The elf shook her head. "I should stay. You need my help."

"Help is on the way. Elin knows where we are. He contacted me," Jeanne said, glancing at Peter. "I wasn't able to tell him about the neighbor, but he knows we need help."

Telynalle was incredulous. "Elin? Kelan's apprentice? What can he do?"

Peter blinked. "A lot!"

"Elin's a wizard now," Jeanne agreed. "He has the Ring of Calada. He'll come. We have to stay near the border. We've promised to protect Twylgalit. If she comes anywhere near the wasteland, the Old One will kill her."

"Then I should stay with you."

Jeanne glanced at Peter. "Can you hide her?"

"Yeah, but why?" Peter turned to Telynalle. "Why stay? That thing knows you. It knows your powers. You said yourself, you were barely able to escape from it before. We've got wizards it doesn't know on the way."

"You are humans. You need my help."

Peter folded his arms. "And you're an elf and it's been tracking you."

"Grandmother is not that far away," Jeanne said. "You could make it there by morning."

"And if it follows me? Would that not put this grandmother in danger?"

"That thing has already killed her family because they're a threat to it. Grandmother is healed now. She'll protect you. And you can help her."

"If you can keep ahead of it and keep out of its reach, then if it follows you, Jeanne and I have time to move closer to the Flood." Peter grinned at Jeanne. "And maybe irritate it some more."

"We just need to hold out until the wizards come," Jeanne said in a persuading tone. "Then you can join us. Wouldn't it be better for you to rest and regain your strength?"

The jay tugged at Telynalle's sleeve. The elf put up her hand to distract it, then paused. "You said that this grandmother holds the Old One on the wasteland. How?"

Jeanne shrugged. "It's some type of binding. Something set long ago. She doesn't understand it, but somehow it's tied to the land she's on. I think the only reason the wasteland has been able to spread is because her people were so sick."

"Wait a minute," Peter said. "The neighbor's been acting weird lately. It walks as if it's fighting against something. Like a wind or something. Do you think that's related?"

Jeanne looked excited. "Grandmother is completely healed. The binding should be so much stronger now."

Telynalle looked out at the wasteland. "Yet still it walks out here— beyond its original prison, if what you say is true. I should examine this binding and see how it can be strengthened."

Jeanne nodded at Peter, and the boy tried to hide his relief. The elf would be safe with Grandmother and the two would protect each other.

The elf gathered up her cloak and the jay shifted on her shoulders.

"The neighbor is heading toward the Flood," Jeanne said. She closed her eyes briefly, then pointed. "Grandmother is in that direction."

"My thanks," Telynalle said quickly. "Take care." The blue jay added a soft comment.

Peter and Jeanne watched as the elf headed into the night. "It hasn't noticed her yet," Jeanne said softly. "That's good."

Peter sat atop a large rock. "I'll just keep it occupied a bit." He pictured another of his memorized portions of the barrier, and then pictured the water flooding through it.

Jeanne turned her head to stare at him. "What did you do? It's totally angry now."

"Oh, just broke the barrier holding the floodwaters back again. It will stop the water—again—but that will take some time. Meanwhile, we should move to another spot; it will come back here first."

Rocks were treacherous underfoot in the dark, but it was not long before they found another hiding place. Peter unslung his backpack and stretched. "So, you're done already? I thought it might take days for you to heal Twyl's grandmother."

"It did take days." Jeanne studied him, and Peter tried not to squirm, knowing that she wasn't just looking at him. He had nothing to hide from her. He suddenly felt the remembered touch of wingtips. "Peter, when did you enter the Lands?"

He shrugged. "Sometime this morning."

"I've been here for three days."

Peter made a disgusted sound. "I *thought* the Watcher was playing games with time. So you arrived several days ago, I arrived this morning—wonder when Twyl and Jody arrived." He peered at her. "They *are* here, aren't they?"

Jeanne closed her eyes for a moment. She sighed and opened them again. "If they are, they're too far away for me to sense." She put her backpack down and pushed her hair back. "The neighbor seemed to be able to detect Twylgalit. It said she was outside of Grandmother's protection."

"That's no help. She'd be that way back in our forest as well."

"Yeah, but it probably wouldn't be able to detect her at all then."

"Point taken." Peter was uneasy when Jeanne folded her arms. He could feel her gaze on him. "What?"

"Jody's your twin," Jeanne commented. "Can't you tell if she's here?"

"Huh?"

"You can. I can sense it."

"What? Oh, you don't mean that twin stuff."

"Yes, I do mean 'that twin stuff.' Believe, Peter!" Jeanne leaned forward and pointed at him. "Where is Jody?"

Peter couldn't help himself. His head turned in the direction of the Flood. In his mind he could feel Jeanne following his awareness, strengthening it so that he could almost sense as Jeanne did as she used his link to his twin.

Jeanne sighed. "She's okay. Twylgalit's with her. And some others I don't recognize." She dropped her head and took a deep breath. "That's all I can tell for now. Sorry to do that to you, Peter, but I knew you wanted to know."

Peter didn't know what to think. He did feel relieved, and he knew it was better to admit that to Jeanne. She would understand. "Of course I wanted to know. She's still my sister, even if she's the biggest pest around."

"Spoken like a true brother." Jeanne grinned. She yawned. "I need to sleep. I could take second watch."

Peter nodded. "I'll take first."

"Thanks." She settled herself next to her backpack and rested her arms atop it. "The neighbor is still busy fixing whatever you did. Tomorrow you'll have to tell me what you've been doing. It's frightened as well as angry."

"Huh." Peter was surprised to hear that. Why would the being be afraid of a little water? He remembered what Telynalle had said about the flood, then shook his head at himself. The neighbor wasn't afraid of the water but of the spells within it. *That means the wizards* can *stop it!* he thought excitedly. After meeting Telynalle and seeing what Armored Guy had done to her, Peter had not been so sure. Now he was.

He turned back to Jeanne to share his finding, but decided from her stillness she was probably sleeping. He settled himself comfortably in a spot where he could watch the night-shrouded wasteland and decided to make some plans for the morning.

The night passed as Peter thought of and discarded several plans. Some included making booby traps using the bags of water, once he could think of a means to trigger the traps. They could fling bags or bottles of water at the neighbor, but that would leave them open to attack as well. *I should have brought elastic rather than duct tape*, he thought. *Something to make a slingshot with!*

Finally he smothered one too many yawns and knew it was time to wake Jeanne for her watch. He leaned forward, then froze, staring out into the darkness. Something had moved against the stars.

Peter checked to make certain his disbelief still shielded them. He might already be visible if whatever it was could see in the dark, but he didn't think he had been spotted. The half-glimpsed silhouette was distant and seemed to be moving in the direction of their previous hiding place. "Jeanne," he whispered softly.

He felt her presence along their link as she came awake with a light wash of fear at the neighbor's nearness. Her hand touched his, and she shared with him what she sensed, the burning hatred and anger of that armored being. He winced from the heat of it, and she blocked more of its intensity. It was afraid, it was angry, but there was also vengeful anticipation growing as it hunted, a gloating eagerness that sickened him. Jeanne abruptly blocked that, and he took a deep breath. *How does she stand it?* he wondered as his stomach unknotted. He was very glad they had convinced Telynalle to go. It would not have been safe at all for the elf to have remained anywhere nearby.

Reinforcing his thought, an angry bellow sounded from their previous hiding place. Jeanne's hand tightened when he was about to make a remark, and Peter stayed silent. He was confident the being would not detect them magically through both his and Jeanne's defenses, but it wouldn't be wise to ignore the being's hearing.

Through Jeanne's awareness he could "see" the hot, anger-filled blob that was the being. He thought it was still near the old hiding place. It moved in the direction of the Flood for a short distance, then retraced its steps and began to circle. Peter wondered if the being was attempting to pick up the elf's scent. *Or however it managed to track Telynalle through a closed faceplate,* he thought. *What if it spots our footprints? Did we leave any? We tried not to.*

The circle the being walked began to widen. The figure paused not far from them, and Peter slowly began to reach for one of the bags of water. There was no change in the emotions Jeanne shared from the being, so Peter didn't think they had been spotted. Yet. But it was still better to be prepared.

Excitement and eagerness surged suddenly. Peter's hand closed on a water bag. He tensed, waiting for the neighbor to come toward them.

Instead, it turned and walked away, heading further into the wasteland.

Peter leaned back in relief when the dark figure had vanished into the night. "Whew!" He kept his voice low still. "Where's Telynalle now?"

"I think... Oh. She's made good speed." Jeanne moved away, and he could hear a rustle from her backpack. "They're close to Grandmother."

They? Peter wondered, then remembered the blue jay.

"Almost safe." Jeanne hesitated. "How fast does the neighbor move?"

"Fast? Walking speed, I guess. Why?"

"Dunno. I never sensed it approaching when I was at Grandmother's. It always just...*pfft*—appeared." Water gurgled as she took a sip.

Peter thought about that and had a sudden worry. "Do you think it knows how to—what did Telynalle call it?"

"Place-shift? Oh, I hope not. That would be very bad. Both for us and for Twylgalit."

"Why?"

"It seemed to be able to sense her. If it notices her entering the wasteland, it could place-shift right to her, and we won't be able to stop it."

"Huh." Peter nodded grimly. "Well, we'll just make sure to spot her first. It's not the only one who can sense people. We can both sense Jody. We'll just stay on the border and beat it at its own game. Right?"

CHAPTER 28

JODY AND TWYLGALIT

You and she are much alike, a deep voice observed.

"I am not like her!"

Both so prickly, 'tis a great shame that each only sees your bad side in the other.

Jody opened her eyes and stared at the dark sky overhead. Maybe that tree sap affected her dreams. She felt as if she kept waking up and hearing voices arguing. She peered into the darkness, careful not to disturb Rafi beside her. The dryad was not visible. *Probably still inside her tree*, she thought, remembering how the girl had left when they settled for sleep. Twyl was on the other side of the furred and feathered circle of warmth that was the gryphon.

"Twyl!" she whispered.

"Yes, Jody?"

"Do you hear someone talking?"

"I hear you, Jody."

"Not me. There's someone else here." Jody shivered. She was cold without her jacket.

Twyl was silent a moment. "I hear no one, Jody."

"I hear you two," Rafi muttered sleepily. "Is it time to start again?" He carefully stretched one wing. "I can't sleep either." He sighed. "I keep dreaming those vines are wrapping around me."

Jody eyed the clearing. Where were those jacket fragments? What if they were coming toward her? She'd never see them in the dark! "I vote for leaving."

"Can you see in the dark?" Rafi asked.

"No," Jody replied. "Can you?"

"Not very well," Rafi replied. "Enough to avoid walking into trees. That's about it. Not enough to see where we're going."

The deep voice suddenly intruded. **No. Now is too dangerous. Wait until morning. Go back to sleep.**

Jody's eyelids were suddenly heavy. She fell back against Rafi. Distantly she heard the gryphon murmur, "I'm so sleepy."

*   *   *

Twylgalit studied her sleeping friends. "Donunay?" she asked worriedly. "What did you do?"

It is for their own protection, the tree replied. **I'm sorry we disturbed your friend. You need sleep as well.**

She remembered the mother grove. "Do you seek to keep us here, Donunay?" Twylgalit asked. She braced herself for the answer. She would not be forced to stay. Her grandmother needed her!

I seek only to keep you safe. Too many dangers walk the Great Woods by night. You will all be free to leave in the morning.

She relaxed, looking at the two sleepers. She had a thought as she studied the gryphon. "You put Rafi to sleep before, didn't you? It was not the plants."

The tree sighed. **My dryad does not make friends easily. She would have pushed you away in her anger, and your other friend would have been taken over by what she carried. She needed to be freed of the small greedy lives. And my dryad had the means.**

"Wait! Don't go!" The dryad rushed up to the group. She stopped and said confusedly to Twylgalit. "I thought I heard them talking."

"You did," Twylgalit agreed.

They decided to wait until morning, Donunay whispered. Twylgalit glanced up at the sweet gum's branches, but did not comment.

"Oh." The dryad turned to Twylgalit. "I am glad. I wanted to talk to you." She looked down. "I am sorry about before. I was afraid and I said things I should not."

Twylgalit was surprised. "You were afraid? Of us? But Jody—"

The girl turned away. "I can't talk to her. She makes me angry."

"She makes me confused," Twylgalit admitted.

The girl laughed and turned back.

"The Watcher of Gates sent me to Jody," Twylgalit explained. "She will help save my grandmother—and the Land." She smiled at the dryad. "You already apologized to her. That is all that was needed."

The dryad shook her head. "I must apologize to you as well." She took a deep breath. "I was jealous. You three are such good friends. I have no friends, except for Donunay."

Twylgalit felt sad. To have no friend... "Then I would like to be your friend," she replied.

"Y-you would?"

"Of course! You have helped us so much already. Please be my friend. You, too, Donunay."

The tree creaked softly. **Thank you, my dear. I would be honored.**

Twylgalit smiled. "I am called Twylgalit." She bobbed her head, and the beads in her hair clattered.

"I..." the dryad seemed amazed. "I am called Yazmin," she replied.

They moved closer to Donunay to talk without disturbing the others. The early morning mists began to gather along the ground, beading their hair with moisture. Within the comforting cocoon of white, Twylgalit talked of her mothers and their home.

"I do not know what happened to my home," Yazmin said sadly. "During the Curse, there were ogres everywhere in the Great Woods. They hurt so many trees with their axes that the older ones began to wake and strike back. Ogres killed my mother's tree."

"And your mother?" Twylgalit asked, horrified.

Yazmin shook her head. "I don't know. She told me to run. I ran and ran until there were no more ogres."

She sat and cried underneath my branches, Donunay reminisced. **So I asked her to stay. How could I not?"**

"Many did not," Yazmin said. "They said, 'Go away. Keep running.'" She sniffed. "I felt so alone."

You are not alone now, Donunay reassured her. **Your home is here, as long as you wish.**

Yazmin leaned over and hugged the trunk. "My Donunay. Do you forgive me as well?"

Always.

Yazmin smiled over her shoulder at Twylgalit. "You said you must continue on, but if you ever come this way again, please visit us."

"I would like that," Twylgalit said with a smile. "I will if I can."

They could both hear stirring within the fog back where the other two slept.

"Is it morning yet?" Rafi asked.

"It's foggy! Twyl, where are you? I can't see!" Jody said.

"Bright growing," Twylgalit responded. "How do you feel this morning?"

"I feel great!" Rafi bounced out of the whiteness. "Thank you, Donunay. I wonder if there's any more frogs around?" He bounded away.

"I feel stiff." Jody slowly walked toward them. "And cold. And damp."

"Hey! There's berries over here!" Rafi's voice cried from somewhere within the mist.

"Keep talking, Rafi," Twylgalit called back. "We shall follow your voice."

"I know where the best berries grow," Yazmin said shyly. "I'll show you."

"Thanks," Jody said, sounding surprised. She glanced at Twylgalit as the dryad led the way. "What's with her?" she whispered. "Why is she suddenly being so nice?"

Far too much alike. Donunay sighed. **From what do you run?**

"I'm not! I—" Jody stopped and looked around. "Did you hear someone?" she asked Twylgalit.

CHAPTER 29

JEANNE AND PETER

Jeanne sensed someone. Outwardly she watched the reddening on the horizon where the sun would appear, but inwardly she scanned for that faint there-not-there trace. It wasn't the neighbor, which now prowled near Grandmother's land. The elf and her blue jay were safely near Grandmother. Which left only—

She turned her head just as a transparent shape appeared nearby. "I didn't expect to see you out here," she said softly.

The ghost grinned broadly. He made an elaborate bow.

Jeanne smiled. "So, is there something you want me to find out here? It was the spring you wanted found before, right?"

The ghost nodded with a smile.

"Can you talk? Do you want us to go back and help Grandmother?"

The spirit shook his head. He held out his hand.

Jeanne was reluctant to touch it. She remembered the visions the Ring of Calada had shown her of the memories of one ghost. Still, this was Twylgalit's ancestor. She didn't detect any threat from him. She placed her hand atop his. She felt only a faint sensation of cold against her palm.

"Now we can talk," the ghost whispered. "I cannot stay long. I came only to warn you. You will need to move on. Once the sun rises, there will be a path leading to you that even the Old One cannot overlook."

"A path? What do you mean?"

The ghost gestured down the way they had climbed the night before. "You could not help it. It is your nature."

"What?" Jeanne looked down the hillside. Scattered among the gray rocks and dust were tiny patches that, in the faint light, looked green or red or orange. She looked back further and saw more. "Oh my. Oh no." She had a sudden vision of even more patches extending along her backtrail, leading to Grandmother. Leading from Grandmother to here. "Oh no!"

"What?" Peter asked groggily behind her. There was a spike of fear from him, and his voice sharpened. "Jeanne, look out! There's a ghost!"

The spirit smiled as he faded away. Jeanne rubbed her cold palm, wishing he could have stayed. There were so many questions she wanted to ask.

Peter joined her. "Are you all right?"

"I—I'm fine, Peter. I was talking to him."

"What, a ghost? Remember the last time a ghost talked to you."

"He wasn't a white hound. He was Twylgalit's ancestor. He came to warn us."

"Of what?"

"I'm afraid it's my fault. I'm leaving a trail." She pointed down the hillside.

Peter looked. "What? Oh. What is that, moss? Jeanne!"

"I didn't know I was doing it!" she protested. She sighed. "The ghost says it goes all the way back to Grandmother. The Old One will spot it."

"Has it yet?"

Jeanne concentrated. The being still seemed to be directing its anger at Grandmother. "Not yet."

"Okay. So we'll eat something and then get moving. Guess we might as well head toward the barrier. Wait until you see the Flood."

They ate quickly and repacked their supplies. Peter used duct tape to hang some of his bottles of flood water on the outside of his pack and one in the loops of his jeans. "Just in case we need them in a hurry," he explained.

As they walked, Jeanne looked out across the wasteland. In the growing light she thought she could see familiar dapples on nearby boulders. Beetles must have flown this way. She smiled at the memory of tiny voices chorusing "Grow, grow!" So some of the lichen patches had survived!

Bigger patches of lichen lined the banks where Peter said a stream had followed. "The water rushed along," he said as they walked. "Armored Guy tried to stop it, but the water just went around." He smiled. "It acted as if it didn't want to get its feet wet. That was funny."

"So that's why you think it might be afraid of bottles of flood water?" Jeanne asked, suddenly realizing why he had the bottles hanging within reach. Did he plan to throw them at the being?

"I dunno. But that water is powerful stuff." He pointed to the dark center of the stream bed. "That certainly doesn't look so dead anymore."

As they walked along the vanished stream, Jeanne told Peter about the lichen patches and the beetles. "I saw one," Peter said, surprised. "It crawled under a rock, then came out and flew away. So that's what it was doing!" He stopped, and Jeanne shared his admiration of a large patch of blue and gray. "You've turned its own weapons against it. I like this!"

"Look at that!" Jeanne crouched beside the stream bed and pointed at faint greenish fuzz atop the dark center. She glanced up at Peter.

"That's new," he said. "I didn't see that in any of the flooded sections yesterday." He peered into the distance. "That's odd. I should be able to see the barrier." He looked down at her.

Jeanne stood up. "The Old One was very frightened about something last night." She felt a shift in her awareness of the being. Uneasiness had touched the anger, sharpened the fear. It was moving. "I think it spotted the trail," she said. "It's started this way."

Peter adjusted his pack, and she could feel his concentration. "Right," he said. "Stay close. It won't be able to detect us magically." He started walking along the stream bed.

Jeanne hurried to catch up. "I had thought I sensed you doing something last night," she said, recalling the being's frustration.

"You had one of your illusions up, too, right?"

Jeanne nodded. "Same one I'll put up again when it gets close enough for physical sight."

"Good." He looked back the way they had come. "I don't see any color where we've walked. Maybe there's a time delay."

"I'm not doing it on purpose!" Jeanne protested.

He grinned at her. "Hey, looks good to me. I think this place needs improvement. C'mon, the Flood isn't much farther."

Soon they reached a spot where they had a clear view of the border between the wasteland and the Great Flood.

But the Flood was gone. In its place was a vast grassland.

"Windgard," Jeanne marveled. "No wonder the Old One was so angry."

Peter shook himself, and she could feel him struggling to accept what he saw. "At least this gives us more places to hide," he said. "C'mon, let's find a few good spots before Armored Guy gets here."

CHAPTER 30

JODY AND TWYLGALIT

The mists dropped slowly while they walked. Rafi seemed to treat them as a big game, bounding off into the whiteness and charging back from a different direction, or hiding in the now waist-high mists only to stand up and startle her when she would have walked right by him.

Jody felt cold and damp without her jacket, but Twyl seemed energized. Even her hair seemed fuller. Jody wondered if her own hair was frizzy by now.

She spotted the black tip of a familiar tail waving above the mist near Twyl. Deciding to beat Rafi at his own game, Jody snuck up on the betraying tail and grabbed it. "Gotcha!"

Rafi's wings emerged from the mist. "Ow!"

A roar came from overhead, and downdrafts flattened the mist to the ground. Jody lost her balance in the sudden blast of air and fell atop Rafi.

"Hey!"

"Ow!"

A large gryphon landed before them. Golden brown feathers covered its front half and its back half reminded Jody of a puma. She scrambled to her feet as large yellow eyes glared at her.

"Get away from my brother, you filthy monster!"

"Monster? Filthy?" Indignant, Jody looked down at herself. Okay, so her clothes were a bit muddy and berry stained, but still...

Rafi brushed past Jody to confront his sister. "Leave her alone!" he snarled, his tail lashing. "These are my friends!"

The golden gryphon blinked. "Your friends? These? Rafi, what would Poppa say?"

Rafi cringed. "I—I'm sorry, Soraya. But—"

Jody couldn't believe what she was hearing. Rafi looked from his sister back to Jody and Twyl and suddenly she knew exactly how he felt. She pointed at Soraya. "You are *so* like my brother. He complained when I hung out with him and his friends, kept telling me to go away and be myself, but the second I get my own friends, they weren't good enough! Well, who are you to decide? You flew away and left him! Rafi can hang out with whoever he likes!"

Rafi glanced at her in surprise. Then he raised his head and turned to his sister. "Yeah!"

Soraya puffed out her feathers. She opened her beak, but Twyl spoke first. "Please, we are looking for help. My grandmother is very ill and our neighbor will kill her. Rafi has protected us against its spells until now. Could you help us as well?"

Soraya blinked. "Rafi...protected you?"

"He was wonderful! He knew exactly what to do!"

"He saved me," Jody chimed in.

"Told you I could do magic, too," Rafi said smugly.

Soraya looked from one to the other. Most of her feathers smoothed down, but those on the top of her head kept raising and lowering along with her ears. Her gaze finally fixed on Jody, but her next question surprised the girl. "So, where's your brother?"

"There." Jody pointed without thinking and then stared in surprise at her hand. Why did she point in that direction?

"Hhn." Soraya snapped her beak a few times. "Lots of water there lately. You sure?"

"That is where Grandmother is as well!" Twylgalit said excitedly. "Past the Great Flood! Oh, we have taken so long! We have to get back to her!"

The golden gryphon studied her brother. "You want to help them?"

"They're my friends! I said I would!" Rafi's black-tipped tail lashed.

The older gryphon sighed. "We could fly."

Rafi's ears lowered. "I'm not strong enough to carry someone and fly. Could you fly with both?"

"No." Soraya reached out with her beak and nibbled his head

feathers. "So we use a spell and make them lighter."

Rafi's ears lifted. "We can do that?"

Soraya studied him. "*I* can. You listen for now." The white dappled gryphon opened his mouth, and Soraya added, "You can try it later."

Rafi's beak shut with a snap. He nodded vigorously.

Soraya turned to Jody and Twyl, and Jody felt as if she was being measured. "You there—" Soraya started.

"I am called Twylgalit," Twyl said with a smile and a bob of her head. "This is Jody."

"You two stand over there," Soraya ordered, pointing with one talon at a spot away from her brother.

Jody glanced at Twyl. The green-haired girl looked excited as she obeyed. Jody wasn't sure how she felt about this. Rafi's sister was awfully bossy. Soraya eyed her as if she knew what Jody was thinking and Jody decided to move to stand beside Twyl.

"I hope this is a spell I can learn as well," Twyl whispered to her as they waited.

Jody mentally sighed. *What is it with everyone and magic?* She glanced worriedly at the green stains in the palms of her hands.

Twyl saw. "So long as you don't call upon that magic, the spell shouldn't affect that," she whispered.

Jody looked askance at her. What did *that* mean? But Twyl didn't explain further. She just smiled at Jody and turned her attention back to Rafi and Soraya.

Soraya raised her wings. "Pronunciation is important," she told Rafi. "Listen closely. And don't sneeze!"

Rafi mutely nodded. He looked to Jody as if he was holding his breath.

Soraya glanced at him, shook her head, then turned back to Twyl and Jody. Her eagle head snaked forward and shrieked at them, and the big wings flapped once, then twice. The resulting breeze washed over the girls. The gryphon lowered her wings. "There."

"That's not one of Poppa's spells," Rafi muttered. "His are all snarly. And long."

"No," his sister replied smugly. "It's one of Momma's. Hers are more elegant."

Jody blinked. That was it? She didn't feel any different. She pushed her hair back into place.

Twyl gasped beside her. "Look!" She bounced lightly in place.

Jody shrugged. She didn't see anything odd about that. She started to move away from Twyl and her bouncing, and was startled to find that she bounced after each step as well. "What-what's happening?"

Soraya clicked her beak. "I might have made the spell a bit strong." She eyed her brother. "Thought it would be best with a new flier." Rafi cringed slightly, and Soraya chuckled. "We'll have time to catch them if they fall off."

"Wh-what?" Jody sputtered.

"You get the short one," Soraya directed Rafi. She turned to Jody. "You come with me."

"Why?" Jody did *not* like this bossy gryphon.

"I need you to direct me to where your brother is."

"Why Peter? We're supposed to help Twyl's grandmother."

"We will. She's past the Great Flood, though. If I'm right, your brother is in the middle of it."

"He's what?"

"I saw someone in the Flood when I was looking for the wizards. That is pure magic and no one but a human would be stupid enough to be standing *in* it."

"Hey!"

Soraya ignored her protest. "I can't find the wizards. I thought at first that Poppa had done something, but he's not *that* powerful." She looked at her brother.

Rafi was busy directing Twyl how to sit on his back. The golden gryphon turned back to Jody. "I can't find any wizards. All I can find is a big flood, and it's got lots of magic in it." The gryphon's ears laid back and her beak suddenly came so close to Jody's face that Jody squeaked and step-bounced back. "Your hair is green and you smell green, but you're not like your friend."

"I'm human," Jody said. She looked down at her green-stained hands and sighed.

"I'm thinking your brother knows more than you about this, so I want to talk to him. You're going to lead us to him. Now get on."

Jody grimaced. Peter would probably get along great with this gryphon. Soraya sounded *exactly* like him.

CHAPTER 31

JEANNE AND PETER

Jeanne looked out over the prairie and smiled. It was *so* wonderful to see green again! She hadn't realized how draining the monotonous gray wasteland had been. She felt energized just looking at the wildflowers and grasses. She marveled at what the wizards had accomplished in such a short time with their spells. The grass was short near the edge of the wasteland, but she could see it was almost knee-high further away from the border. In the distance saplings stretched their branches to the sky. She took a deep breath. Despite the dusty smell of the wasteland, there was also the faint fragrance of flowers wafting from the prairie.

"What's keeping it?" Peter asked, watching the interior of the wasteland from their vantage point. "It should have reached here by now."

Reluctantly pulling her gaze from the recovering Windgard, Jeanne looked back the way they had come, scanning with her other sense as well. The neighbor was still headed in their direction. "I don't know—it seems to be walking very slowly." It was intent on something. She tried to figure out what seemed so familiar about what she sensed. "It feels so mean. Deliberately nasty, like—" An old memory of a very young Amy Evans squashing a line of ants hit her, and she rapidly threw up a block, stopping herself from going deeper. "Omigosh, it's killing all those little plants." *The lichen!* she mourned. *It's my fault you hurt. I'm so sorry.*

"Block, Jeanne!" Peter said. She could feel his worry and concern. "Focus on something else. Concentrate on Windgard."

"It—it's okay. I blocked in time." She brushed at her eyes and took a deep breath.

"Maybe we'd better cross into Windgard and hide there."

"Yeah." Jeanne looked at the tiny spots of green around them, realizing with a sinking heart that she couldn't protect any. *I'm so sorry.*

She followed Peter toward the border of the wasteland. She wondered at the large stretches of dark soil covered with a light dusting of green extending into the wasteland from Windgard. "This is one of the spots where I broke the barrier and let the Flood in," Peter said. She sensed a mixture of guilt and sadness as he sighed. "I suppose it's going to try to kill this as well."

Jeanne looked back to the interior of the wasteland, noticing a change in the being. "It's moving faster now."

"Do you think it's spotted us?" Peter asked.

"I don't think so," Jeanne said. But the being was now excited about something. Something anticipated... She scanned outward. "Peter, I can sense Jody and Twylgalit!" She turned to look out across Windgard. "They're coming this way."

"Where's our friend?"

"I think it senses Twylgalit. It's excited. It's starting forward to meet them."

"If they're coming across Windgard, we'll meet them before it does. Let's go."

Peter walked into Windgard, but Jeanne stubbed her toes against something when she attempted to follow. She didn't see anything there, but she could feel it. She couldn't cross the border. "Peter, wait!"

"What?" Peter turned and came back.

"There's something here." Jeanne put her hands out, attempting to find the barrier. Nothing stopped her at shoulder-height, and she tested lower. Just below knee-height, she felt a wall.

"The barrier is still there?" Peter asked. "It didn't stop me."

"Did it stop you before?" Jeanne gingerly tried to step over the invisible barrier. She sighed when both feet finally were on the grass.

"C'mon, let's hurry," Peter said. He glanced worriedly back at the wasteland. "Which way are they coming?"

"Answer it yourself, Peter," Jeanne chided. "Where's Jody?"

"I don't know!" Without looking, he flung out a hand toward Windgard. "She's out there!"

Jeanne's awareness of Jody and Twylgalit agreed with the direction. But they were coming so fast—much faster than if they were walking. And there was an impression of height. She looked up and saw distant specks in the sky that seemed to be growing larger. "Look up, Peter!" she said, pointing.

"What are those things?" Peter asked, shading his eyes.

"Gryphons," Jeanne said in amazement. She felt envy rise in her. "Jody's riding a gryphon!" She began to run toward them.

Peter ran as well. "Can they see us?"

"Unless you're shielding against them, too." Jeanne waved and saw the tiny figures wave back.

Peter looked around the open grassland. "We're too close to the wasteland. We've got to get further into Windgard."

Jeanne suddenly sensed blazing anger and hatred behind them. She turned and saw an armored shape at the border. "It's here!"

Peter turned as well. "How did it get here so fast?" He waved at the approaching gryphons. "Go away! Get back!"

The being raised its hands.

"It sees us!" Jeanne warned.

A ball of violet rocketed toward them. Jeanne waited for it to hit, but the ball suddenly splattered into nothingness a short distance away. "It can't hurt us," Peter said beside her. Jeanne hoped he could continue to believe that.

Jody felt Jody's fear spike overhead, and a familiar scream came closer. A furry shape shot by, flipped in midair a short distance above the ground, and dumped a screaming Jody onto the grass. As she bounced, the large gryphon angled its wings, flapped, and rose back into the sky.

Jody sat up. "Ow," she complained.

Jeanne blinked. Why did Jody have green hair? She looked only long enough to check that Jody was unhurt, then returned her attention to the Old One.

The armored being fired a violet bolt after the departing gryphon. The gryphon swerved and screamed at the bolt as it passed. The ball promptly shattered into tiny sparkles.

"Sweet," Peter commented. "So that's a wizard?"

The Old One bellowed in anger, and Jeanne could feel its frustration. She could feel something else as well, a welter of various emotions growing stronger and stronger.

Rainbows flickered on the border of Windgard a short distance away and suddenly a crowd of wizards stood there. Jeanne recognized Graylod holding his blazing staff at the front of the group, with Salanoa standing right beside him. As the spell-light died, several others brushed past Graylod to stand protectively before him. She could feel his exhaustion amid the determination of the others. Her attention was caught by the gray and white spotted Windkin that had just moved to the front of the group. Elin was here!

The Old One roared and flung a bolt at the group of wizards. Elin half-reared, and violet energy exploded against a suddenly visible shield of rainbow-colored light before the wizards.

Jeanne grinned at seeing the Ring of Calada in action. She remembered how it had protected her when she had worn it.

The smaller gryphon and its passenger had almost reached them, despite Peter's wave-offs. Jeanne could hear the angry cries of the larger gryphon overhead. Slowly, awkwardly, the smaller gryphon began to circle and fly back the way it had come.

A large blocky wizard gestured, and a boulder lifted from the wasteland. Meanwhile, the Old One flung a handful of violet at the gryphons. The larger gryphon shrieked just as the smaller one sneezed. Part of the violet bolt disappeared, but the rest struck the smaller gryphon's wing.

"Rafi!" Jody cried.

The gryphon twisted as he fell, and his passenger tumbled off his back. The larger gryphon dove after the smaller. Jody started forward. "No!" she protested. "Save them!"

The hovering boulder shot toward the Old One and shattered against its fist.

Jeanne was startled to hear a Windkin's challenging scream from the midst of the wizards. The black figure of the Windrunner suddenly appeared, rearing above them. "To me, Winds!" he ordered.

Winds swirled up from the ground, flattening the grass and blowing the wizards' cloaks and robes about. The spiraling air circled the falling girl and lowered her gently to the ground beside the stallion.

Jeanne started forward, but Peter blocked her path. "Stay here."

"But she might be hurt. And the gryphon—" She watched as the larger gryphon helped the smaller one to land.

"So will you be if you try to reach her. There are wizards over there; let them see to her. Jody, get over here!"

"No!" Jody continued walking across the grass toward the group of wizards. "Those are my friends over there!"

The Old One gathered the broken bits of rock with a gesture and fired them at the wizards

The violet encased missiles ricocheted off the rainbow-colored shield back at the armored being.

Jody stopped and threw her hands over her head. "What is going on?"

"She's leaving my shield," Peter muttered. "She'll be in the open!" He raised his voice. "Jody, get back here!" he ordered.

Jeanne hesitated, sensing a new addition approaching. She looked past the Old One just in time to see Telynalle appear behind it. *Place-shift!* she thought. The elf held a roughly trimmed branch as if it was a staff, and Jeanne realized she could sense Grandmother's magic about it.

The Old One whirled and growled as it flung a bolt at Telynalle. The elf batted the energy away with one swing of the staff. "I am no longer defenseless, Evil One," Telynalle said.

"You think so, elf?" The being took a menacing step toward her, reaching out with one hand. A gryphon missile screamed out of the sky and struck. Claws flashed and the thing shouted in pain.

"Don't ever touch my brother!" the gryphon screamed in reply as she swooped back out of reach.

The armored being began to raise its uninjured hand, then lowered it as Jeanne sensed a shift in the level of its anger. It slowly backed away and turned to view all of its opponents. "So," it said. "The mighty Wise have come to invade my land."

"No." The Windrunner stepped forward. He pawed the ground with one hoof. "That is not your land. You have encroached upon the land of my people, nibbling away at its borders year by year. That stops now."

"Animals. Animals masquerading as intelligent beings. You have no lands," the Old One said.

"And what are you beneath that armor?" Peter asked. "Not-life impersonating life, huh? What's the point of that?"

The blank helmet face turned in his direction and Peter stood straighter, glaring back at it. Jeanne, feeling an increase in the anger and rage, blocked completely. Jody made a faint squeak as the being's regard passed over her.

The being turned back toward the wizards. "This would have been mine long ago. I have made it mine. You are not welcome."

"Nor are you," Graylod replied. "Return to your own place."

"No longer will you spread your poisons and destruction of life," Telynalle added.

Jeanne felt the other wizards' confusion at her words *Hadn't they come to stop it?*

"You think to stop me?" the Old One asked, echoing her thoughts. "The Old Ways are more powerful than any you so-called Wise can draw upon. Death is final." With that, it flung violet at both Telynalle and the wizards.

As those bolts were deflected away, the armored being gestured toward the three humans. Jeanne expected another bolt to shatter against Peter's defenses, but instead, Jody screamed. The girl flew through the air as if pulled and landed before the Old One. It closed a large armored hand about her arm and there was a flash of light, gone so fast that Jeanne wondered if she had imagined it. The Old One laughed.

"Jody!" Peter yelled.

"No!" Twylgalit protested from behind Elin's shield.

"The last link in my binding is severed," the Old One gloated. It turned toward Telynalle. "Not even you can stop me now. Tell the tree that."

Jody struggled in its grasp. "Ow, you're hurting me!"

The armored figure looked down at her as if surprised. *It is surprised!* Jeanne thought. "You are not dead," it said.

"Let go!" Jody replied, tossing her hair. Jeanne blinked. Was there a blonde streak shining amid the green?

"You are not of the blood." The being was puzzled.

"No, but I am."

Jeanne looked to where Twylgalit stood among the wizards. This wasn't the shy and fearful girl she remembered. Twylgalit dug her toes into the ground and raised her hands. "Release her."

The Old One turned toward Twylgalit, radiating such rage that Jeanne almost blocked completely again. *No,* she stopped herself, *now's the time for some uncertainty in that arrogance.*

"Let her go," Peter demanded. Jeanne could feel his concentration as she began to focus on her own powers.

The armored figure studied first one group and then another. Telynalle hefted her staff. Salanoa, Graylod, and the other wizards raised their staffs as well. "Let me go now!" Jody demanded, trying to kick the armored legs.

The being abruptly took two quick steps toward Twylgalit and the sheltering wizards. It stopped and looked down at its feet. The helmet looked up at the waiting wizards. The being chuckled and vanished, taking Jody with it.

Peter and Jeanne ran to join the wizards. "Where did it go?" Peter demanded. He looked down at where the being had stood, where the new grass curled and died in large brown circles.

Elin stepped forward to greet Jeanne. She flung her arms around his neck and leaned into him. "Where could it have gone?" the Windkin wizard asked.

"Back to its source of strength," the blocky wizard guessed.

"But why then take a hostage with it?" Telynalle asked, hurrying across the border to join them as well. "It wants to be free. There is only one thing holding it captive."

"Grandmother!" Twylgalit said. "Oh, we have to save her!" She touched the branch Telynalle held and looked up at the elf. "This is hers! You have seen her?"

"Why did it take the girl?" another wizard pondered.

"Why Jody?" Peter asked.

"It grabbed the wrong one," Jeanne said swiftly, releasing Elin. "It meant to kill Twylgalit."

"And that is?" Graylod asked.

"Me," Twylgalit said in a small voice.

Graylod and the other wizards glanced at her.

"Her people have held the Evil One bound for many years," Telynalle explained. She ran one hand along her branch/staff. "It is a powerful binding."

Graylod smiled to reassure Twylgalit and nodded. "So instead it captured an unrelated human," the wizard mused.

"She's related to me!" Peter argued. "We're wasting time! That thing has my sister!" He looked at the wasteland.

"Wait," Elin said, as others turned toward the wasteland. "There is another place it could have gone. The Gate is nearby." He looked from one wizard to another. "The Windlords' Gate. It tried to steal it once before. Before the witches invaded." He stopped and looked at the Windrunner. "I'm sure that is where it has gone."

"I thought it couldn't leave the wasteland," Peter commented.

"It shouldn't be able to," Jeanne agreed. She looked at the dying grass. "But Jody doesn't know that." Her eyes widened. "She thinks it can. She *believes* it can! Peter, she's got your power!"

Graylod nodded. "That is why it took the girl with it. With her, it is almost free. Jeanne, can you sense it?"

She closed her eyes and concentrated, trying to shut out the maelstrom of emotions swirling around her. If only everyone would calm down! She looked for sullen anger and blazing hatred, but that was all around them, as if the being had splattered the area when it had departed. She shook her head, opening her eyes. "No, it's too diffuse." But there was a faster way. "Peter, where is Jody?"

"Not again!" Peter protested. Sighing, he took a deep breath, closed his eyes and pointed into Windgard. "Out there."

"That is what the Winds now whisper." The Windrunner nodded. "I will go to the Gate."

"And I as well," Elin said. He glanced toward the gray wizard.

Graylod shook his head and leaned on his staff with a sigh. "I cannot transport everyone so soon."

"There is no need," Telynalle said. "It may go back to revenge itself." She placed her hand on Twylgalit's shoulder. "We will go back to Grandmother."

"I'll stay with the gryphons," Salanoa said, from where she tended the smaller one's wing. The larger gryphon paced back and forth, occasionally looking over the wizard's shoulder. "We'll catch you up."

"Rafi?" Twylgalit asked worriedly.

The injured gryphon lifted his head. "I told you we'd help with your grandmother," he said to Twylgalit. "We'll be there."

The older gryphon muttered something that sounded like "sneezing" and nodded. "He's tough. Just a few singed feathers, hey, Rafi?"

Telynalle swung her staff, and the elf and Twylgalit vanished.

Elin nudged Jeanne. "Get on, Jeanne. You, too, Peter."

The Windrunner looked at Graylod. "Coming, old friend?"

Jeanne didn't hear the reply. As soon as Peter joined her on Elin's back, the gray and white spotted stallion surged forward, galloping over the grassland.

"Peter?" Elin called over his shoulder. "Why does your sister have green hair?"

*   *   *

Peter had forgotten how fast the Windkin could run. The prairie seemed to flow under Elin's hooves. Peter barely noticed when the Windrunner and Graylod joined them. The blocky wizard flying on their other side did catch Peter's attention for a moment, however. Perhaps it was because the wizard was sitting cross-legged in midair.

Before too long Peter could see the small hillside with the ruins in the distance. Elin moved to the forefront of the group as they approached, and Peter realized why when a violet bolt hurtled toward them from the ruins. The Ring of Calada flashed its rainbow-colored shield, blocking the blast. Peter hurriedly set up his own defensive shield around the group as well.

Another bolt exploded against their shields. Peter could see the armored being standing before the ruined wall. Jody, visible beside it, appeared to be unharmed. He didn't see why Elin had thought Jody's hair was green. It did look darker than her usual blonde, but no way could it be green.

"It's really angry and it's feeling very frustrated," Jeanne warned the group.

Peter almost felt like laughing. So the Old One had found out that it wasn't easy to get the Gate to work.

The two Windkin and floating wizard stopped at the base of the hillside.

"Release the girl," Graylod ordered.

"Open the Gate and I will release her," the Old One replied.

Graylod shook his head. "The Watcher of Gates controls the Gates. Only he can do so."

The Old One hit the grayish panel of wood with a fist. "I will kill her if you do not open the Gate."

Jeanne slid off Elin's back, and Peter followed. "It's so stubborn," Jeanne whispered. "I'm having a hard time influencing it."

"We have no power over the Gates," Graylod repeated.

"I know that place," Peter whispered. "I could sneak up and get Jody away from it."

Jeanne shook her head. "Peter, I can't control it. It could kill you."

"No, it can't," Peter said firmly. She looked about to protest, and he added, "You told me to disbelieve every thing it says."

The being shook Jody. "This human came through a Gate!"

"Ow!" Jody protested. "I told you, I don't know how it works!"

The helmet face turned from her to view the wizards. "You." Its free hand pointed at Peter, and he braced himself to disbelieve any bolt. "Human. Give me that." The finger shifted.

Peter looked down and realized that it was pointing at his wristguard. "This?" He held up his wrist, and heard shocked murmurs from the wizards. "And you'll let her go?"

"Give me that or I will kill her."

Peter grimaced. Some bargain. How did it know about the wristguard?

He started up the hill, keeping his shield of disbelief tightly about him. Perhaps he could expand it around Jody as well and get her away. As he drew closer he became aware of every tiny detail. Jody's face was tear-streaked, her face pale against her grass-stained hair. The Old One's armor seemed to be made of overlapping flat plates, and those on the arm gripping Jody seemed to have discolored patches.

He stepped onto the pavement, and the tall figure backed up, pulling Jody with it. It held out its free hand. "Give me that band or I will kill her."

"P-Peter," Jody whimpered.

Peter pulled off the wristguard. He looked down at it, seeing the silvery-gray carvings and wondering if he could booby-trap it somehow.

"Give me that!"

Peter shrugged. "Sure, why not. It doesn't work for me." *It doesn't work*, he repeated mentally to himself. He tossed it to the thing.

"No! Peter!" Elin protested.

The Old One caught the wristguard. It laughed, then turned and walked through the panel, dragging Jody with it.

"No!" Peter reached the panel just as the shimmer died. He banged his fist futilely against the unresponsive wood. "No! Jody!"

"Peter," Elin said.

Peter glared at the wizards. "It had my *sister!*" He turned back to the silvery wood. "I didn't think the Watcher would let it through, okay?

Jeanne scrambled up the hill. She grabbed Peter's hand and placed her ring hand against the wooden surface. Closing her eyes, she said one word. "Please."

The brown shimmer of the portal reappeared. Peter nervously tightened his grip on Jeanne's hand as they stepped through. Now was not the time for any side trips.

CHAPTER 32

PETER

They emerged from the Watcher into the familiar clearing before the haunted tree. Dropping Jeanne's hand, Peter looked around the forest, finding no armored being, no Jody, and, even more surprising, no changes from what he remembered from before they had entered the Land. "They're gone? " Jeanne asked.

"No," Peter disagreed. "Look at the ground. No tracks, except for ours heading into the Watcher. They haven't stepped through yet."

Jeanne looked at him. "The Watcher sent us through first? But we followed them. How do you know they didn't end up somewhere else?"

Peter shook his head, remembering his previous experiences. "I don't. But the Watcher controls the gates. You remember last time how we left it seconds after we had entered? It's trying to help us rescue Jody." He looked at the tree. "You stand on one side of the Watcher. I'll be on the other. When they step through, whoever is closer to Jody grabs her and gets her away from the thing."

"Right."

They had barely taken up positions on either side of the tree when suddenly the trunk shimmered. The Old One emerged first, dragging Jody behind it. Peter and Jeanne both tried to grab the girl, but somehow the being was aware of them. It turned and swung Jody out of their reach as they passed.

The armored figure stood in the center of the clearing, Jody struggling in its grasp. Around its feet plants were withering and dying in a circle that fanned outward as they watched. Peter thought he could almost hear the screams of the nearby trees. Looking at Jeanne's grim face, he suddenly realized that she did.

"Let her go!" Peter demanded.

The blank helmet face turned from side to side. "A new world. One soon to be wiped clean of all life. A whole world."

Peter tried to think of something to free his sister. If only it had taken *him* hostage! He could have hit it with disbelief and— Something Jeanne had said abruptly clicked. He knew what to do. He knew what to *say*. "Oh well, Jody, I guess that's enough," he said, trying to sound casual.

"Wh-what?" Jody asked, peering through a curtain of her pale blonde hair.

Jeanne was staring at him as if he was crazy. He nodded slightly to her and mouthed the word "block."

Peter focused the whole of his attention on the Old One. He had to believe what he was about to say. "Jody, it's just a man in a rubber suit."

Jody stared at him for a moment. "I hate you! You always spoil it for me!" she shouted. She turned on the astonished creature. "I don't believe you! You're not real! You're mean and awful and I don't believe in you!"

Cracks appeared in the armored hand gripping Jody, and the being abruptly released her. Peter grabbed Jody and shoved her behind him. He stared hard at the being, at the discolored patches spreading up its arm. "I don't believe in you," he said firmly. The patches raced up to the being's shoulder.

"I'm not sure why we're always so worried about things escaping into this world," Jeanne muttered softly. "The second they run into either of you they're done for."

The Old One raised its fists and roared at them. Jeanne and Peter exchanged glances.

Peter wondered how the being could still be standing. Maybe his disbelief wasn't strong enough here. Water bottles gurgled as he bumped into Jody behind him. He pulled one bottle free. *What if this doesn't work either?* he worried.

The Old One took a step toward them.

The three backed up together. Suddenly the Watcher creaked loudly. They stared as the old tree shuddered, its top swaying back and forth. There was an ominous cracking noise.

Peter's eyes widened as he looked from the thing approaching them to the tree swaying behind it. "Get out of the way!" he shouted, turning and pushing the girls ahead of him. "Move, move!"

The being laughed behind them as they ran. It was still laughing when the Watcher fell over on it with a mighty crash.

Bits of twigs and bark continued to rain down in the silence. Peter stared at the massive fallen tree. Dirt pattered down from what he could see of the exposed roots. There was no sign of the being. Where it had been standing was completely covered by the trunk and tightly crossed thick branches. Jeanne raised a hand to her head.

"Jeanne?" Peter asked.

"I don't sense it anymore," she said, her eyes closed. "There were sharp pains—piercing"—she took a breath—"but something blocked the rest. It—it could be dead. I don't know. I can't feel its anger anymore." She opened her eyes and looked down at the tree. "I can sense the Watcher though."

Jody looked again at the unmoving tangle. "That tree is still alive? But it fell."

"Deliberately," Peter said. "That 'tree' can move, Jody. That's why there're legends about it. Wanna bet that was the Watcher's plan? Lure it into this world where it could be killed?"

Jeanne silently stared at the tree.

"Unless the Watcher sent it through to somewhere else," Peter mused, remembering the army and the force-shielded trees, "but I doubt the Watcher would be that nice. I remember what it did to a witch hound. Turned it to green dust," he said to Jody.

"You!" Jeanne suddenly shouted. She glared angrily at the massive trunk. "I think you're right, Peter. It's so proud of itself. You planned this, didn't you! Did you let Twylgalit's family die for your plan?" she yelled at the Watcher.

"But it fell," Jody repeated.

Peter looked thoughtfully at the fallen tree. "Half the roots are still in the ground. Betcha it'll right itself when it's good and ready."

Jody stared at him. "But—"

Jeanne looked around the clearing. "You let them all die," she muttered angrily. She unslung her backpack. Rummaging within it, she pulled out a water bottle with a scratched label. She began pouring water near some of the injured trees.

They froze as something rustled in the twisted and broken limbs of the fallen Watcher. Peter held a water bottle ready.

A branch slowly edged up through the tangle. On it was Peter's wristguard.

Jody raised her hands and backed away. "Don't look at me," she said quickly. "I'm not touching that."

CHAPTER 33

JEANNE

Jeanne snuggled under the covers that night with a happy sigh. It was *so good* to be back in her own bed. As comfortable as Grandmother's branches had been, she felt much more secure surrounded by her room and her family and the familiar creakings of her family's old house.

She sighed again, this time with the contented sense of accomplishment. It had taken the rest of the afternoon, but all the trees Twylgalit had contacted within the forest and Peter's development had been checked for disease and given small doses of the water from the spring or the Flood just in case. She had even given a big dose to the fallen Watcher before they had left the clearing, reasoning that the Old One had thought its touch would kill Twylgalit and the Watcher had done more than touch the being by falling on it.

She turned over, wondering why she had a slight nagging worry that she had left something undone. She puzzled over what it was as she fell asleep.

Jeanne dreamed she stood in the Watcher's meadow. The green-leaved tree rustled gently before her. **Would it comfort you to hear that I was not aware of the problem until the one you know as Grandmother contacted me?**

She eyed the tree, feeling anger she had not been aware of draining away. "The Old One was that sneaky?"

The Old One was very old and very sneaky.

Jeanne smiled as she reached up and touched the waving leaves. "Well, you're very old and very sneaky, too. I'm sorry I was angry at you."

A Sensitive has every right to be angry at suffering and death. Do not blame yourself for those you could not help.

Jeanne nodded, feeling tears well. "Twylgalit's family. All those small plants."

They gave their lives willingly, knowing that others would live by their sacrifice. Come, see what the wasteland will become once the wizards are done.

The rest of her dreams were filled with images of grass-swept plains and small forests stretching to Grandmother's spring.

*   *   *

Jeanne stared blankly at the clothing in the store window. She had forgotten the shopping trip interrupted by Twylgalit's appearance yesterday. Nothing there looked suitable for riding in, and definitely not for mucking out the stable. But her mother insisted that she needed new clothes.

She sensed someone approaching her and braced herself. "That turquoise would look good on you," a familiar voice said in an unfamiliar way. "It would bring out the color of your eyes."

Jeanne glanced up. Jody was being friendly? And meaning it? Two stores away, she could see Amy Evans and the rest of her crowd walking away radiating disapproval, one or two glancing back in disbelief. Jeanne looked back at the top. "It looks too dressy," she disagreed.

Jody tilted her head. "Too dressy for riding? I don't think so. And for town it should be fine. You need to sharpen up your image, Jeanne. And I'm just the one to help you with that."

Jeanne looked at her. "What about Amy?"

Jody glanced at the departing group and shrugged. "They're not for me anymore. They reminded me of some people I met. I didn't like those people or what they wanted me to be. I think I need to decide what I want to be. Meanwhile, um…"

Jody was uneasy about something. Jeanne waited, wondering what she would say next. This was so unexpected.

"Uh, I was wondering. Could I maybe come with Peter the next time he helps out at the stable? Not to ride! Just to watch. You two looked so cool when you rode up on that big horse." She frowned. "That *was* real, wasn't it? Peter tried to tell me I was dreaming."

Jeanne smiled and nodded. "That was real. You rode a gryphon. What was that like? I was so jealous when I saw you."

"You were?" Jody smiled and tossed back her hair, which, Jeanne was glad to see, was back to its normal pale blonde color. "Oh, look at that caramel top. Do you think that would look good on me?" She froze, looking past the window display into the store. "Is that your mom? Oh no, don't let her buy that for you!"

Peter caught up with them at the food court. He looked at Jeanne and tilted his head at Jody.

Jeanne smiled. "It's okay. We're good." She could sense her partner's relief. But there was a lingering worry. She nodded toward her mother by the coffee bar. "And we're okay to talk. What's wrong?"

Peter sighed. "Not wrong, exactly. You'll never guess what happened to my wristguard a few minutes ago. I thought I broke it." He held out the wristguard. A narrow band had separated at the top. He pulled off the separated band and handed it to Jeanne.

She studied the silver-gray band. It was slim enough to be a nice bracelet, and as she turned it in the light she could make out a delicate pattern of leaves. Jeanne smiled and handed it to Jody. "I think this one's meant for you, Jody," Jeanne said.

KATHRYN SULLIVAN

Kathryn Sullivan has been writing science fiction and fantasy since she was 14 years old. The world set up in *The Crystal Throne* has been developing since then, although some of the short stories have escaped into fan zines, print zines and ezines. *The Crystal Throne* won the EPPIE Award in 2002 for Best Fantasy Book!

Kathryn's stories have appeared in *Short Trips: Repercussions, Flights of Mind, Professor Bernice Summerfield and the Dead Men Diaries, Twilight Times, Anotherealm, Shadow Keep Zine, Fury,* and *Minnesota Fantasy Review.* Some of the short stories in *Agents and Adepts* are those from the world set up in *The Crystal Throne* that had escaped into print zines and ezines. *Agents and Adepts* won the 2003 Dream Realm Award for Best Anthology!

Kathryn is Distance Learning Librarian at Winona State University in Winona, MN, and coordinator of the library's webpages. She's owned by two confused birds—one small jenday convinced that he's a large guard dog and one large cockatoo convinced that she's a small lap dog with wings.

The list of her stories is at...http://kathrynsullivan.com.

AMBER QUILL PRESS, LLC
THE GOLD STANDARD IN PUBLISHING

QUALITY BOOKS
IN BOTH PRINT AND ELECTRONIC FORMATS

ACTION/ADVENTURE	SUSPENSE/THRILLER
SCIENCE FICTION	PARANORMAL
MAINSTREAM	MYSTERY
FANTASY	EROTICA
ROMANCE	HORROR
HISTORICAL	WESTERN
YOUNG ADULT	NON-FICTION

AMBER QUILL PRESS, LLC
http://www.amberquill.com